NO ONE WILL EV

Jessica assured herself as she lifted her sweater and fumbled for the catch of her bra. The moment her hungry infant son found her breast, his wailing ceased.

She breathed a sigh of relicf and watched out the car window for Brody returning with the take-out chicken. The lineups must be long, she thought and turned her attention to her child.

Suddenly the car door was yanked open. "Sorry I took so long." Brody leaned across the seat and dropped a bag into the back, then eased into the driver's seat. "There was a mix-up with the orders. And you'll never guess who I saw on the way out—"

His voice dropped off abruptly. It was by complete accident that his gaze slipped down. His eyes jerked up immediately to confront Jess's startled expression—which he was sure mirrored his own.

But more surprising to Brody was how moved he was by the sight before his eyes.

ABOUT THE AUTHOR

Oregon author Sandra James would love to say that her green thumb gave her the idea for *Spring Thunder*. Unfortunately the only plants that survive in the James household are the silk variety! The family member with the true horticultural flair is her sister-in-law, who works at a local nursery. She's delighted to know that she planted the seeds for Sandy's fifth Superromance.

Books by Sandra James

HARLEQUIN SUPERROMANCE
205–A FAMILY AFFAIR
249–BELONGING
277–STRONGER BY FAR
306–GUARDIAN ANGEL

Sandra James

SPRING THUNDER

Harlequin Books

TORONTO • NEW YORK • LONDON
AMSTERDAM • PARIS • SYDNEY • HAMBURG
STOCKHOLM • ATHENS • TOKYO • MILAN

Published December 1988

First printing October 1988

ISBN 0-373-70335-X

PROLOGUE

JESSICA CULVER WAS COLD. So cold she thought she'd never be warm again.

She sat huddled silently in the back of the taxi, oblivious to the steamy August night. She had flown into Medford an hour ago, called her cousin Maggie Howard to let her know she was on her way there, then climbed into the only cab sitting outside the airport's tiny terminal.

The cabdriver must have sensed her need for solitude. Only once had he questioned her. That was when she reminded him to turn off the main highway toward Silver Creek.

He cast a quick look at her in the rearview mirror. "Not much up that way except an old abandoned lumber mill. Most folks moved away when the mill shut down."

Not everyone, Jess countered silently. "There's a lodge near there," she said. "It's a couple of miles past Silver Creek. If you turn right onto Indian Hill Road, it'll take you straight to it."

This part of southern Oregon had always been Jessica's second home. She and her parents had made the drive south countless times, and Jess had always spent at least three weeks here every summer. It was shortly after Maggie had lost her husband that the mill had closed its doors. Maggie's father was one of those who had moved. He and his wife had retired in eastern Oregon. Jess wasn't surprised that Maggie, widowed and with a daughter and son to raise, had chosen to stay. Her cousin's tiny stature masked a fiery courage. Maggie was a fighter, and she wouldn't back down until the last card had been turned.

Would Maggie have run away...as she had? Jess couldn't stop the niggling little voice. Yet she knew she couldn't have stayed with Eric. She had played out their sham of a marriage far too long, already.

Her head dropped back against the vinyl cushion, and her eyes closed wearily. She was tired. So tired of pretending. And after what she had seen...

A shiver ran through her as she recalled Eric's words. *When you walk out that door, it's the end for me. You know that, Jessica.*

Jess knew. But she was so caught up in her own shock and misery that she really didn't care.

You can't divorce me now! It's less than three months before the election. Dammit, I've already talked to two reporters this morning who wondered why you weren't at that dinner last night. You can't do this, Jessica. If you walk out on me, you'll rob me of my life, my career.

His life. *His* career. It was typical, so very typical of Eric, to think only of himself.

When that ploy failed, threats followed.

You'll regret leaving me, Jessica. I'll make you sorrier than you ever dreamed.... And I'll get even with you, Jessica. Somehow, someday, I'll get even with you for ruining me....

"This the place, lady?"

Jessica's eyes snapped open. A large, rambling structure filled her vision, caught in the hazy moonlight. The wooden sign by the huge metal mailbox was weathered and gray but the lettering was clear: Welcome To The Trail's End Lodge.

Welcome. It was silly to be so sentimental over that word. But Jess's throat grew unbearably tight as she stared at the sign. The first time she had seen this lodge had been after Steve's funeral. Maggie and Steve had bought it only a month before he died. But crazy as it was, this was the first time in years that she actually felt welcome.

"This is it," she confirmed. She reached for the door handle and got out of the car on shaky legs.

The driver pulled her suitcase from the trunk. Jess had just pressed the fare into his hand when one of the lodge's huge double doors flew open. Like a wraith in the night a barefoot Maggie Howard flew down the steps, her long red-gold hair spilling about her shoulders, her thin cotton robe billowing out behind her.

"Jess! Oh, Jess, it's been such a long time. I couldn't believe it when you called. I could have come for you. There was no need to take a cab all the way out here.... Oh, God, I'm so glad to see you!"

Jess found herself seized and folded into Maggie's surprisingly strong embrace. When she finally drew back, she found herself under the scrutiny of a very concerned pair of sea-green eyes.

"How are you, Jess?" the other woman asked softly. "I've been on edge ever since you called. You sounded...different." Her gaze moved searchingly over her cousin's pinched, white features. A dawning comprehension crept into her voice. "Oh, no." Her fingers gripped Jess's more tightly. "Something's happened.... What, Jess? What?"

For a moment Jess couldn't speak. There was a cold hollowness inside her, a terrible numbness that threatened to consume her.

She wanted to cry. She *needed* to cry. But all her pain was tightly locked inside, and she had the craziest sensation that if any of it broke free, she would shatter into a million pieces.

"It's Eric," she finally whispered. "I've left him, Maggie. I saw a lawyer and started divorce proceedings this morning." She was vaguely aware of Maggie's shocked gasp. "You always said I had a terrible sense of timing," she added on a deep, shuddering breath. "And I guess you're right, because I—" her voice was woefully thin "—I'm pregnant."

CHAPTER ONE

BRODY ALEXANDER straightened his tie, then wondered why he'd bothered. The contemptuous little smile on his lips was reserved solely for himself. Old habits died hard, it seemed. He'd always hated wearing a tie, and the fourteen years he'd spent in the good old U.S. Army hadn't cured him of that dislike.

Of course it wasn't every day that he had an appointment with a California Supreme Court justice or rather, an *ex*-supreme court justice. The call had come through late yesterday afternoon. A cool, disembodied female voice that identified herself as Miss Matthews requested he meet with Mr. Eric Culver at ten o'clock the next morning—which was why he was sitting in Eric Culver's office right now.

It had been on the tip of Brody's tongue to refuse. He was at no one's beck and call these days, and he disliked the woman's uppity manner. Even more, he resented that the once high-and-mighty Eric Culver couldn't be bothered to make the request himself.

"Why?" he'd asked bluntly.

He'd been politely informed it was regarding a matter of mutual interest.

Mutual interest? That was a laugh. Eric Culver was probably the last man on earth Brody had anything in common with.

Presumptuous though she was, the woman must have had some inkling of his thoughts.

"I can almost *promise* this meeting will be to your advantage, Mr. Alexander." There was a brief but significant pause. "Financially speaking, of course."

Of course, he echoed mockingly. Money was the operative word here. Why didn't she just come right out and say so?

"Can we expect you here at ten tomorrow, Mr. Alexander?"

Brody didn't miss the heavy note of expectancy in her voice. If prissy Miss Matthews could see him now, sitting in his cramped little office practically waiting for the phone to ring, she wouldn't even be asking. "I'll be there," he said curtly.

To his surprise, she didn't hang up. "The business Mr. Culver wishes to discuss with you is of a rather personal nature. Naturally," she continued in honeyed tones, "he prefers that you not mention this visit to anyone."

There was a subtle warning in the sleek voice. For the first time, Brody found his interest piqued. Personal business, hmm? It wasn't all that unusual for someone to want to keep a meeting with a private detective on the quiet side. He was used to late-night meetings in smoke-filled restaurants on the wrong side of the tracks.

But meeting with ex-justice Eric Culver might prove more interesting than most of his cases. He'd had his fill of trailing errant spouses to seedy motels for a little afternoon delight. But why, he wondered silently, should Eric Culver need a private detective in the first place?

He wasn't about to refuse, though. He could use a case he could sink his teeth into. Business had been lean lately. Very lean. He'd had an offer just last month from Alan Winters, an attorney who was planning his defense of a sleaze bag with underworld connections. Winters had wanted him to cough up a little dirt on the key prosecution witness. That

Brody had hesitated even a second before telling Winters what he could do with his offer was proof of just how bad things were. He still had the tidy little nest egg he'd managed to put away during his army stint. But somehow he'd always thought of that money as Murphy's, and it seemed almost sacrilegious to even think of dipping into it.

Now, looking around once more at the plushly furnished Oakland office that belonged to attorney Eric Culver, he wondered again just what Culver wanted of him. He glanced at his watch and grimaced. Ten-twenty. He'd give Mr. High-and-Mighty ten more minutes and then Culver could . . .

"Mr. Alexander?"

Brody looked up to see a tall, elegant blond sweep past the receptionist to stand before him.

"I'm Miss Matthews, Mr. Culver's assistant." She didn't bother to extend a hand. "He'll see you now."

Brody got to his feet and began to follow her. "About time," he muttered under his breath.

Her pencil-thin eyebrows rose in haughty inquiry. "I beg your pardon?"

Miss Matthews, Brody decided in disgust, was an ice cube. She'd surely crack if the slightest bit of warmth got under her skin.

"Nothing," he said in as pleasant a voice as he could muster. "Could we get on with this, Miss Matthews? I have another appointment soon." And that was a bald-faced lie if ever he'd heard one. His calendar for the entire week—for the next month, in fact—was as empty as a blank sheet of paper.

Miss Matthews opened the door to an inner office and motioned him through. Brody stepped inside. The door closed noiselessly behind him.

The room Brody found himself in was four times the size of the waiting area. An entire wall of glass afforded a bird's-

eye view of San Francisco Bay. The last whispery traces of
rain and fog had disappeared hours ago, leaving behind a
world that glinted in the morning sunshine. The waters of
the bay looked like a shimmering sheet of silver.

Brody scarcely gave the view a second glance. It was only
a facade—the pretense of goodness and light, with darkness lurking just under the surface.

Nothing was ever as it seemed, and no one—*no one*—
should ever be taken at face value. It was a lesson to be
learned early; a lesson to be remembered well, and often.

That was Brody's first thought as he stared at Eric Culver.

Culver stood near the window, hands behind his back,
gazing out at the vast panorama below. There was such a
hint of drama in the pose that Brody felt his mouth curl with
cynical amusement. It reminded him of a plantation owner
of old, arrogantly surveying and relishing his domain.

Culver turned then. He wore a conservatively cut dark
blue suit, a fastidious white shirt, a plain, dark tie. He was
tall and not muscular, but nonetheless he seemed very fit.
Brody guessed his age at somewhere near fifty, though he
looked ten years younger. Pale gold hair lay sleek and
smooth against his head; not a single strand was out of
place. Brody saw that Culver's aquiline features were almost classically perfect. Deep-set eyes, high cheekbones,
thin, straight nose.

"Mr. Alexander? I'm glad you could make it on such
short notice." Culver sounded as smooth and polished as
Brody had anticipated. Brody was waved to the leather
armchair opposite the massive desk.

But while Culver's voice was pleasant enough, his eyes
were as cold and hard as flint. Brody didn't flinch but met
the other man's gaze head-on. "I understand you wanted to
see me."

Culver smiled. "I certainly do," he murmured, taking a seat behind the desk. "You've been a private investigator for how long, Mr. Alexander?"

"Two years." Brody's reply was easy. He watched as Culver picked up a folder from the desktop. But his eyes narrowed when he saw his name typed in bold, capital letters across the top.

"I see." Long, slender fingers flipped open the folder. "Are you good, Mr. Alexander?"

Culver's mildness was anything but placating. Brody had the sudden feeling he was on trial here, and he didn't especially like it. Folding his arms across his chest, he regarded the other man with a hint of wariness. "I usually get the job done," Brody stated, pausing slightly. "One way or another."

Pale blue eyes were slowly raised to meet his. "Actually," Culver said softly, "it's the 'One way or another' that brought my attention to you in the first place." He pretended to study the contents of the folder, but Brody wasn't fooled. If Culver was trying to make him nervous, it wasn't working. Brody had played by the rules for a while, but he'd never had a great deal of respect for authority figures, especially self-imposed figures. If Culver didn't stop his tap dancing, he'd soon find that out for himself.

"I see that you were in the military for a number of years. You started out as an MP, eventually went through officer candidate school and ended up in the Criminal Investigations Division where you did quite a lot of undercover work."

Brody stared at him a moment. "So you have friends in high places," he said finally. Culver might have access to what was supposedly privileged information, but his "friends" hadn't been able to salvage his judicial career.

"I noticed that along with your commendations, you managed to accumulate quite a number of reprimands." There was a faintly amused expression on Culver's handsome features. "One can't help but wonder," he murmured, "why you went back to civilian life when you did. In only six years, you could have retired—at thirty-eight. And a military pension these days is nothing to sneeze at."

Brody sat very still. Only the slight narrowing of his eyes betrayed his anger. "You seem to have all the answers," he said shortly. "Why don't you tell me?"

The blond man shrugged. "I suppose it has something to do with the disagreement you had with the commanding officer at your last post." There was a brief but significant pause. "I assume you know who I mean. The general that you—"

"Decked," Brody finished succinctly. His smile was one of grim satisfaction. "The high point of my career."

"The *end* of your career," Culver pointed out. "How you managed to keep from being court-martialed is beyond me."

Brody's smile vanished. "I resigned my commission," he clarified, his tone gritty. "And the general had it coming."

Culver opened his mouth; Brody suspected he was about to offer another unwanted opinion.

He fixed the other man with a stare. One look at his steely expression and Culver's jaw snapped shut. "I had my reasons," Brody said tightly. "And I know for a fact you won't find them in that file. Besides, I'm here to get a job done. My past has nothing to do with it, so I suggest you make your point now, Mr. Culver, because I don't especially care for people snooping around in my past."

Culver spread his hands wide. Brody noticed immediately that they were a gentleman's hands. Smooth, uncallused, dusted with a faint sprinkling of fine gold hair.

Culver's eyes flickered. "I had no idea you were so touchy about your background," he murmured. "For you to achieve the rank you did, your career must have been right on course until it backfired. My only point was to assure you that I have no objection to whatever methods you choose to employ. And you've worked undercover in intelligence. I like that. It seems your mode of operating was occasionally rather unorthodox, but you were quite effective. You struck me as a man who has few scruples."

Brody's lips compressed into a thin line. Scruples? The runaway sixteen-year-old whom Police Sergeant Cullen Murphy had hauled off the street certainly had none. He'd changed since Murphy had taken him into his home and under his wing, and while Brody never pretended to be a saint, he wasn't sure he appreciated the picture that Culver was painting of him.

Culver picked up a small ivory figurine from the corner of the desk and studied it. Just like a lawyer, Brody thought disgustedly. Dragging out everything in order to gain the most effect. Why the hell couldn't Culver cut the court-room theatrics, look him straight in the eye for once and say what was on his mind?

"As I said, Mr. Alexander," he finally continued in his soft-spoken voice, "it doesn't bother me in the least that you're a man who doesn't go by the book."

Brody got to his feet. Eric Culver could save his speeches for the courtroom. He'd heard all he cared to.

"Oh, I wouldn't leave yet if I were you." Culver's voice stopped him at the door. "Not if you want the job I'm about to offer you."

Brody half turned, but he left his hand where it was, curled around the doorknob. "Is that what this is about?"

His sarcasm wasn't lost on Culver. For an instant the lawyer's mouth tightened, then he appeared to relax.

"You're a direct man, I see." He rested his hands on the desktop, tapping his fingertips together. "Very well, then. I'll come right to the point. I'd like you to locate my wife for me. Or rather, my ex-wife." Culver waved him back inside and once again indicated the chair across from him.

Their eyes met, one pair wary, the other ripe with expectancy. If Brody could afford to be picky, he'd be halfway across town by now. Unfortunately, he couldn't. He hesitated, then moved across the room.

Culver was speaking again. "You're aware of my background, Mr. Alexander?" For some reason, the air of certainty about him grated on Brody's nerves.

He knew of Eric Culver, of course. He came from an elite, moneyed family in San Francisco. A former district attorney, Culver had later served as a superior court judge before the governor appointed him to the state supreme court. Culver had served his initial term; then, in accordance with the law, his name had been placed on the ballot to be confirmed by the voters for his next term. Culver had thought the confirmation was merely a formality, that he was destined to serve out another term as justice. But that was before his name hit the news.

In late summer, not long before the upcoming election, Culver's pretty, seemingly adoring wife had walked out on him and filed for divorce. The resulting exposure and speculation had ruined Culver's bid for confirmation, the confirmation he'd thought was already in the bag.

He vaguely recalled that Culver's wife had never publicly stated her reasons for leaving her husband. Nor had there been a scandalous divorce trial; not that it mattered, since the act alone proved to be more than enough to send her husband's career toppling.

Brody nodded. "I assume you mean your judicial background. It ended some months ago, didn't it?"

Culver's face seemed to freeze over. "Thanks to Jessica." His voice was bitter.

"Then why do you want to find her?" The question was blunt and direct. "It's a little late to reconcile, isn't it?"

"Our divorce is already final. I have no desire to reconcile." Culver stared into space, his face closed and expressionless, then his eyes finally swung back to Brody. "It's not Jessica I'm interested in so much as her child," he added quietly.

Brody's face must have reflected his surprise. This was the first he'd heard about a child.

Culver smiled at his reaction, but it was a smile that held no humor. "Yes, Mr. Alexander. My dear wife had just learned she was pregnant when she divorced me. She'd only found out for sure the week before she left. I still find it extraordinary, but that was the one thing the press never got wind of. Probably because Jessica disappeared so fast after I was served with the divorce papers." He was silent for a moment. "Jessica should have become a mother sometime in the last few weeks." Culver pulled a picture from a drawer and handed it to him. "This is Jessica."

The photo was one that had been clipped from a newspaper. Odd, he speculated silently. If this clipping was any indication of Culver's feelings for his former wife, this marriage had probably not been a match made in heaven. He also noted by the date that the shot had been taken shortly before Jessica had walked out on her husband. The photograph was grainy and small, but he could tell that Jessica Culver was one hell of a good-looking woman.

"Pretty, isn't she?"

Brody didn't realize he'd been staring until he glanced up to find the other man's eyes upon him. Pretty? he echoed silently. That didn't even begin to describe this woman.

"Any idea where she is?" He handed the photo back to Culver.

"A fair idea, but I can't be absolutely sure. She wasn't needed here while the proceedings were going on. I believe she stayed with a cousin in southern Oregon, somewhere near Medford. At least that's where she was when the decree was finalized."

"That's where she's from?"

Culver shook his head. "She's from Oregon, yes, but farther north. A town called Amity."

"It's not unusual for a woman to go back to her family." A mocking smile touched Brody's lips. "That's the first thing they usually do—pick up and run home to Mama."

"She has no close relatives in Amity," Culver said quickly. "Just her cousin Maggie in Medford. The last I knew, her mother was living in Reno. But somehow I don't think she's with her mother." He rose and moved to stand before the wide pane of glass. "No, I'd say she's in Oregon somewhere. She was always so anxious to go back, but I'll never know why."

Brody's eyes were on Culver's slender, well-formed back. There was something hidden and elusive about the man that he couldn't quite put his finger on. He shrugged, and decided it was probably just his imagination.

"So what do you want done once she's been located?" he asked bluntly. "You mentioned the baby. You may think I have no scruples, but I draw the line at kidnapping. If that's the kind of dirty work you want done, you might as well do it yourself. I'm not having my tail thrown in jail for you or anybody else," he finished flatly.

"Kidnapping?" Culver turned slowly. "Really, Mr. Alexander, I think you're forgetting that I'm a member of the legal community. I'll admit that since I've been in private practice again I've stretched the law to its limits, but I still have a healthy respect for the system.''

Which was just another way of sugarcoating the pill, Brody concluded grimly. Culver had no intention of getting his hands dirty, which was why *he* was here.

"But you still want the kid." It wasn't a question. It was a statement of fact.

Culver neither agreed nor disagreed. "What I want," he said with a faint smile, "is to know for certain whether or not Jessica's child is mine."

"You have reason to believe it isn't?"

The lengthy pause was incriminating, yet Brody found himself waiting for Culver to speak. When he did, all his earlier bitterness was gone. It almost seemed as if he were apologizing.

"Jessica has always been a woman whose appetites..." He stroked his chin thoughtfully. "Let's just say my lovely ex-wife is a woman with an extremely healthy interest in the opposite sex. Especially older men, I'm afraid. I'm an example, you see. Jessica is more than twenty years younger than I."

"She was unfaithful?"

"I can't be certain." He sighed. "If you're asking if I have proof, I don't. But since she divorced me so unexpectedly, what else can I believe?"

"And that's why you want to find out if the baby is yours."

"Yes. I want to make a motion for temporary custody so that I can have the baby tested to see if I'm the father."

Brody's eyes narrowed. He had the feeling he was being led around by the nose. "So why can't you have the tests done sometime when you have the kid for—" He broke off when he saw that Culver was shaking his head.

"Jessica would never allow it. I have no visitation rights, you see. It was part of our divorce settlement that Jessica have sole custody and control of the unborn child. And before you ask why I didn't have all this settled months ago, admittedly it was because I didn't fight it. Jessica had my neck in a noose and she knew it. I couldn't risk any more publicity because of the election, so I gave her everything she asked for. My reconfirmation should have been merely a formality, but because of the divorce, it wasn't. My name was all over the gossip columns as it was."

"So the divorce was uncontested?" Brody lifted his brows in question.

Culver nodded. "If I had contested it, gone to trial and fought her at every turn, it would have made matters worse. My hands were tied. I was in a vulnerable position because of the election. Jessica knew it and used it to her advantage. I decided it was best to let the divorce go through as quickly and as quietly as possible. If I petition for visitation rights, Jessica will use the fact that I conceded all rights to the child as part of the settlement." He paused. "Nor did I feel I was in a position to challenge custody while she was pregnant. I was afraid she'd run and I'd never find her. But now, not knowing if the child is mine... This may be the only chance I'll ever have to be a father. I have to know, Mr. Alexander. I have to."

Culver sounded sincere and convincing, and it all made perfect sense. Eric Culver, Brody reflected, seemed to have anticipated every question he might have posed.

He straightened in his chair. "If you want custody, even temporary custody, you're going to need a damn good reason."

"I know." There was a heavy silence as Culver resumed his place behind the desk. "That's why I want you to watch Jessica, watch for anything that might give me the leverage

I need to make a motion for a change in custody. That shouldn't be too hard, since Jessica is a very physical person—something of a clinging vine at times. It shouldn't take her long to find someone to keep her warm at night—if she hasn't already."

For just an instant, there was a hard light in his pale eyes, but then he grimaced. "I truly regret having to resort to such sleazy tactics, but Jessica has left me with no other choice."

There was just the right twinge of regret in his voice, just the right touch of hurt. He was smooth, Brody decided. Maybe too smooth? He had the strangest sensation that maybe—just maybe—Culver wasn't telling him everything.

He glanced up to find Culver watching him closely. "This could be a rather dirty little affair, but I'm willing to pay you extremely well for your services. I'm also willing to throw in a substantial bonus if I'm able to succeed through your efforts. Knowing Jessica, she probably won't make it too difficult for you." He paused, then asked softly, "Do we understand each other, Mr. Alexander?"

Brody understood, all right. As a kid growing up in the Mission district, he'd thought nothing of playing dirty. He'd cleaned up his act—Murphy had seen to that—but that was before he'd been confronted with all the petty little intrigues, the political manipulations and maneuverings in the military. And that was before the brass had given a veteran cop like Murphy such a raw deal.

But that Brody Alexander had been a different man—and he was used to playing hardball again.

He got to his feet. "How much time do I have?" he asked evenly.

For some unknown reason, the other man's slow-growing smile grated on Brody. He almost wished he hadn't asked.

"I'm interested in results," Culver answered blandly. "Take as much time as you need, Mr. Alexander. As much time as you need." He pulled open a drawer and handed Brody a file folder. "I think this information on Jessica will answer any questions you might have."

Brody was halfway through the door when Culver's voice halted him once more.

"Don't be overly troubled by your conscience, Mr. Alexander. In spite of how she looks, Jessica is a woman who can take care of herself. She proved that when she divorced me."

In other words, when it had come time to talk money, Culver's divorce had cost him a bundle.

Brody's nod was terse. Oddly, he wasn't inclined to be particularly sympathetic.

HOURS LATER, Brody sat at the tiny Formica-topped table in his kitchen, long legs sprawled in front of him. A half-full cup of coffee, cold and untouched, sat beside his right hand.

For a curious moment, Brody almost felt sorry for the woman who had once been Eric Culver's wife. Her life—all that she was, all she had ever been—was spread out before him, illuminated by the stark-white light shining above the table. She had been shaped and molded by the man whose life she had shared for six years.

He'd memorized almost every word on the bio Culver had given him, not that there was much to tell about Jessica Ryan Culver. She was twenty-nine years old; born in Amity, Oregon. An only child, she had lived her entire life on a farm there until she was twenty years old, when she'd spent her last year of college in Sacramento.

There she had met Eric Culver.

Brody glanced down at the series of photos and newspaper clippings in front of him. The case wasn't so very different from others he'd handled—wronged husband or wife checking up on the other. But Brody was intrigued almost in spite of himself.

He had to admit that Jessica's dark-haired loveliness was a perfect foil for Eric Culver's blond good looks. Brody had never been partial to brunettes, but with her slender curves, Jessica Culver possessed an earthy sensuality that called out to the raw, primal male within him. This was one time he wouldn't mind mixing business with pleasure.

It was easy to go through the sequence of events in her life. Young, naive child-woman meets older, sophisticated charmer. A story-book wedding followed, complete with a blushing bride clinging to the arm of her much more worldly husband. In her wedding photo, she was radiant, her eyes full of starry hopes and golden dreams. He detected a hint of shyness, as well, and a look of such unadulterated adoration as she gazed up at her new husband that it made him scoff.

Subtle changes followed. She was more composed and poised as she adjusted to her new position in life. Brody could almost see her steady ascent in growth and maturity. Yet hers was the face of a Madonna, and a part of him wondered if anyone could possibly be as sweet and pure as she looked.

Brody rearranged the pictures without conscious thought. Jessica Culver still smiled, but those lovely eyes were haunted. Brody's gaze dropped to the caption beneath the clipping. Justice Culver, as confident and self-assured as ever, was accompanied by his wife as he spoke to the graduating class at Stanford University. It was dated early June.

Two months before Jessica Culver had walked out on her husband.

Abruptly he gathered up the photos and clippings and stuffed them back into the envelope. For some reason, he couldn't stand to look at Jessica Culver's lovely face for another second. But even when the kitchen table was once again neat and orderly, Brody still couldn't forget her expression in that one particular photo. She had looked so unhappy. Disillusioned, perhaps?

With a grimace, Brody rose and dumped the muddy remains of his coffee in the sink. Staring out into the darkness, he absently kneaded the tightness in his neck and pondered the events of the day.

The portrait Eric Culver had painted of his wife was anything but pretty. If Culver was to be believed—and he had no reason *not* to believe him—Jessica was a cold and calculating woman. And she had been pregnant when she left him, he reminded himself. Culver might be right; it was altogether possible that her child was not fathered by her husband, which could have been responsible for that haunted look in her eyes. It also could have explained *why* she left him. She could have been afraid, fearful of his reaction. Fearful of the resulting scandal, should the truth be revealed.

Brody's hand dropped to his side. Was he defending her? It irritated him that he had to remind himself that the reasons behind Jessica's desertion were none of his business. He wasn't being paid to find out why. He was being paid to find Jessica, and so what if she *looked* as innocent as a newborn babe?

Outward appearances no longer carried any weight where Brody was concerned. He remembered his first night on guard duty in Vietnam. An officer had tried to smuggle a young Vietnamese girl into the base. She had the sweetest, most innocent liquid brown eyes he'd ever seen. The senior MP on duty wasn't going to search her, but he changed his mind at the last minute. Hidden under her tunic, the girl had three grenades taped to her waist. Rough and seasoned as his life had been, that had been a shocker, a real eye-opener for Brody.

He glanced around his living room, experiencing a spurt of restless dissatisfaction and discontent. It had started long before he'd resigned from the army. By now he should have been used to it. With a muttered curse, he switched off the light and headed for bed, absently fingering the cleft in his chin as he left the room.

Still, the image of Jessica Culver's sweet-faced innocence danced behind his eyelids. Again he envisioned her face, so full of hopes and dreams, the way it had been on her wedding day. He remembered a time—for an instant it seemed like just yesterday—when Murphy had dreamed of going back to the life he'd had as a kid, before his father had lost his vineyard. Murphy, the closest to a father figure *he* had ever had, had wanted to buy some land, become a grape grower and maybe even bottle a little of his own wine someday. Brody had been thrilled, proud and curiously humbled when Murphy included him in that dream.

If Brody felt any guilt, it was swiftly thrust aside. All he needed to do was find Jessica and keep tabs on her for a while. If she had already landed tidily in the lap of another man, well, that wasn't his fault.

It had been a long, long time since Brody had allowed himself to dream. He'd been living a hand-to-mouth, day-to-day existence when Murphy had caught him shoplifting at sixteen. Full of furious resentment, Brody had cursed both the man and the life that had brought him so low, not realizing that the glowering, redheaded cop would be his salvation. Cullen Murphy had let him spend one unforgettable night in jail, but then he'd taken him home and cleaned him up. Murphy had cared . . . as no one else had cared.

But after Murphy had died, Brody had once again come to hold the view that dreams were for the foolish and the very young, and he was neither. But with the money Eric Culver was willing to dish out, he could at least begin to hope. Maybe it was time to look ahead again, to erase the past and start all over; maybe find a sweet, loving woman to take care of him, to fill the bleakness inside. Maybe.

CHAPTER TWO

THE ANCIENT TREE CAST a looming shadow across the driveway. Like a silent sentinel, the massive oak stood guard at the edge of the lawn. Lazy morning sunshine yellowed the faded clapboard of a rambling two-story house, a massive barn and several smaller sheds. In the distance, the rolling hills of Oregon's Coast Range rose misty and green.

Inside the house she now called home, Jessica Culver pushed a trailing strand of dark hair behind her ear as she peered out the kitchen window. Jess couldn't have been more proud of her newly purchased property, the property she hoped to turn into an ornamental-plant nursery. But at this particular moment, there was a deep frown of worry etched between her slender, arched brows. Despite the fine-boned delicacy of her features, her jaw was firm and resolute, her blue eyes dark with disapproval as she let the lacy curtain fall back into place.

Lord, but the man was stubborn. Jess had known Lucas Palmer all her life, but she'd never realized just how frustrating he could be! She'd told Lucas yesterday that there was still plenty of time to start on the seedling frames. In that respect the unseasonably cold, dry winter that Oregon's Willamette Valley had seen this year was a blessing. But Lucas's pickup had just rumbled down her gravel drive, weighted down with a full load of lumber in the back end.

Jessica hurried out onto the back porch and down the steps. The screen door slammed behind her.

She heaved an eloquent sigh as the pickup rolled to a halt. "You," she reprimanded with her hands on her hips, "should still be home in bed. You shouldn't even be *thinking* about being up this early."

Lucas Palmer stepped down from the driver's seat. "At seven in the morning?" he scoffed. "I've been up with the sun longer than you've been on this earth. Besides," he muttered, carefully avoiding her censoring gaze, "I've got a few things to do here."

"That," Jessie countered with quiet deliberation, "is my problem, not yours."

Lucas pointedly walked around her toward the back of the pickup. "Now, look here, Jessie," he said gruffly. "Just because you're too proud to ask a body for help doesn't mean I'm going to sit back and not give a hand when it's needed—and you with a little one, yet. I watched you grow up, young lady, and if your father were still here, I don't think he'd approve of your pigheadedness! You—" he finished on a blustery note "—should be inside the house. Do I need to remind you that you've been out of the hospital less than two weeks?"

If Lucas had been six inches taller, he'd have been peering imperiously down his nose at her. As it was, he was doing his damnedest while looking her straight in the eye.

"Three," Jess corrected, smothering the laugh she knew he wouldn't welcome. "And Nathan will be sleeping for at least the next two hours, so there's really no need for you to strain your back when I'm perfectly capable of—"

"No need?" Shaggy brows the color of a rainy, wintry day drew together over faded blue eyes. "Jessie, I'm far more likely to strain my back *inside* your house than out, trying to find my way around all the boxes you've yet to unpack."

Jessica gave a feeble, lopsided smile. Her mother had sold the farm last summer and moved to Nevada to be near Jess's aunt. Since Jess had just split with Eric, her mother had offered to put some of the furniture from the farm into storage until the time Jess set up permanent housekeeping. She had found this place just over a month ago, and thankfully, the sale had gone through okay. Jess had signed the mortgage papers at the bank in Amity just before her son was born.

But her loan approval had taken so long she'd begun to think the bank intended to turn down her application. She'd finally stopped looking over her shoulder for Eric, but she wouldn't have put it past him to stand in the way of the one thing she had always wanted: to establish her own nursery.

At the thought of Eric, a shiver traced down her spine. She told herself it was silly to be so apprehensive. Months had passed since she'd filed for divorce; surely if Eric was hell-bent on some sort of revenge, she would know it by now. But he hadn't called her. He hadn't followed her. He hadn't done anything.

And that was almost more frightening than anything he *could* have done.

Jessica let her breath out slowly, dismissing the unwelcome memory. One thing she couldn't dismiss was the certainty that Lucas was right; there *was* too much to do, even with Lucas's help. As for the trail of boxes he'd complained about . . . well, she'd only had time to unpack what was necessary. If she and Lucas hadn't planted the Christmas trees during her first week here, she'd have been forced to wait until next year. Then Nathan had arrived earlier than expected. . . . But she'd been living out of a suitcase for so long now, it didn't bother her half as much as it apparently did Lucas.

She wouldn't let herself feel that she had taken on too much. Starting a nursery was the dream she had nurtured since she was a child. Now that the chance had finally come her way, she wasn't about to give up because of a few stones thrust in her path.

Maybe Lucas was right that she was pigheaded. Her cousin Maggie certainly thought so. She'd done her damnedest to convince Jess to wait until after her baby was older before starting such a venture. But for the first time in her life, Jess was looking out for herself. It didn't matter that it had taken twenty-nine years for that opportunity to appear. It only made her all the more determined to see her dream become a reality—for herself and her son.

She sighed and moved to the back of the truck where Lucas had unhooked the tailgate. "You went to the lumber-yard last night to pick this up, didn't you?" Her frown reappeared as Lucas clambered onto the bed of the pickup. When he didn't answer, she went on, "You know I could have had this delivered, don't you?"

"No reason to," he grunted. "You might as well save a dollar wherever you can."

Jess slid her hands beneath several of the stacked boards Lucas shifted forward. It wasn't the thriftiness of a lifetime that prompted the man's concern, and she knew it. "What I can't afford," she countered lightly, "is to lose *you*." Together they lifted the boards and laid them near the corner of the barn.

Jess followed Lucas back to the truck, and he grumbled all the way. "Do you know how long it'll be before this nursery is a paying operation? And you won't take a cent from that damned man you were married to. The least he could do is support his son!"

Jess resisted the urge to shake her head. She loved Lucas Palmer as dearly as she loved her own family, but she and

Lucas had been having the same argument at least once a week since she'd decided to buy this house and the surrounding acreage.

Jess alone knew the secret that had led to her divorce from Eric. Even Eric had no idea that she knew.... She hoped that secret would remain locked inside her forever. It was too humiliating, still too shattering for her even to think about.

Lucas, like her mother and Maggie, had accepted her explanation that being married to Eric was no longer tolerable. They all knew of the life she'd led during their marriage—she had put up with his long work hours, endured the social commitments she had never liked. But with a man like Lucas, there was no fine line between right and wrong, good and evil. Everything was cut-and-dried; one way or the other. Eric was Nathan's father, and as such, Lucas felt he was still financially responsible for the child. But Jess wanted nothing to do with Eric, even if it meant struggling through the next few years. She didn't dare admit it to Lucas, though.

"Lucas," she told him very gently, "I knew very well what I was getting into. I know it will be five years before the Christmas trees will be ready to harvest. I know it will be two years before I see any profit on the rhododendrons and azaleas—"

"Once the cuttings are planted."

"Once the cuttings are planted," she agreed.

"And you can't do that until the frames are made."

"And I can't do that until the frames are made." Jess placed another pile of boards on the ground, secretly glad Lucas had stopped for a minute. It had been over three weeks since Nathan's birth, but she wasn't as strong as she'd hoped to be.

Jess dusted off her hands and faced Lucas over the pile of lumber. "The situation with Eric is exactly the way I want

it,'' she said again. "I don't want any child support. I got
half of everything Eric and I owned, and luckily it was
enough to put a substantial down payment on this property.''

"I'll bet if he'd had his way, you wouldn't have."

Jess tightened her lips. It was true, but she didn't say so
to Lucas. Eric had made a few unreasonable demands, but
it hadn't taken long for him to back down. Jess was well
aware that the reason their divorce had gone through so
quickly was because he hadn't dared risk the publicity of a
court trial. In the end it hadn't mattered. She truly regretted that he'd lost his post in the state supreme court, but she
refused to accept the blame.

There was also a measure of truth in Lucas's observation
that she had to get by until she eventually saw a profit. But
she would not give voice to the doubts and went on lightly, "I
wouldn't have bought this place if I didn't think I could get
by until I see a profit—'' her eyes began to dance "—barring
any unforeseen acts of God, like a typhoon or an earth-
quake—''

"This isn't the time to make fun of your Maker, Jessie!"

Jessie. Only her father and Lucas had ever called her that.
Her mother preferred Jess. Eric had the dubious distinc-
tion of being the only one to call her Jessica—even in the
heat of intimacy. But to think of such moments only invited a wealth of pain and bitterness, and Jess had had
enough of both in that one, disbelieving moment when she
had seen Eric and . . . But no. No!

She forced her attention back to Lucas, and met the old
man's snapping blue gaze. He wasn't much bigger than she,
and with his semidefiant stature, his fierce indignation, it
almost seemed as if he were indeed venting the wrath of
God. But Jess had practically grown up at this man's knee.

At times he was all bluff and bluster, but beneath the some-times gruff exterior, he possessed a heart of gold.

"I don't think there's ever a good time," she said with a flash of wry humor. "But there is time for us to finish this later—" she caught his eye and raised her brows warningly "—after breakfast."

Lucas scowled at her.

It was almost as if Jess could see him digging his heels into the ground. Not to be dissuaded, Jess seized his elbow and turned him toward the house. "Not another word," she said firmly. "I'm not letting you outside again until after we've both eaten. Is that understood, Lucas Palmer?"

"Never thought I'd see the day, Jessie, but you've turned into a bossy little thing, haven't you? You stayed a mite too long with your cousin Maggie this winter. I think some of her sassiness has rubbed off on you."

His disgusted look didn't fool her in the least. Jess hid a grin. Lucas was right. Even as a child, Maggie had never been one to hold back, and age certainly hadn't mellowed her. Her cousin was outspoken and feisty, particularly in Jess's eyes, since she herself had always been on the shy side. And like Lucas, there were no half measures for a woman like Maggie. All that she was, all that she believed in, Maggie felt with her whole heart and soul.

Jessica's thoughts sifted back through time. Seven years ago, both she and Maggie had been on top of the world. She was the ecstatic, blushing bride of Eric Culver, just discovering what life and love were all about. And Maggie, ever worldly and ever wise, already *knew* what it was about; she had an adoring husband and two lovable, energetic children to prove it.

Now, both women stood alone. Both were struggling, both trying to make a new life for themselves and their children.

For just an instant, the distant spell of days gone by called to her; days filled with carefree laughter and a future that promised more of the same. With the innocence only a child possessed, Jess had never thought she'd see the day when her parents would leave this valley. They were as much a part of it as the old-growth cedars behind the house she'd grown up in, the only true home she had ever known. But now her father was gone, and her mother had moved away. And Lucas...

He was aging, she thought with a pang. Lucas Palmer was aging. The years that had seen her grow from child to young girl to woman had never seemed to affect Lucas. In Jessica's mind, he had always looked the same.

Almost fearfully, her gaze swept over him. Even now, his face appeared more weathered than old. He'd had his thatch of iron-gray hair for as long as she could remember, but it was thinner now, lying flat against his head beneath the faded blue cap he always wore.

When Jess had returned to Amity this past winter, she had somehow expected the same man she left behind. His farm had become too much for him to handle—even he had recognized it. An adjacent landowner had bought up the prime farmland and Lucas had moved to a small house in town.

She remembered the day she had first seen him again. The emptiness she had glimpsed in his eyes, the barrenness of spirit, had shocked her. She had foolishly blinded herself to the changing seasons of life. But with her care and prodding—and from simply feeling needed—Lucas was once more himself. But he insisted on doing so much—*too* much.

"You gonna stand there and gawk all day, Jessie? You're a sight for sore eyes, I'll give ye that, but I got better things to do."

"Like eat?" she asked dryly, pretending to give him a rather thorough once-over. "I did say something about breakfast, didn't I? And you don't look as if another pound or two is going to matter."

Lucas squinted at her from the corner of his eye. "You're the one could use some fattening up."

Jess chuckled. "Why? So I'll look like Betty Mead?"

His eyes lit up. "Now, there's a thought."

How Jess stopped her jaw from dropping open, she was never sure. Betty Mead had been a schoolteacher at the local elementary school for over thirty years. She'd retired several years ago and done a little traveling, but this winter she'd taken a job as a part-time office clerk at the garden-and-farm supply store in town. Betty was in her fifties and a handsome woman for her age.

Jess's mother had often teased Lucas that the woman who could put up with him was probably extinct. Whatever the reason, Lucas had never married.

Once, when they were in the store to pick up some tools, Jess had asked Lucas, tongue in cheek, who could be a better match than the town's oldest bachelor and the town's oldest spinster? At the time, Lucas had stalked off, blustering and turning so red and purple she'd thought he'd lost his sense of humor. But it occurred to her now that it might have been for another reason entirely. Now there was a thought.... Maybe a bit of matchmaking was in order.

Together they mounted the steps and went inside. Jess's house was much the same as many others in these rolling hills. It was an unremarkable two-story country home, perhaps thirty years old. The exterior needed a few minor repairs, but the inside was in blessedly good shape. The previous owners had replaced the floor coverings throughout and added a half bath and laundry room off the kitchen. But Jess groaned every time she walked into the L-shaped living and dining room. The walls were painted a dark, depressing shade of green. And she winced every morning when she opened her eyes. Her bedroom was an audacious shade of purple.

Besides Nathan's bedroom, the huge country kitchen was the only part of the house Jess had managed to put in order. It was sunny and airy, with dainty yellow-and-white muslin curtains at the windows that added to the overall cheeriness of the room.

Lucas set the table while Jess quickly stirred up a batch of buttermilk pancakes. When the two of them sat down to eat, Jess hid a smile as he piled four pancakes on his plate, then smothered them with butter and thick, warm syrup. Another four followed in short order. During the time she was married to Eric, she'd seldom had occasion to cook for either of them; he had preferred his housekeeper's cooking to hers. Jess wasn't ashamed to admit that Lucas's appreciation for her simple efforts, whether it was spoken or unspoken, filled her with pleasure.

While they ate, Jess pondered her dilemma. These last few weeks, it had become increasingly clear that she was going to need more help if her business was to get off the ground. What little she and Lucas were able to do simply wasn't enough. She really needed someone full-time, five days a week, for at least a month, maybe two.

She stole a quick glance at the calendar. Today was Friday. As soon as she had a chance, she would call the employment office in McMinnville to see if they could place someone with her. If that didn't work out, she'd simply have to run an ad in the weekly newspaper.

But how was she going to break the news to Lucas?

She had just opened her mouth to ease into the subject when a thin wail sounded from the room at the top of the stairs. Babies, Jess decided wryly, were as unpredictable as life itself.

She glanced across at Lucas, her eyes still reflecting her surprise. "Oh-oh, Nathan's awake already." She started to scoot her chair away from the table, then stopped, hands down on the table. "You think if I let him cry a few minutes, he'll go back to sleep?"

Lucas hooted with laughter. "You're askin' the wrong person, Jessie. You're the only baby I've ever been around, and look how long ago that was. Besides, I thought you said Nathan would sleep another two hours."

The few minutes she'd planned to wait lasted about ten seconds. Jess jumped up from the table the moment Nathan's cry became more insistent. "I'll have you know I'm not yet thirty," she announced primly, then wrinkled her nose at him. "And this just goes to show how much *I* know about babies."

But she was learning. Oh, yes, she was definitely learning, and it was one of the most profound pleasures of her life. Her step light, she hurried up the stairs. Nathan's screams had reached a feverish pitch by the time she reached the nursery. His hands were balled into tiny fists, and he drew his legs up under his tummy as he gave another hearty wail.

She strode gracefully across the room. As she reached for her son, a sensation that was almost painfully sweet rushed through her. Jess had wanted her baby; she loved and adored him beyond anything she had ever known in her life. But seeing him for the first time, knowing that he was hers, that he was a part of her, had touched something inside Jess that made her want to pinch herself to see if such bliss was real or imagined. When she held her son in her arms, it was as if the nightmare of the past year had never happened.

The baby's crying lessened as soon as she lifted him from the crib. After changing his diaper, she snapped his one-piece sleeper back in place and slid her hands under his small body. Nathan screwed up his face and began to fret once more.

Jess lifted him to her shoulder, patting his back gently. "What is it, love?" she crooned softly to him, smoothing the soft fluff of midnight down that covered his scalp. "Did you get lonely up here, all by yourself—"

The baby burped, a surprisingly loud and lusty sound to come from such a tiny package.

Jess was still smiling as she made her way back to the kitchen.

Lucas was carrying their breakfast dishes to the sink. He turned on the faucet, then held a sticky plate under the warm rush of water. "What gives, Jessie?" he chided over his shoulder. "I heard you torturing that young man all the way down here."

"'What gives,'" Jess chuckled, shifting the baby to the curve of her arm, "is gas."

"Gas!" The old man's booming laughter filled the kitchen. "Now that's something I know a thing or two about." He turned and started to step back to the table, then paused to wave a callused brown finger under the baby's nose. Nathan's tiny brows straightened in a frown as he attempted to focus. Lucas ran the tip of his finger down the baby's button nose; Nathan's mouth immediately opened.

"Guess what this little man's after," he said with a chuckle. "I don't expect he woke up just because of a little gas, after all."

Still holding the baby in the crook of her arm, Jess carried the cups to the sink. "But he can't be hungry already," she protested. "I just fed him at six o'clock, and it's not even eight yet. I know that all a baby is supposed to do is eat and sleep, but don't you think—"

"That's more your department than mine," Lucas said cheerfully. "And you can't say Nathan doesn't have his priorities straight.'' He took the cups from her and dropped them into the sinkful of sudsy water. ''You just go in the other room and take care of that little guy. I'll finish these dishes and then go outside and get started.''

Jess sighed. ''But I should be out there with you.''

''No, Jessie,'' he said, and there was a trace of stubbornness in his tone. ''You're right where you belong, with that little man of yours.'' Lucas glanced back to find her looking at him helplessly.

He turned back to his soapy task, all the while fuming silently. It wasn't right that Jess should look so torn in two. It wasn't right that she should be so worried, and it wasn't right that she couldn't spend long, idle days with her son.

And it wasn't right that she was so alone. She needed a man behind her—a man who loved and needed her the way she needed to be loved; not an old, decrepit man who did what he could, and hoped it was enough, even while he knew damned well it wasn't.

Lucas sensed her hesitation. He heard the slight rustle of her clothing as she rose. He glanced back to see her hovering near the table, the baby over her shoulder.

''Jessie.'' He cleared his throat awkwardly.

''Yes?'' He still found it hard to believe that his Jessie, the Jessie he'd loved as much as his own daughter, had grown into the sweet, lovely creature behind him. Silently he cursed Eric Culver, the man who had put such shadows inside her. He shifted his feet, again confining his attention to carefully rinsing the suds from the plate he held in his hand.

''Jessie, I . . . you know I've never been much for words, but I . . . I'm glad you decided to come home and settle.''

Jess stared at him. In the instant before he turned his head aside, she could have sworn there was a sheen of moistness in his faded blue eyes. But more than anything, it was the rustiness in his voice that gave him away.

Hearing it made Jess fight a sudden rush of tears. Her throat tight, she walked across to him and gently kissed his lined cheek. "So am I," she murmured unsteadily. "So am I."

Five minutes later, Jess sat in the rocking chair in the living room. Nathan nursed contentedly at her breast. From her place near the window, she saw Lucas leave the house and head toward the barn.

He stopped for a second to pull off his hat and wipe his forehead. The brisk early-April breeze tossed his iron-gray locks in a wild, haphazard tempo that made Jess want to smile. If it weren't for the slight catch in his hip, he might have seemed twenty years younger.

The affectionate smile on her face disappeared. This time Jess wasn't fooling herself. Lucas was no longer a spry young man of thirty, and it was time he realized it. He wouldn't be pleased when he found out she intended to hire another pair of hands. Jess knew that it was up to her to let him down as gently as possible.

Coming home so beaten and disillusioned herself, then finding Lucas much the same way, had almost been more than she could bear. But Jess had found a hidden strength she didn't know she possessed, and it was that strength which led her to believe that brighter tomorrows were just ahead.

Lucas's words drifted into her mind once more. *I'm glad you're home....*

She'd had such hopes and dreams when she married Eric. Someday they would come back here, make this sleepy little Oregon town their summer home, a place to go to get away from his pressured life. She'd always known that she'd come back, if only for a while. She'd just never dreamed it would happen the way it had.

But that no longer mattered. She was back where she belonged, and she was here to stay. She glanced out once more at the brilliant blue bowl of sky high overhead, and a much-welcomed sense of peace stole over her. She was home, home in this lush, fertile valley; and that alone would heal her as nothing else could.

CHAPTER THREE

THE FLOURISHING GREEN landscape was the first thing that struck Brody about Oregon. Never before had he seen such richness of color. It lay in every direction: in the huge, towering evergreens that crowded the side of the road, the lush grassland that dipped and curved into fir-covered rolling hills, the miles and miles of virgin timberland he'd glimpsed on his way north.

He made good time on the twelve-hour drive from San Francisco, though he hadn't gotten started until noon Sunday. Ordinarily he wouldn't have given a second thought to pulling off the road and snatching a few winks, but as long as Eric Culver was footing the bill, he decided he might as well be comfortable. He spent the night at a motel in Northern California and pulled into Amity early Monday afternoon.

Nor had Culver given him a bum steer when it came to locating his ex-wife. He'd called an old friend of Murphy's who was still with the San Francisco Police Department and asked him to run a motor vehicle registration check in Nevada, where Jessica's mother lived. Pete had come up empty on that one, so Brody asked him to send a Teletype to Oregon and bingo!—he hit the jackpot. There was a Volvo station wagon registered to a Jessica Culver. Unfortunately there wasn't an address listed in the return Teletype. That was no problem, though; if necessary, he could walk into any Motor Vehicles office in the state, and for a small fee, find out the address to which the car was registered.

It was so incredibly easy that Brody wondered if Culver had known where to find her all along. The thought made him just a little uneasy.

He hoped his journey might end in Medford, just across the state line. Culver had told him that Jessica had a cousin who ran a vacation and hunting lodge near there. Early that morning, Brody called the lodge and asked for Jessica. The voice of what he suspected was a young girl told him that Jessica had moved back "home" a couple of months ago. Feeling rather smug, Brody hung up the phone, got back into his Firebird and resumed his journey.

His car needed gas when he finally arrived in Amity. While the attendant filled up the tank, Brody idly asked if the man knew where Jessica Culver lived.

To his surprise, the man turned and pointed in the opposite direction. "It's the old Thompson place," he told Brody. "You go back up the highway there about half a mile. It's set back from the road a ways, but if you watch for the filbert orchard on your left, you can't miss it. It's the first house after that. Nice place, too. Hear she's starting herself a nursery."

Brody blinked. He really hadn't expected much of a response, but after hearing the man's ready answer, he was almost surprised the man hadn't offered to drive him there himself. But what in the hell were filberts?

He managed to find her place with no trouble at all and parked at the edge of what he guessed must be the filbert orchard. Taking advantage of the shelter the small trees offered, he walked in the direction of Jessica's house.

It was a tall, two-story house with clapboard siding and a wide veranda at the front. A tan Volvo station wagon was parked in the drive. Behind it was the oldest, most beat-up pickup truck Brody had ever seen in his life. Between the dirt and the rust, he couldn't tell what color it was.

An odd smile curled his lips. He tugged at a loose branch blocking his vision and found it already severed from the limb. Even as he watched, a man walked around the side of the barn toward the pickup. It was impossible to guess his age at this distance, but when the man lifted his cap to run his hand over his forehead, Brody spied a flash of gun-metal gray.

His gaze narrowed. If this guy was as old as Brody suspected he was . . . Eric Culver's snide voice drifted through his mind once more. *My lovely ex-wife is a woman with an extremely healthy interest in the opposite sex . . . especially older men.* Surely *he* wasn't Jessica's lover!

A woman came into view as well. It was Jessica. She and the man appeared to be engaged in a rather engrossing conversation. The man shook his head occasionally, while Jessica stood with her hand on his arm and then his shoulder. She finally bent forward slightly. Brody would have sworn she kissed the old man.

He thought of his Nikon with the zoom lens tucked away in the trunk of his car. But it was too late. Brody watched as the old man got into the rusty pickup and drove away.

Slowly he walked back to his car, considering what he had just witnessed. Like a pebble in his shoe, he had the feeling that even if he'd wanted, he couldn't ignore the image of Jessica Culver with that old man.

His lips curled. *Smitten.* Why the word entered his mind so easily, Brody was never sure. But even while a part of him recoiled, he could see how a man might become totally smitten by a woman like Jessica Culver. Distant as he was, her slender gracefulness hadn't escaped his attention.

A loud crack intruded on his consciousness. Brody realized his fingers had snapped the slim young branch still in his hands. He was aware of a slow, simmering feeling burning inside him. For the life of him, he didn't know why. Because Jessica Culver was like so many others he'd seen in his lifetime—a user? What she did with her life was none of his business, or who she did it with, for that matter.

Nor was he angry because Eric Culver had been duped. With the fee Culver had offered, Brody knew better than to believe Culver's ex-wife had milked him dry. He hadn't batted an eyelash when he'd named a figure that equaled Brody's modest profit over the past year.

Yet for the first time, Brody admitted to being more than mildly curious as to why Jessica hadn't gone back to her mother. Just as he'd told Culver, it was a rather typical scenario when a wife found herself on her own after a divorce, with no immediate family nearby. But then, Jessica wasn't a wife wronged or a woman scorned. Or was she?

Nor had she elected to remain with her cousin in Medford. Because there was a man waiting for her here in Amity? Once again, Brody's stomach knotted at the thought. Was Culver right? Had there been a man in Jessica's life even before she'd divorced Eric—the man he had just seen? No. It couldn't be.

Brody suddenly found it odd that he was so willing to give the benefit of the doubt to Jessica, a woman he didn't even know. Very odd.

WHEN BRODY WOKE UP the next morning, he parted the drapes to find a ceiling of low-hanging gray clouds hugging the earth. A faint drizzle misted from the sky. But by the time he stepped outside his motel room an hour later, he was amazed at the change in the weather. The moisture clinging to the hood of his car glistened like a sea of winking diamonds, but the threatening storm-clouds had been buffeted to the east by a strong wind. In its place was a glorious canvas of clear blue sky, but there was still a hint of rain in the air and a sharp bite that made him grab his jacket.

He'd checked into a motel north of Amity, closer to McMinnville. The last thing he wanted was to arouse any suspicion, and after what the gas station attendant had said, he decided Amity was the kind of place where everybody knew everybody else's business.

But he intended to ask a few questions, keep an eye on Jessica and find out if there really was anything to Culver's theory that Jess had left him for another man. Jess. His shortened version of her name caught him by surprise. Then he realized he'd already begun calling her by her first name in his mind, and he wondered at it.

The contemptuous little laugh he gave was directed at himself. No one would have called Brody Alexander a soft touch, but it seemed that Jessica Culver had gotten under his skin already. But then, why worry? There was really no reason for their paths to cross. He was here to do a job, no more, no less. On that note, Brody opened the car door and slid inside.

His attention wandered to the view outside the window. Topping a slight hill, he found himself admiring the foothills, swept along like a huge wave against the western horizon. When he passed again through Amity's sleepy main street, he decided it looked much as it might have a hundred years ago, during horse-and-buggy days.

He'd had coffee and a roll at the restaurant adjacent to his motel, so he headed straight on to Jessica's. Again he stopped his car at the edge of the road near the filbert grove and weaved his way through the gnarled orchard. He'd just gotten comfortable, his back perched against a narrow tree trunk when he saw Jessica emerge from the house. There was a tiny blanket-wrapped bundle in her arms, which she stowed in the passenger seat of the car before climbing in on the other side. She backed the car out, then drove down the highway.

The rusty old pickup wasn't around today. Brody waited a full five minutes, then picked himself up and dusted off his jeans. Quick, purposeful strides ate up the uneven terrain to her house.

Hands on his hips, he paused to survey his surroundings. A huge oak tree towered near the front porch, its branches spreading onto the rooftop. On the other side of the drive, there was a small grove of what he guessed was some kind of fruit tree. It was a pretty sight, the trees filled with delicate white blossoms that lent the two-story house and grounds a quality of gentility.

He suddenly remembered what the gas station attendant yesterday had mentioned—that Jessica was starting a nursery. In the far corner of the property, Brody spotted row after row of tiny evergreens. Walking around the monstrous barn, he paused near the far end. The field that stretched before him had obviously gone untended for some time. Unlike the dark, freshly turned tracts he had glimpsed so often in the past day, the ground looked as hard as clay, cluttered by patchwork tufts of grassy weeds.

Brody wondered briefly if Jessica really knew what she was doing. But maybe she and the old man had decided to go into partnership together—he provided the know-how and she the money. Convenient for everyone but Eric Culver. Not that it looked as if Jessica were living high off the hog. The house and barn certainly looked sturdy and structurally sound, but there were spots where the paint was cracked and peeling. Both could use at least a touch-up job.

Brody suddenly felt as if an invisible hand were squeezing his heart. Murphy would have loved this place, he realized, battling a sense of helplessness. The retirement Murphy had dreamed of was only a means to an end. He'd planned to sink every dime he had into a piece of land, nurture it and watch it grow, ripe with the fruit of his work and determination. Brody's gaze swept the area once more, penetrating and intense. It was almost as if he were searching for something.

He found it halfway between the house and the edge of the orchard—a trellis, perhaps ten feet long.

His feet carried him those few steps before he realized it. His eyes bleak, he reached out to touch the woody vines that clung to the wire mesh. In all likelihood they were table grapes, not wine grapes, but Brody found himself wondering what mysterious god of fate had chosen to bring him here. The rare, fanciful thought might have made him laugh if it weren't for the feeling twisting him inside out. Memories of Murphy were the last thing he'd expected to find here. In the end, Murphy's dreams were just that—useless, wasted dreams.

But those dreams had given comfort to the lonely, empty reality of Murphy's life. And strangely enough, it didn't stop Brody from wishing he could achieve that same dream. Not just for himself—for the cynical, uncaring side of himself he sometimes hated but couldn't deny—but for Murphy. Money might be the root of all evil, but it was useful. Especially now, when it could give him at least a fighting chance to drag himself upward. Someday, he and Murphy had promised each other . . . Someday.

That someday was now, and it was one more reason to seize the opportunity Eric Culver had given him. Maybe it was time to start fighting for those dreams.

A sound snatched him back from his reverie. Behind him, a car door slammed. Brody turned and found himself standing not ten feet away from Jessica Culver.

JESSICA'S MIND WAS FULL as she drove back from the market in town. When she'd called the employment office in McMinnville on Friday, she hadn't been terribly encouraged by the conversation. There was usually no shortage of seasonal labor available. It usually picked up drastically in June, but this was only the first week in April. The man she had spoken with, Mr. Williams, had told her that most of the men they were trying to place at present were skilled workers or at least interested in acquiring a viable skill. He would try to locate someone who might be interested in her job, but he couldn't promise anything.

Mr. Williams had gotten back to her late yesterday afternoon and told her not to get her hopes up. Everyone he'd called so far had given him a flat "Not interested."

But then she had an unexpected surprise. He'd called this morning and said he'd finally located someone at least willing to be interviewed.

Jess was desperate. She had to find someone. She didn't know how to make digging around in the dirt sound exciting or interesting to someone who didn't possess the blood of a farmer or a nurseryman, but she would do it somehow.

Maybe then she could manage to get to the numerous odds and ends outside that needed to be taken care of. One of these days, she would have to borrow Lucas's old push mower and mow the lawn. The house, the fence and the barn needed to be painted. The garden needed to be cleared and the floorboards of the front porch needed to be replaced, she reminded herself for the hundredth time. She rounded a curve and spotted her house, and in spite of the list she had just recited to herself, she experienced a thrilling pride in the knowledge that it was hers . . . and that this was only the beginning.

She had just turned into the lane that led to her house when she noticed him. Her heart lurched. Her fingers tightened on the steering wheel as she glimpsed the figure of a man standing in the yard. For just an instant all her mind was able to register was that he was tall, blond.

Eric!

You'll regret leaving me, Jessica. I'll make you sorrier than you ever dreamed . . . and I'll get even with you. Somehow, someday, I'll get even with you for ruining me. . . .

The car slowed almost to a halt. Her eyes closed. *God, no!* her mind screamed. *It can't be him! Please, it can't be Eric!*

It wasn't. She could see that for herself, now that she was closer, and she suddenly recalled the reason she'd been so anxious to hurry through her shopping. This must be the man Mr. Williams had promised to send out at eleven sharp this morning. Lord, and she'd almost missed him!

She drove ahead and stopped the car in its usual spot and jumped out. "Hi," she called out. "I'm Jessica Culver. Sorry I'm late."

Late? Brody, thinking he'd been caught virtually red-handed, suddenly began to experience an entirely different sensation. Surely she wasn't *expecting* him.

Jess's eyes ran quickly over him as he turned. On close inspection there was certainly no mistaking this man for Eric. His hair was darker, tawnier than Eric's pale gold, and shaggier. The wide shoulders, covered by a scarred leather bomber jacket, could have been achieved by Eric only through padding. And Jess knew that the always fastidious Eric wouldn't have been caught dead in the worn, faded jeans that clung almost lovingly to this man's leanly muscled thighs.

Jess glanced around. "Where are you parked?" she asked curiously.

"I . . ." For once in his life, Brody found himself floundering. She seemed almost friendly. He didn't understand it. He didn't understand it at all. "I—I'm parked by the . . . the filbert orchard." Mastering the art of speech was almost impossible.

She sighed. "Couldn't find the address, right? I'm sorry. The house numbers were so rusted I took them down, and I'm afraid I don't have new ones yet." She was on the verge of saying more when she suddenly heard Nathan crying. The trip home had lulled him to sleep, but now he seemed to have finally noticed the car had stopped.

Jess darted over to the car. Brody's eyes followed her, his mind still reeling from trying to make sense of Jessica's reaction. If he didn't know better, he'd think she knew him.

He watched as she untethered the car seat. "I hope I haven't kept you waiting long," she said over her shoulder. "But I'm really glad you're here. I was beginning to think I wouldn't find anyone until Mr. Williams called this morning to tell me you'd be by at eleven."

Mr. Williams? Who the hell was Mr. Williams?

"I hope this job is one you're interested in. I'm really desperate to find someone." She straightened, pulling a squalling infant to her shoulder.

All at once it clicked in Brody's mind. The nursery. She thought he was here about a job! He thought of his binoculars and thanked God he hadn't looped them around his neck as he often did.

She had clearly mistaken him for someone else, but Brody wasn't about to enlighten her. This was a heaven-sent opportunity. Maybe his luck had begun to change, after all.

Holding the squirming, fretful child was a juggling act in itself. He saw the despairing glance she flashed at the back seat of the station wagon as she started to reach for her purse while trying to keep the infant's head covered by the blanket. Following the direction of her gaze, he noticed two grocery sacks resting on the floor behind the front seat. He was quick to seize the moment.

"I'll get those," he told her. Silently he scoffed at himself, wondering a little at his actions. Brody Alexander, white knight and rescuer of damsels in distress? It didn't quite fit the image he'd carved out for himself over the years.

A bag in each arm, Brody followed her into the house.

"Thanks." Jess's voice was breathless as she watched him deposit the bags on the counter. "I'm sorry things are so hectic around here, but I'm afraid I still haven't adjusted to life with a newborn. If you'll just give me a minute to find Nathan's infant seat, I'll be right back."

She disappeared through an arched doorway. Brody's keen gaze followed her for a second, then he turned his attention to the room. The kitchen he was standing in was large and sunny, its cozy, homey atmosphere undeniable. He was reminded of Culver's cold and sterile office in Oakland.

Jessica hurried through the doorway once more, the whimpering baby over her shoulder, gaily patterned infant seat in hand, a fleecy white blanket looped over her elbow.

Brody had the strangest urge to try to wipe that harried expression from her face.

She plopped the seat in the middle of the table and proceeded to tuck the blanket into it. Brody leaned against the counter, oddly content to watch her.

She was far lovelier than he'd ever imagined. The photos Culver had provided didn't do her justice at all. Her body was slender to the point of thinness, with the exception of full, rounded breasts that kindled an extremely healthy male interest. Though she was simply dressed in jeans and a shell-knit sweater, she radiated more than a hint of earthy sensuality. The smooth, polished veneer of sophistication she had acquired during her marriage to Culver might never have existed.

She finished by easing a pacifier into the baby's mouth, whispering softly to see if he would accept it. "I hate this as much as you, Nathan, but please, try it one more time."

It was obvious that motherhood was a totally new experience to her. Brody was tempted to laugh, until his eyes drifted to the baby. The fuzz covering his head was dark like Jessica's, his eyes a deep, murky blue. Whether or not this was Eric Culver's child was probably something only the mother knew.

The pacifier was vehemently rejected but Jessica tried again. This time the baby's tiny eyebrows drew together in a puzzled frown at this new taste, but he began to suck tentatively.

Jessica gave a heartfelt sigh of relief. Nathan had been such an angel these past few weeks, nursing and falling immediately back to sleep. But there had been a few times, like now, when he wasn't at all pleased about having his normal routine interrupted.

She turned her attention to the man patiently waiting behind her. He was lounging against the counter, arms crossed over his chest, long legs stretched out before him. Her gaze bounced up to his, and she formed a fleeting impression in her mind. In spite of the relaxed stance, he seemed all tough, hard male; a little like a diamond in the rough. His skin was like smooth leather pulled over sharply defined cheekbones. The slight cleft in his chin softened an otherwise strong jawline, but the thin, carved line of his mouth was both firm and sensuous. He was good-looking, yes. But it wasn't the elegant, suave sort of handsomeness that Eric possessed, she thought, wincing inwardly. The man before her was very much a man's man.

But that hard mouth was curved in a faint smile now. "How old is your baby?"

Her hand moved lingeringly to the soft downy head. There was no denying the love she felt for her son. "A month next week," she said proudly.

"A boy?"

She nodded. "Nathan." Nathan James, she almost added, but didn't. It had just occurred to her that she hadn't yet learned who this man was.

She raised her head and glanced at him. "I don't think I caught your name yet."

Her clear blue eyes stared straight into his, and Brody thought they were the most beautiful eyes he'd ever seen.

Her hair was longer now than it had been last summer. He remembered that from the clipping at Stanford. It was loose and free, skimming her shoulders every time she moved her head. He also remembered her haunted expression that day. That, too, was gone, but the reasons behind it were not forgotten. Brody knew it instinctively. It showed in the faint lines etched in her forehead, the pale shadows beneath her eyes. Yet in some way he couldn't quite define, she still looked as sweet-faced and innocent as she had when she'd married Eric Culver.

All this was noted, considered and stored in the fraction of a second before he spoke. "My name is Brody. Brody Alexander." He let another smile curve his lips. "I lived in Northern California until about a month ago."

She started slightly, but recovered so quickly Brody almost thought he'd imagined the reaction. But the hand that had been idly caressing the baby's head froze for a moment before resuming its stroking. It was the only outward sign that his words might have bothered her.

"So you're new to this area?" Her voice was smooth and even.

It was Brody's turn to nod. "I'm between jobs," he went on boldly, "or I wouldn't be here. I came up to visit an old service buddy of mine in McMinnville, but I didn't know until I got here that he'd moved. There's nothing tying me down in San Francisco, and God only knows this is a change of pace from California, so I decided I might as well stick around and look for a job." Brody held his breath and waited. He'd practically been caught in the act once already. If it happened again...

The pacifier slipped from the baby's mouth. He started to draw an indignant breath but Jess popped it back into his mouth just in time.

"So you're staying in McMinnville?"

He nodded. "At a motel there—the Golden Eagle."

She hesitated briefly. "Are you looking for any kind of job in particular?"

Damn, but a force from above should be striking him dead! Brody took a deep breath and looked her straight in the eye. "I've been here for almost three weeks already and things are looking pretty thin. Frankly, I'm not in a position where I can afford to be choosy."

Nor, Jess realized, was she. She had the vague sensation that Brody Alexander was not a typical drifter, but she also liked his directness. His statement that he was from California had shaken her momentarily, but that was probably because she'd been so nervous again about Eric. No, she decided, she and Brody Alexander certainly seemed in need of each other.

She relaxed and smiled at him. "Then maybe I should tell you a little about this job. It's nothing to write home about, believe me. In fact, it's going to involve a fair amount of physical labor."

He wasn't at all perturbed. "I understand you're starting a nursery."

"Maybe. Then again, maybe not, if I don't get down to business soon. I just bought this house and acreage a little over a month ago, and there's so much to do!" She threw up her hands, but her face had taken on an animated glow.

"What kind of nursery are you planning?"

"I'll be raising mostly ornamental plants—flowering shrubs, rhododendrons, azaleas, that kind of thing. This should be an ideal location since I'm planning to whole-sale. I should be able to sell to retail outlets in Portland and Salem." She rose and gestured toward the window over the sink. "I just finished planting Christmas trees before Nathan was born. Lucas told me I was crazy for wanting to wait five years until I'm able to harvest them, but a nursery just isn't a nursery without Christmas trees, especially in Oregon—"

She broke off when she saw his puzzled frown. "Lucas is your husband?" he asked. His eyes met hers. He was careful to conceal all expression from his face and voice.

A faint shadow crossed her face. She seemed suddenly nervous. "No." She cleared her throat. "Actually, I don't have a husband.... I mean, I no longer have a husband. I'm divorced. And Lucas is a very old, dear friend of mine who has made my problems his own." She sighed. "His intentions are good and he has sixty-plus years of knowledge and experience behind him, but I'm afraid he can't handle it all, much as he'd like to."

Brody surveyed her closely, without appearing to do so at all. Indeed, the urge to appreciate the way the sunlight weaved through her dark hair was tempting, but he forced himself to concentrate on what she was saying. Lucas must be the old man he'd seen yesterday. Was he more than "an old, dear friend"? A part of him scoffed at the thought, but he intended to find out.

"So that's why you're looking for someone to hire?" He spoke softly. "To take the load off your friend?"

Her expression sobered. "Lucas still thinks of himself as thirty years younger. He's always telling me he isn't ready for the rocking chair yet. And he isn't," she hastened to add. "But he needs to ease up a little, and I want to make sure he doesn't overdo it. But I need to have a greenhouse built, and a shade house and a storage shed put up. I've got cuttings to be planted, but the frames for the seedling beds need to be put together first, and there's land that needs to be worked up when the stock is ready to be transplanted. What I need is a little male muscle and brawn, and I'm afraid that's something a new mother doesn't have."

And that, Brody thought grimly, was as it should be. He had the impression that Jessica had been doing far too much already.

"I want to make this work," she added. She seemed to be speaking more to herself than to him. "I *will* make it work."

Brody said nothing. Culver had painted Jessica as a scheming shrew, and whether he believed it or not, when he'd come here, he'd half expected her to be living with the man she'd jilted Culver for. He was still a little surprised that she owned this place, and that she was so determined, as well.

"I'm not a carpenter," he said slowly. "And I've never worked at a nursery or even a farm in my life."

Jess waved a hand. "That's not a problem," she told him before he could say more. "Lucas farmed for years and years before he retired last year. Most winters he spent doing odd jobs for people around here, doing exactly the kind of thing I need done. I'm sure he can teach you everything you need to know." She appeared to hesitate. "There's only one thing. Once I really get my feet off the ground, I should be able to handle the day-to-day operations without too much help, since it will be mostly a matter of waiting until the plants are ready to cultivate." Her gaze met his. "I should only need someone full time for a month or so. Two at the most."

She had walked back to her place at the table and stood with her hands on the back of her chair. There was just a hint of a question in her tone. Brody discovered her expression was one of tentative hope. A twinge of guilt stabbed at him but he swallowed the feeling and smiled slightly. "I'm in no hurry to return to California, if that's what you mean. Maybe by the end of that time I will be."

"So the fact that it's short-term doesn't bother you?"

"Not at all." He shrugged, then looked up at her. "Are you offering me the job, Mrs. Culver?"

"It's yours if you want it, yes." Her voice was clear and steady. "I'm willing to pay the wage I discussed with the employment office."

Whatever that was, Brody thought wryly. Her job offer couldn't have worked out better if he'd planned it himself.

He gave her his most disarming smile. "I want it," he said softly.

"Good. It's yours, then." Her eyes strayed to Nathan, who'd lost his pacifier for the third—and last—time. He began to squirm and whimper. Jess reached for him and patted the baby's back, trying to soothe him.

"When do you want me to start?"

"How about tomorrow? Eight o'clock?" She had to raise her voice slightly to be heard.

Brody nodded. "Sounds fine."

Nathan was crying in earnest now; Jess knew he wouldn't be satisfied with anything less than her breast. "Good. I'll see you tomorrow morning, then." She began to edge toward the door. "Do you mind seeing yourself out, Mr. Alexander? Nathan seems to have decided he's waited long enough for his lunch.''

Brody watched as she left the room, then let himself out through the back door. He grinned his satisfaction as he walked down the long lane, hoping his newfound employer wasn't watching. Going to work for Jessica Culver was a damned good way of keeping an eye on her. Maybe some- one upstairs was watching out for him, after all.

He had nearly reached the main road when he saw a car pull over to the shoulder. A man got out.

"Hi,'' the newcomer called tentatively. "Do you know if Jessica Culver lives there?'' He pointed to Jess's house. "I've been driving around for an hour trying to find this address.'' He waved a small piece of paper.

Brody looked the man over carefully. He was short and almost painfully skinny. No muscles. No brawn. How Brody stopped a full-fledged grin from appearing, he was never sure. This was more than good luck; this was an all-out miracle. *Here* was the man Jess had been expecting.

"You're here about the job?'' Brody drew himself up to his full height.

The man stepped back. Eyes wide, he nodded.

"Sorry,'' Brody said mildly. "It's just been filled.''

CHAPTER FOUR

AS LUCK WOULD HAVE IT, Nathan had just finished nursing when Jess heard a knock at the back door. From her spot in the corner of the living room, she'd seen Lucas's pickup rumble past the window. A few seconds later the screen door slammed, and she heard his footsteps march across the kitchen floor.

At least, Jess reflected wryly as she pulled down her sweater, her sense of timing—or maybe her luck—was improving. Lucas hadn't shown up while Brody Alexander was still here. She had the feeling Lucas would have had a few choice words for both of them. It was even possible he might have influenced Brody to turn down the job. But was Brody Alexander the kind of man to back down at the first sign of trouble? Somehow she didn't think so.

A low sigh escaped her lips. As it was, Lucas wasn't going to be pleased.

Lucas stopped short in the doorway, his expression sheepish when he spotted Jess with Nathan. "Sorry," he apologized in his usual gruff tone. "I keep forgetting there's a baby in the house."

Jess merely smiled, her gaze immediately drawn to the infant nuzzled against her breast. Nathan blew out a bubbly sigh of contentment, his stomach full, his eyes closed.

Lucas started to pick his way through the clutter of boxes. Jess could almost see him clamp down on his tongue, but his eyes were on Nathan.

"How'd he sleep last night?"

"Oh, he's regular as a clock, all right." Jess's tone was dry. She was tired but she wouldn't admit it. "He got me up at two and six in the morning, almost to the minute."

Lucas frowned and sat down on the corner of the sofa, the only other vacant spot in the room. "Shouldn't he be sleeping all night by now? Maybe you should ask the doctor about it."

He sounded so much like a worried mother hen that Jessica laughed. "Little as I know about babies, I think it's still a little early for that yet. Maggie keeps telling me to take my cues from Nathan. When he's ready for whatever comes next, he'll let me know."

Jess had worried herself sick the first week and a half she was home, in tears and on the phone with Maggie more times than she could remember. Nathan had nursed for only a few minutes at a time before promptly falling back to sleep. She'd been worried that her milk hadn't begun to flow yet or that he wasn't taking enough, and that he would lose what few precious ounces he'd gained. Then those spots had erupted on his tiny bottom and...

Lucas nudged the bill of his cap slightly higher. "What's on the agenda for this afternoon?"

Jess eased the baby up over her shoulder. "I thought maybe you'd run down to the farm store and pick up the lime and the fertilizer I ordered."

"Sounds to me like you're just trying to throw me together with Betty again." Lucas folded his arms across his chest and attempted to fix her with a glare. Unfortunately the twinkle in his eye diluted the effect. Jess was truly beginning to wonder if there was something going on that she didn't know about.

"And you don't seem to be objecting too strenuously." She wrinkled her nose at him.

Lucas didn't deny it as she had half expected him to. "Betty happens to be fifteen years younger than I am."

It was on the tip of Jess's tongue to retort that the age disparity between herself and Eric had been even greater. Instead, she teased him softly. "My, my, you are making progress. You even know how old she is! What else aren't you telling me, Lucas?"

A slow flush crept up the old man's neck. He opened and closed his mouth twice before Jess laughed delightedly. With a look that might have been withering if it weren't for the twinkle in his eye, Lucas yanked his hat farther down his broad forehead. "Guess I'd better get a move on so I can work on those frames this afternoon."

Jess sobered abruptly. "Lucas, I... Before you go, there's just one more thing."

His shaggy brows met in a frown.

"Lucas, about those frames—" she hesitated "—actually, I was thinking maybe you could wait until tomorrow to start on those."

His look was downright suspicious. "What's so special about tomorrow?"

Jess bit her lip. "Remember last week, when we were talking about how much work there is to do yet?"

"Sure do. Which makes me wonder why you're keeping me from it."

A tempest was on its way. Jess could see the warning signs in his face. She took a deep breath and decided to take the bull by its horns. "I've hired someone to help. Someone who'll be able to lend you a hand and take the burden off your shoulders—"

"Is that what this is about, Jessie?" He glared at her. "You hired some fresh-faced youngster who doesn't know one end of a hammer from the other just because he's fifty years younger than I am?"

That made Jess smile, at a time she suspected wasn't particularly wise. "He isn't some fresh-faced youngster," she said softly. "And I have no intention that he replace you, Lucas. You have the know-how. He's just going to provide the manpower." She paused. "But this is my responsibility, and I know how hard you've been pushing yourself because of me. I'd never forgive myself if something happened to you because of my problems."

"So you think this old goat's about to keel over any minute now, eh?"

Jess was beginning to think sheer stubbornness would prevent that from ever happening. "Of course not," she said calmly. "But when was the last time you saw a doctor?"

"Don't need to see a doctor 'cause I ain't sick!"

His response was just what Jess expected. "You sold the farm because it got to be too much for you," she reminded him.

"You'd have sold it too if you'd been up before the sun all your life. A man's got a right to take it easy if he wants to."

Jess couldn't help but note he hadn't denied it. "But you're not taking it easy. And you should go in for an exam at least once a year," she pointed out. "Even I do that, and I'm not sixty-eight years old."

The old man hitched his thumbs into his belt and began to prowl the room. Gently patting the baby's back, Jess could hear Lucas muttering under his breath. She had him on that one, and he knew it. Behind her, he stubbed his toe on a carton. Jess could almost feel his gaze boring into her back.

Finally he halted in front of her. "If I go see a doctor, would that make you feel better?"

Jess swallowed her triumphant smile. "It would. Can I make the appointment for you?"

"Might as well. I know you'll give me no peace until the deed is done." He scowled at her. "I suppose you'll insist on going in with me and holding my hand, too."

Her expression was completely innocent. "Maybe Betty would like to."

Lucas planted his hands on his bony hips. "Now I know for sure you stayed with your cousin Maggie too long," he muttered. "You're just as cheeky as she is." With that, he turned on his heel and stalked from the room.

Jess merely shook her head. The day was turning out better than she had anticipated. Lucas had relented much more easily than she'd expected and—Lord, what a miracle!—she'd talked him into seeing a doctor. It seemed she had scored not one, but two victories. Quite a coup where Lucas Palmer was concerned.

BRODY LET HIMSELF into his motel unit an hour after he'd left Jessica's. He'd stopped for lunch, then headed back to the Golden Eagle. Out of habit, his eyes swept quickly around the room before he stepped inside.

Tossing his keys on the cheap, veneered dresser, he picked up the phone and punched out a number. He sat down on the edge of the bed and waited.

The line was picked up by a sugary sweet voice that made him grimace. "Eric Culver's office."

"I'd like to speak to Mr. Culver, please."

There was a slight hesitation. "Mr. Culver is tied up at the moment. Is there something I can help you with?"

Her air of boredom grated. He should have identified himself, Brody realized. But he wasn't particularly disposed to be nice to Miss Matthews; she was too damned condescending. "That's too bad," he said mildly. "I just thought he might be interested in knowing the whereabouts of his ex-wife."

"Mr. Alexander?" The boredom had all but vanished. "Is that you? You've located her?"

"Yes, yes and yes."

"Just a moment. I'll get Mr. Culver for you."

Eric Culver came on the line a second later. "Alexander? You've found Jessica? Where is she?"

"Right where you figured she'd be. She came back to Amity. Bought herself a house and some land just before the baby was born. She's starting a plant nursery."

"That sounds just like Jessica." Disgust was ripe in his voice. "She was always after me to give up our town house and buy a place outside the city."

"There's more," Brody said slowly. He went on to tell Culver that he'd been hired on by Jessica. He wasn't quite sure of Culver's reaction, but he wasn't about to let Culver tell him how to do his job, either.

The last thing he expected was a low burst of laughter. "That's rich, Alexander. It couldn't have worked out better if I'd planned it myself. Jessica would never dream that I'd have someone practically planted in the garden with her."

The conversation lasted several more minutes. Brody had decided it was best to simply play it by ear. And Culver agreed.

Yet Culver's parting comment was disturbing. "Alexander, I think I'd better warn you . . . Don't let Jessica's looks deceive you. No one knows better than I how sweet and innocent and eager she seems—a clinging vine, in fact. Just remember, it's all an act. She's a charmer, all right. A deadly one."

Brody said nothing. This was the second time Culver had warned him about Jessica. He wished he were convinced of

Culver's motivation. Somehow he had the feeling Culver had his own best interests in mind.

But it wasn't until the connection was broken that Brody realized Culver hadn't asked about the baby even once. True, maybe he wasn't the baby's father. Then again, maybe he was. Culver hadn't even asked if the child was a boy or a girl.

Brody let out his breath slowly, carefully replacing the receiver in the cradle. He was suddenly glad his contact with Culver was a business one only. He didn't think he liked the ex-judge. No, he didn't think he liked him at all.

JESS HAD JUST FINISHED laying Nathan in his crib when she heard the sound of a car door slamming. Thinking it was Lucas on his way out, she waited for the familiar roar of his pickup. Instead, she heard a knock at the back door.

Her eyes widened at whom she saw there. "Why, Betty," she exclaimed. "What brings you all the way out here?" Jess smothered a laugh when she found herself straining to find Lucas over Betty's shoulder.

Betty Mead stepped inside. She was of medium height, and her figure was good but with just the slightest tendency toward plumpness. Her wavy dark hair was styled loosely, with only a few fine threads of gray woven throughout.

"Hello, Jess." The newcomer smiled, the expression in her velvety brown eyes tentative. "I know I should have called first, but I have this afternoon off and I was on my way home. I thought I might as well bring out the supplies you ordered yesterday." Her smile widened. "I also wanted to bring this by." She held out a small, gaily wrapped package decorated with ribbons tied around a bright red rattle.

Jess took it, then leaned forward and impulsively hugged the woman. "Thank you, Betty, but you really didn't have to."

"Oh, but I wanted to. It's not often I have the chance to choose a baby gift." Betty's eyes gleamed. "Why don't you open it?"

Jess stepped back into the kitchen and seated Betty at the table. Then she tore into the package with all the eagerness of a three-year-old at Christmas, finally unrolling a long, narrow swatch of material. For a moment she stared at it in bemusement.

"Why, it's a growth chart," she cried. The chart was fashioned of gaily patterned quilting in the shape of a giraffe. At the top was a loop of twine so that it could be hung on the wall like a banner. "Wherever did you find it?" she asked Betty delightedly. "Not here in town, I'll bet."

Betty smiled, clearly pleased at Jess's reaction. "I made it," she said proudly. "I've seen them in catalogs, and it really wasn't that hard." She frowned suddenly. "You don't have one already, do you?"

Jess shook her head vehemently. "Between my mother and my cousin Maggie, I'm loaded down with sleepers, undershirts and diapers." She pulled a face. "All those practical things. But I don't have anything half as cute as this."

There was a twinge of regret in Betty's voice. "You won't be able to use it till the baby can stand. You don't mind, do you?"

Jess shook her head. "Not at all." She leaned forward and kissed the woman's plump cheek. "I love it, Betty, and I know Nathan will, too. Speaking of Nathan, would you like to see him?"

"I would, but if he's sleeping, I'd hate for you to wake him up.... Maybe I could just take a little peek."

Jess was just as eager to show off her son as Betty was to see him. Apologizing profusely for the confusion in the living room, she led the way to Nathan's room where Betty whispered adoringly over the sleeping child.

"He's so tiny," she exclaimed once they were back in the kitchen.

Jess was in the midst of making a pot of coffee. "He was almost two weeks early," she admitted. "But he weighed in at just under six pounds, so I was able to take him home with me."

When Jess had moved back into town, she'd made no secret of her divorce. Considering her advanced stage of pregnancy, she'd expected a few snide remarks, but thankfully there had been none—at least not to her face. She found herself holding her breath, wondering if Betty might be inclined to ask questions she really wasn't prepared to answer. But the subject turned elsewhere, and both seemed to welcome the chance to chat with another woman.

Nathan was still sleeping when Betty got up to leave half an hour later. "You know," she said with a smile, "I have most afternoons off, so I'd be glad to watch Nathan for you if you've got errands to run. Then maybe I'd get a chance to see him awake."

They were outside by now, and Jess noticed the way Betty's eyes sneaked past her toward the barn. She wondered if perhaps Betty didn't have a hidden motive for baby-sitting— not that she minded. Not only would it give Betty the chance to see Nathan awake, but more than likely, Lucas would be around as well.

Her suspicions were confirmed a few seconds later.

Betty's eyes widened innocently as Lucas ambled from the barn and started toward them. "Oh," she called out. "You're still here, Lucas. I was hoping you would be. Could you help unload these things for Jess?" She hurried around toward the trunk of her car.

Lucas closed the last few steps. "Couldn't very well go anywhere with you parked right behind me, now could I?"

Jess looked from one to the other. Judging from his cheerful tone, he certainly wasn't complaining. And hadn't his step turned just a little livelier at the sight of Betty?

Hiding a smile, Jess turned to go back inside, leaving the pair together behind Betty's car. Somehow she didn't think her matchmaking efforts were going to be necessary, after all.

Her foot on the first wooden step, Jess heard the phone ringing in the kitchen. She sprinted and picked it up just in time.

"I was just about to give up," said the throaty, feminine voice that belonged to her cousin Maggie Howard. "Did I catch you in the middle of feeding Nathan?"

"No." Jess laughed. "It's just been rather busy around here today."

"Is that good or bad?" Maggie inquired cautiously.

Jess smiled into the receiver. "Actually, it's good. There's still so much to be done, and Lucas and I just can't handle it. That's why I hired a man—his name is Brody Alexander—to help Lucas with the odd jobs."

"Migrant workers who come with their families are fine—" Maggie sounded worried "—but if this guy is a transient—"

"Oh, it's nothing like that," she said with a laugh. "He came up from California to see an old army buddy. But his friend had moved, and he decided to stay in the area for a while and see if he could find a job. The best thing is that he doesn't object at all to it being short-term."

There was a long silence. "I don't want to tell you how to run your business," Maggie said finally. "But what do you really know about him?"

Nothing, Jess realized numbly. The word seemed to swing out of nowhere to slap her full in the face. Maggie hired temporary help at the lodge every summer. Her concern made Jess realize just how inexperienced she was. There was suddenly a huge knot in her stomach. Her smile disappeared.

"Not much more than his name," Jess admitted, her tone very low. "Pretty dumb, eh? I didn't even have him fill out an application, although the employment office in McMinnville did send him over."

"Hopefully there won't be any problem, then." Maggie still didn't sound entirely convinced. There was a brief hesitation before she added, "Listen, I don't want to worry you, but I thought you should know that early yesterday morning a man called here for you."

"Who?" Her voice was sharp.

"I'm afraid I don't know." Maggie sighed. "I'd have called you sooner, but I just found out myself. Anna told the caller you weren't here anymore, that you'd moved home. He didn't say who he was or that he'd call back, and he didn't ask her any questions. He just thanked her and hung up."

Jess's mind was racing. Who would have called her at Maggie's? She knew it wasn't her attorney in Sacramento. She had made certain he had her new address and phone number. So who could the caller have been?

Jess knew intuitively what was on Maggie's mind; Maggie wouldn't have bothered to warn her otherwise. A prickly unease trickled down her spine. Could she really deny the same thought was winging through *both* their minds?

Eric.

Maggie sounded agitated. "I'm really sorry, Jess. I'd have let you know earlier, but Anna didn't tell me until she got home from school today. She wasn't home last night, either, and it must have slipped her mind this morning."

Jess could tell from Maggie's disapproving tone that her cousin was still having trouble with her fifteen-year-old daughter. Maggie had mentioned it when she was visiting just after Nathan was born. Anna was cute and pretty, maybe a little on the shy side, especially compared to her mother, but she was a good kid. Whatever problems mother and daughter had, Jess didn't think they would last long. And she didn't want to make things worse for Anna.

"It's probably nothing," she murmured, not wanting either Anna or Maggie to feel guilty. But all at once, a thought occurred to her. Brody had said he was from California. And now the phone call and Eric. Was there a connection? Or was it just coincidence? Still, Brody had been very open about divulging where he was from. Surely that was a point in his favor.

"I wouldn't worry about it if I were you," she told Maggie. Jess wished she felt half as convincing as she sounded.

There was a brief silence. "Jess," Maggie said slowly. "You can tell me this is none of my business if you like, but does Eric know about Nathan?"

"I didn't notify him when he was born, if that's what you mean." Jess's voice had turned uncharacteristically harsh. "Eric made his feelings about my pregnancy very clear. He didn't care one way or another about the baby." She paused. "I doubt it was Eric who phoned, if that's what you think, Maggie." Her laugh was brittle. "Chances are he wouldn't have been half so polite. So don't give it another thought, okay?"

"All right." Maggie agreed reluctantly. "But I'll let you know if anything else comes through. And if it *was* Eric, you can be sure I'll give him a piece of my mind. He's done enough damage as it is."

This time Jess's laugh was genuine. Knowing Maggie's fiery nature and fearlessness, she didn't doubt her cousin's words in the least.

It wasn't until Jess hung up the phone that she realized this was the second time today that the thought of Eric had shaken her composure. Perhaps she was being paranoid—about Brody *and* Eric. Months had passed since her decision to end their marriage. She had come home to start her life over. Wasn't it time she stopped looking over her shoulder for him?

Nevertheless, she had to remind herself that she had nothing Eric wanted. The thought was faintly colored by bitterness; there had never been anything about her that Eric had *ever* really wanted.

She also knew Eric a little too well. He was a man who held a grudge, who did not easily forget a wrong done to him.

It was a sobering thought. And a less than perfect way to end what had been a rather good day.

CHAPTER FIVE

IN THE MORNING LIGHT, with the shades pulled down, Jessica Culver's house looked empty and lonely. Brody cut the car engine and sat for a moment, succumbing to a whimsical curiosity. Somehow it had surprised him that Jess had returned to this part of Oregon. As Eric Culver's wife, surely the world she traveled in had been vastly different from this. Most of the women he knew would have been bored out of their minds in this sleepy little town. Why not Jessica Culver?

There was a cynical twist to his mouth as he pulled the keys from the ignition. He really knew very little about Jessica Culver, he reminded himself. Nothing but what Eric Culver had told him. But after his conversation with Culver yesterday, he realized he'd be wise to harbor a little wariness—where Jess *and* her ex-husband were concerned.

The day promised to be a blustery one. A mass of dark, threatening clouds skidded along the western horizon, swept ahead by a steady north wind. Brody turned up the collar of his jacket as he got out and started up the path toward the house.

Before he'd even raised a hand to knock, Jessica opened the door.

"Hi there. I saw you drive up."

Her voice was the same rich velvet he remembered. She was dressed much as she'd been yesterday—in jeans and a simple cotton sweater. Her dark hair was loose, spraying lightly over her shoulders. Her incredibly blue eyes were framed only by the natural length of her sweeping dark lashes.

His earlier thoughts returned in full force. But whatever else she was, Jess was a damned desirable woman. He wondered how that soft mouth would taste against his.

His own mouth turned up lazily. "I'm early," he said by way of apology.

"That's okay." Jess opened the door wider. "Actually, I'm glad."

"Oh?" Brody stepped into the kitchen. He briefly noted the baby sitting in the infant seat on the counter. He was glad she'd turned aside to dispose of the dish towel in her hand. He wasn't sure she would appreciate his less-than-innocent thoughts.

But even those were wiped from his mind when she turned back to him. She seemed subdued. Tense? Or fearful? His guard went up like the sudden slamming of doors and windows, but he forced himself to wait until she spoke. Brody didn't know what, but something had definitely changed since yesterday.

"I'm glad you came early," she repeated. Her eyes met his, then flitted away. "Because that way I'll have a chance to talk to you alone."

Brody said nothing, but every nerve inside was as tight as a wire.

Jess cleared her throat. "I have a cousin—Maggie Howard—who lives near Medford. She owns a vacation lodge there. I was talking with her yesterday...."

At the mention of her cousin, Brody's heart began to thunder. Christ! Had he been found out already?

"She's had a good deal more experience than I have with hiring procedures—"

"And you've decided to let me go." His statement was flat and abrupt.

Her gaze flew to him. "I . . ." She was flustered and handling this badly, she knew. "No," she added. And then it all came out in a rush. "It's just that Maggie asked me what I knew about you, and I realized I know absolutely nothing about you, or your work history."

"You said it didn't matter that I had no background in carpentry or nursery work," he reminded her.

"It doesn't," she assured him quickly. "But what kind of background do you have?"

She was looking at him quizzically, but there was also a faint wariness in her expression. Brody hadn't really wanted to tell her about his work in the army, since it so closely paralleled his civilian job of private investigator. But he also realized that she couldn't foster any suspicions of him, especially at this early stage.

He made a lightning-quick decision. "Military." He schooled his features into a frown. "I thought I told you that."

"You mentioned you'd come to Oregon to look up an old army buddy."

"I'm sorry," he apologized. "I guess I should have explained. I started out as an MP, did a little military intelligence work in Vietnam and ended up in the CID." And that, he decided wryly, was making a long story short.

"CID," she echoed. "What's that?"

"Criminal Investigations Division. Handling base security and internal investigations."

Jess slowly relaxed. If he was hiding something, surely he wouldn't have been so accommodating. Besides, she sensed he was telling the truth.

She let a faint smile curve her mouth. "That does sound a long way off from being a carpenter." She paused. "But since you're here, maybe I'd better tell you about Lucas."

Brody was only too willing to accept the change in subject. "Lucas," he repeated. "The man I'll be working with." His eyes were once again on her face, his mind on her body. She was tall for a woman, but slender and small-boned. Beneath the fabric of her jeans, there was a very slight rounding of her abdomen; if Brody hadn't known of her recent pregnancy, he'd never have noticed it.

"Yes." She paused, seemingly at a loss for words. Finally she said slowly, "I think I should warn you, Mr. Alexander—"

"Brody," he interrupted. "Call me Brody."

She smiled absently. "Brody, then. And I'm Jess." A slender hand lifted to tuck a stray curl behind her ear. His eyes tracked the movement. "Anyway, I just wanted to warn you that Lucas may seem a little hostile at first."

Brody smiled indulgently. "He thinks you hired me to unseat him?"

Jess hesitated. "In a way," she admitted. "You see, he's had a hard time adjusting to retirement. It's understandable, really. He's sixty-eight years old, and he's worked nearly every day of his life. His help here is beneficial for both of us. I need to get things rolling, and this is just what he needs to feel useful again. But I'm afraid he's rather touchy about his age, and I can't help but worry about him because of it."

She stopped for a moment, then pointed to a plant sitting on the counter. He noticed a tiny pair of cutting shears, a bag of soil and a pot laid out on a newspaper next to it. "You see this?" she asked.

Brody nodded, a little puzzled. The plant looked horrible. Most of the long branches were bare and spindly looking. The soil was littered with tiny yellow needles that had apparently fallen from the shoots.

"It's an asparagus plant," she went on. "They're grown mostly by florists and used in floral arrangements. I found it the other day in the shed. I know it looks half dead now, but all it really needs is a sunny east window, misting every day and plenty of fresh air—they don't like a humid, close environment crowded with other plants."

"A little like Lucas."

"A little," she agreed quietly. "I hope I can revive it, but it needs some tender loving care first. It's like the filbert orchard next door. Ten years ago there wasn't much of a harvest on those trees. But then someone else bought the property, trimmed and sprayed the trees—" She shook her head. "Lucas said the yield last fall was unbelievable. Anyway," she added softly, "I guess what I'm trying to say is that if you could take the load off Lucas without him being aware of it . . ."

Brody's smile deepened. "In other words, it's not done right unless *he* does it."

"I'm afraid so." She sighed. "I know it's a tall order. But I just wanted you to know that if his attitude seems . . ."

"Hostile," he supplied, holding back a grin.

She smiled weakly. "I see you've got the full picture. But please bear in mind that his bark is worse than his bite."

Their eyes met, and Brody didn't think he could have resisted the plea in her eyes even if he'd wanted to. "I'll give it my best shot," he said softly.

Jess was relieved. "That's all I ask."

"I do have a price, though."

Her eyebrows lifted. "Oh?" she inquired cautiously.

"What in the hell are filbert trees?"

He sounded so absolutely confounded that Jess burst out laughing. "I'm sorry," she apologized finally. "You know what hazelnuts are, don't you?"

"Of course," he started to reply indignantly, then blinked. "*That*'s what a filbert is?"

She nodded. "I'd never heard them called hazelnuts until I was in college."

Just then they both heard a noisy engine sputtering up the drive. Seconds later, Lucas Palmer stomped up the back steps. Nathan had begun to fuss, so Jess scooped him up in her arm and hurriedly introduced the two men.

Lucas wasted no time in raking his fierce blue gaze over the taller man facing him. "So you're the wise young cuss thinks he's gonna show me a thing or two about my business, eh?"

Brody was more amused than anything else over the old man's defensiveness. Lucas's face was more worn than old, seamed with lines that only added character. He suspected that was exactly what this man was—quite a character. At least no one could ever accuse Lucas of not saying what was on his mind. Brody respected that. In his line of work, it happened far too infrequently. Lucas Palmer had pride, as well; that, too, he could respect.

He met Lucas's steely regard with a steadiness of his own. "I expect it'll be the other way around. Jess may have told you I'm not a carpenter."

Lucas snorted and sent an I-told-you-so look to Jess. From the sick expression on Jess's face, Brody had the feeling he'd just made a blunder. "But I *am* willing to learn," he added quietly.

That didn't seem to impress Lucas. He jerked his head toward the driveway, which was visible through the window over the table. "That your car, boy?"

Boy? A feeling close to pain grabbed hold of Brody's heart. Murphy was the only one who had ever called him "boy" and gotten away with it. It wasn't until later, when Brody had gone through the slow-going and sometimes volatile struggle to earn the respect he wasn't sure he wanted or deserved, that Murphy had called him "son."

He neither wanted nor understood the feeling that single word aroused, but he managed a terse nod. "It's mine," he said briefly.

"Got one of them noisy, hot-rod engines in it?"

No more than yours, Brody was tempted to retort. He glanced at Jess and met her horrified gaze. "I don't happen to think so," he said mildly. Opening the back door, he stepped aside and let Lucas precede him through it.

"Well, even if it doesn't, just remember there's a baby in the house here, so you better take it easy comin' and goin'."

Behind the two men, Jess closed her eyes. Nathan, as if sensing something in the air, let loose a single, protesting wail.

On the bottom step, Lucas squinted at Brody's car once more, his eyes on the license plate. "You from California?" It seemed more an accusation than a question.

Brody's earlier amusement had returned. He was glad the old man didn't look around to catch his smile. "I am," he answered calmly. "But as I just told Jess, I spent a lot of years in the military, so I've done a lot of traveling. Gets pretty tiresome. Who knows?" He shrugged. "I may decide to stick around here for a while."

"Well, we don't much like strangers around here," the older man grumbled. "Especially Californians. Had a governor here a while back wasn't afraid to say so, either!"

Brody opened his mouth, then thought better of it. Judging from the mutterings going on ahead of him, he'd just stirred up a beehive.

Still patting Nathan's back, Jess closed the back door with a groan. If Brody put up with Lucas throughout the day without quitting on the spot, it would be a miracle.

JESS PEEKED CAUTIOUSLY from under her lashes at the two men sitting on either side of her at the kitchen table. They had just finished lunch, and she was still finding it difficult to believe that warfare hadn't erupted. Lucas hadn't been particularly talkative, but he hadn't been openly antagonistic toward Brody, either. Still, Jess wasn't sure she was ready to count her blessings yet.

Brody and Lucas had been outside all morning, nailing and setting up the frames. Jess was unable to see them from the house, but when she'd called them for lunch, she'd been amazed at how far along they'd come. Clearly they hadn't spent all their time arguing.

The chair scraped against the floor as Lucas pushed back from the table. He cleared his throat. "Think I'll run home after my mail, Jessie. I won't be long."

"Lucas?" Her voice stopped him at the door. "I made that appointment for you to see Dr. Olsen. It's next Tuesday at four in the afternoon. Don't forget to mark your calendar."

Lucas muttered something under his breath. All Jess caught was "interfering woman" before the screen door slammed shut. Jess was sorely tempted to call after him that there was a baby in the house. Picturing his reaction made her chuckle.

She dropped her napkin on her plate and looked up to find Brody's eyes on her face. "There's more than what you told me this morning?" he asked quietly.

The question caught her off guard for a moment, until she realized he was referring to Lucas's appointment with Dr. Olsen. "Oh, no. At least I hope not," she added quickly.

"But it's been years since he's seen a doctor, and I finally got him to agree to go in for an exam."

Brody's gaze followed her slender form as she walked to the sink. Somehow he didn't doubt that statement at all. Jessica Culver was a woman who could probably spin a web around any man she chose without even trying. He recalled the stack of photos sitting in his motel room. As Eric Culver's wife, she had become a sleek, sophisticated woman of the world.

She's a charmer, all right. A deadly one. The words Culver had spoken just yesterday drummed through Brody's mind. *She's also a beautiful one,* Brody added silently, thinking that he much preferred the simple, unadorned woman before him now to the woman in the photos. At least he ran no danger of being caught in the web. His inbred caution was like a second skin now.

Jess placed the dishes on the counter and turned around. "Mr. Alexander, I—"

"Brody." His voice was soft, insistent.

She acknowledged his correction with a slight smile. From the way she smoothed her hands on her jeans, Brody sensed she was rather embarrassed. "I'm glad Lucas didn't scare you off. The way he charged in and out of here this morning, I wasn't sure you'd last the hour. I appreciate you at least giving him a chance."

Not for the first time, Brody realized just how much Lucas reminded him of Murphy. Why, he couldn't have said. Because of his pride and staunch self-reliance? Perhaps. He also sensed that it probably wouldn't be easy to fool a man like Lucas. Murphy had always known when he was lying.

Would Lucas?

It didn't help that Lucas was so protective of Jess. He was going to have to be careful around the old man. Very careful.

But Jess's approval made Brody want to squirm in his seat. God knew he wasn't a saint. He passed the comment off with a shrug. "No harm done. He's not half as bad as you warned me. Besides, I wouldn't be much of a man if I couldn't put up with a little criticism. Speaking of which, I'd better get outside before Lucas comes back."

Jess nodded absently, her mind was on his preceding statement. *I wouldn't be much of a man.* Perhaps it was his choice of words that inspired Jess to look at him in another light—that of woman to man. She almost wished she had forgotten just how ruggedly handsome Brody was. She hadn't, but her mind was slower to accept that realization than her body. Her heart had already set up an erratic rhythm. With an awareness she couldn't deny, she watched as he finished the last of his coffee, then rose with lazy grace.

But along with that sensation came another, entirely different from the first. Despite his military career, Brody Alexander was a drifter. He had no plans, no commitments. There was a wealth of intelligence in his eyes, and a world of experience, too. She suppressed a shiver. The feeling was almost frightening, though she couldn't say why.

His jacket draped carelessly over one shoulder, Brody strode across the room to put his cup in the sink. For a fraction of a second, they were so close his body brushed hers.

He stepped back. "Thanks for the lunch." His eyes, dark and secretive, held hers as he shrugged into his leather jacket.

Jess nodded wordlessly, feeling curiously short of breath. Her heartbeat didn't slow until he was out the door and out of sight.

NATHAN STAYED AWAKE for a surprisingly long time that afternoon, so it was nearly four-thirty when Jess slipped into a coat and headed out behind the barn.

Rounding the corner, she caught a glimpse of Brody bent over his work farther down the field. Lucas was closest. He straightened at the sound of her footsteps. "Checking up on us, Jessie? You're a little late, I'd say."

He sounded so cheerful that Jess nearly stopped in her tracks. Then her eyes slid beyond his shoulder.

"You're finished already?" Her jaw dropped. "I thought you'd be hard at it through tomorrow, at least. Maybe even Friday."

"Well, we're not completely through," he drawled as his grin slowly spread. "But another five minutes and we will be."

"You think so, eh?" Jess teased him lightly. "What about the coverings for the frames? And you're forgetting the rhododendron and azalea cuttings."

Lucas nodded toward Brody. "He can work on that tomorrow. Then I can help you plant the cuttings in the compost."

Brody came up behind them. Judging from his expression, he was a little puzzled at the conversation. "Coverings?" he asked with a frown.

"We're going to hook some wire mesh and burlap to strips of wood to cover the tops of the frames for the rhododendron and azalea stock," Jess explained. "The seedlings are pretty fragile and delicate for a while and can't resist strong sunlight, frost or wind. Or birds and small animals that may decide they'd make a tasty meal," she added.

"So the frames are mainly for protection?"

"That's right. Hopefully they'll resist everything but a hurricane." She chuckled. "The covering we can roll back as needed, exposing the seedlings gradually to normal light.

They'll be transplanted into bigger, plastic pots as they mature."

"So you'll use the frames again and again?"

"That's the idea," she agreed. "I'll just leave them in place. Once I have my greenhouse up, I'll be able to do a lot of the initial sowing inside in the fall or winter and move them to the frames in the spring after they've been transplanted."

Brody glanced around curiously. "How much land do you have?"

"Twenty acres."

"Twenty acres!" His jaw dropped. "That's a hell of a lot of land for one woman to manage."

Jess's eyes flashed and her chin went up. Brody quickly realized his mistake. He suddenly had the feeling that this was one woman who could give him a lesson in independence.

"I know it won't be easy," she said stiffly. "But at least now I feel I'm finally on my way. We should be finished with the cuttings sometime next week. And Lucas and I planted the Christmas trees last month, so—"

"Wait a minute," he said slowly. His eyes swung briefly to the tiny evergreen trees in the distance before returning to her face. "Last month? *You* planted those trees last month?" His gaze fell almost accusingly to her stomach.

Lucas had been quietly listening to the exchange. "That she did," he put in grimly. "It's no wonder Nathan saw fit to come into this world early."

"It had to be done," Jess said quietly.

"And *I* could have done it!"

"And you just expected me to sit around and do nothing? Lucas, I think you know me better than that."

"That I do, Jessie. But I wish you'd let me worry more about getting things done around here."

"You worry too much, as it is," she told him firmly.

It was clear this was a bone of contention between them, but Brody heard them arguing as if from a distance. His jaw tightened. He was still doing a slow burn as he thought of Eric Culver sitting in his plushly furnished office while his ex-wife—nearly nine months pregnant—was out planting trees.

His gaze came back to Jess to find her glaring at Lucas, her stance as militant as the old man's. Somehow Brody expected that she would be the first to give in, but she wasn't.

It was Lucas who dropped his eyes and scuffed the ground with the toes of his boot. "Seems to me," he said gruffly, "we should be celebrating instead of arguing."

"You're right," she said with a sigh. "But at least we're off to a good start. A *very* good start, thanks to Brody." Her lips began to twitch as she laid a hand on Lucas's shoulder. "Not bad for a man who wasn't supposed to know one end of a hammer from the other."

With that, she laughed lightly and spun on her heel. The two men stared after her, one with an expression of utter confusion in his eyes, the other with a grudging admiration.

CHAPTER SIX

THE REMAINDER OF THE WEEK continued with the routine established on Brody's first day of work. He and Lucas worked steadily throughout the morning until Jess called them in for lunch. Then it was back to work again. There was no shortage of chores for Jess, either, and she planted cuttings in the barn whenever she was able to. She had purchased a portable monitor for Nathan's room and carried the receiver with her when she had to be outside during his nap.

Brody expected to be bored out of his mind, and it had been years since he'd done any kind of hard, physical labor. So no one could have been more surprised than Brody that he wasn't itching to set foot back in California. Or was he? He'd wanted a change as much as he needed it. The truth was, when this case was wrapped up he wasn't sure he wanted to go back to being a private investigator.

He liked the feel of the sun on his face, the wind in his hair. He also had the feeling that Lucas would be the perfect person to squeeze for information about Jessica. But he knew it was too soon. Just as he'd suspected, Lucas was sharp, and he didn't dare ask too many questions. Lucas had eased off in his hostility, but Brody knew Lucas had yet to trust him.

So far, Brody's only complaint was that his hands still hadn't gotten used to the sudden abrasive treatment. His palms were a mass of reddened calluses and blisters.

But by the time Saturday rolled around, Brody had learned that Lucas was just as fiercely protective and concerned about Jessica as she was of him. It would have been easy, so easy, to implicate the two of them as being involved in an illicit affair.

So why didn't he?

It was just the kind of sordid situation Culver wanted—an old man like Lucas and a sweet young thing like Jessica. Brody was well aware of that, yet something inside made him balk at the prospect. Because he had no proof? He didn't, he reminded himself. But he also knew instinctively that while Jess and Lucas might love each other, they weren't lovers.

His sudden attack of conscience was frustrating. Brody had lost his mother at ten; his father had had a nightly love affair with a tall amber bottle and scarcely knew his son existed. Brody had grown up tough, and he'd grown up hard. It was a way of life that continued into his military career. There was no softness in him. With the exception of Murphy, no one had ever given him a break. So why was he even tempted to give Jessica Culver a break? Especially with the kind of money he had at stake here. Maybe he wasn't as uncaring or unconventional as he'd thought; this possibility provided little comfort.

Brody also learned that he had accumulated a hundred questions he hadn't expected to have to confront. Who was the father of Jessica's baby? Eric? Or some unknown lover? If the latter, where was her lover now that she no longer had the encumbrance of her husband? Why wasn't he at her side? And what the hell kind of man could walk away from a woman like Jessica? She was beautiful—both captivating and innocently sensual. A man would have to be a eunuch to walk away and not look back.

It was these questions that nagged at Brody most of all.

A hand clapped him on the shoulder, rousing him from his abstraction. He glanced up to find Lucas hovering just above him.

"About done with those frames?"

Brody pounded the last nail into the wood. "That does it." He rose to his feet next to the old man.

Lucas squinted against the sunlight. "You weren't handing me a line this morning when you said you used to tinker around with engines and machinery, were you, boy?"

Brody clamped his jaw shut. At times like this he longed to lash out at Lucas, but something always held him back. Suspecting it was his unwilling comparison of Lucas to Murphy didn't help matters.

"No." His voice was tight. "It was a hobby."

Lucas gave a grunt of approval. "Then come with me."

Brody followed him to the barn. Lucas threw open the wide double doors, sending a halo of sunlight creeping toward the shadows in the rear. The pair stepped inside, and Lucas spread one arm wide to indicate the various equipment that occupied most of the huge barn.

"Where did this pile of junk come from?"

Brody flushed when he realized he'd voiced the thought aloud, but Lucas surprised the hell out of him by giving a rusty chuckle. "That's exactly what I said when I first saw it. Don't let Jessie hear you say it, though."

Brody glanced at him speculatively; there was an underlying seriousness in his tone.

"Jessie inherited all this when she bought the house," he explained. "I expect the previous owners left it because they knew they'd never sell it elsewhere. I doubt it's worth what it would cost to have it moved."

Brody silently agreed. He pointed to the far side of the barn where a rusty, muddied assortment of machinery was spread against the wall. "What are those?"

"Attachments for the tractor. There's the disk, the plow, the rake and the Rototiller." He pointed them out one by one, then quirked a shaggy eyebrow. "Not much good without a tractor, which is why I brought you in here, boy." He nodded toward the hulking shape of an aged tractor in the far corner. "I can't get the damn thing to start. Think you could take a look at the engine?"

Brody didn't dare do anything to alienate Lucas. This could be the "in" he needed. "I don't see why not."

Lucas dropped a key into his hand. "Good. I'll get those frames moved while you have a gander at this monstrosity."

"Monstrosity" was certainly the word for it, Brody decided grimly when Lucas returned half an hour later.

Lucas took one look at his face and shoved back his cap. "Couldn't get it started either, eh?"

Brody shook his head. "Not even a whine."

The man slapped one of the huge wheels. "Any idea what's wrong?"

"It could be anything." Brody frowned. "The entire engine looks shot to me. I'm not sure it's worth the effort."

"That's what I thought, too." Lucas's voice was troubled. "But Jess needs it in order to get the rest of the nursery stock in. There's no way it can be done without it. I've got a friend comin' over Monday to look at it. He should know if the tractor is worth salvaging or not. I hope we're wrong, for Jessie's sake, but I'm not—"

Suddenly he broke off. Brody's eyes veered quickly in the direction of his.

Jess was standing in the doorway, one hand braced on the frame, the other gently cupping the bottom of the sling looped around her shoulder and back. He caught just a glimpse of a tiny knit cap and fine, dark, baby fuzz.

For just an instant, he could have sworn her expression was stricken. But when she advanced farther into the barn, her face was curiously void of any emotion.

"Go on, Lucas." Her voice was even. "What's this about being wrong, for my sake?"

Lucas shifted his feet uncomfortably. "Jessie, I didn't want to have to tell you this until I knew for sure—"

"Lucas." The merest hint of a smile touched her lips, but her eyes were grave. "I'm a big girl now. I can take a little bad news."

"This could be more than a little bad news," he said slowly. "Brody and I were just talking about this tractor."

"And?"

"And I'm afraid it might not be the deal you thought it was. Neither one of us can get the damn thing to start. But don't worry just yet, 'cause I already asked Ray Hansen to take a look at it Monday. But at least that flatbed truck seems to be working fine."

"That flatbed truck isn't going to get my land tilled and raked." Her voice was as grim as Lucas's had been moments earlier. "I know what it costs to replace one, even a used one." Her soft mouth tightened. "I should have known something like this would happen."

Lucas stepped forward, curling a wiry arm around her shoulders. "Now don't get yourself worked up just yet. Ray hasn't even seen it yet."

"I'm not getting worked up." She sighed. "I'm just disappointed." And boy, was that an understatement, Jess decided sourly.

Lucas glanced back at the younger man, still standing in the shadows. "Besides, Brody here may be able to fix it up just fine. Why, he told me just today how handy he is when it comes to fine-tuning an engine."

Her eyes sought Brody's for confirmation.

It was Brody's turn to shift uncomfortably. Damn! What had Lucas gotten him into. "I'm not a miracle worker," he began slowly.

"You said you weren't a carpenter, either. But you did just fine and dandy with those frames, boy."

Surely that wasn't a compliment. But it appeared that it was, if Lucas's beaming expression was any indication.

And he was a sucker for a pretty face and a cantankerous old man who was as changeable as the Oregon weather. What a sap! Brody thought disgustedly. "If necessary, I'll do what I can," he finally relented.

Lucas and Jess went back outside, and Brody turned his attention to the "monstrosity." The tractor looked to be as old as Lucas, he guessed dourly. Finding parts would be almost impossible. Secretly he hoped Lucas's friend would agree with them that Jess would be better off with a newer one.

The sun was waning when he finally finished poking and prodding. Grabbing a nearby rag, he tried wiping some of the grease from his hands and arms. It was no use. All he succeeded in doing was smearing the sticky mess even further.

It was then that he noticed Jess standing nearby, watching him with a slight smile, the baby sling still around her shoulder. "Where's Lucas?" he asked.

"Gone home," she said with a lift of her brows. "Half an hour ago."

Brody finally gave up and tossed the rag onto the tractor. "I guess I lost track of the time." His tone was sheepish.

"I guess you did," Jess commented dryly. Her eyes flitted to the tractor, then back to his face. There was something rather odd in her expression—not quite curious, not quite suspicious.

"Anything wrong?" he asked.

Her hesitation was fractional. "I was just wondering how you knew so much about engine repair."

"I did a lot of it while I was in the army."

She stiffened visibly at his ready reply. Her eyes swerved accusingly to his. "I thought you said you were an MP."

"I was," he said quickly. Damn! She *was* suspicious of him; he was going to have to do something about that, and soon. "It was a hobby, mostly. I had a buddy who was a mechanic. I'd go in on weekends sometimes and give him a hand in the motor pool."

"Working on what? Car engines?" He detected a hint of skepticism.

"Some." He shrugged. "A few tanks and jeeps and a lot of heavy-duty trucks."

"Was this the same buddy you came here to see? The one in McMinnville who moved away?"

For an instant Brody said nothing. He'd forgotten that particular little white lie, and he disliked the twinge of guilt that pricked at him. "No. This was a different one. His name was Walt. Walt Miller. He was from New Orleans." That, at least, was the truth.

His reply must have satisfied her, for she seemed to relax. Her gaze dropped, encompassing his grease-stained hands and arms. "Would you like to come in and wash?" she asked quietly.

He nodded.

There was a small utility room off the kitchen, and it was there that Brody thoroughly soaped his hands and forearms. He could hear Jessica moving around in the kitchen, but when he happened to glance over, she was standing in the doorway, holding the baby over her shoulder.

"I appreciate you coming in to work today." Her smile was apologetic. "I really hadn't planned on having you come in on Saturdays."

Brody carefully rinsed the soapy film from his skin. "It's no problem. I didn't have anything else to do anyway." Nothing but think about her. He seemed to be doing quite a lot of that lately, and he really didn't think it was such a good thing.

"No, I don't suppose you do." He could feel her eyes on him and wondered what she was thinking. "I mean, not knowing anyone, and all.... And there certainly isn't much to do at a motel at night except watch TV."

Watch TV? With Jess so near, Brody could think of a very specific—and pleasurable—way to idle away the night at a motel. A half smile curled his mouth. "Amen to that," he agreed.

"That is where you're staying, isn't it? The motel in McMinnville?"

Brody turned to look at her. Their eyes met, and in that instant, Jess became aware that she sounded more than curious. After all, Brody was a man, and it hit her right in the pit of her stomach how very attractive he was. To him, she probably sounded rather forward—perhaps even suggestive.

"I'm sorry," she said quickly. She switched the baby to the other shoulder, patting his tiny back furiously. "I certainly didn't mean to pry."

Brody smiled slightly at her nervousness. The obvious dismay in those big blue eyes was almost childlike.

"I mean, where you live is really none of my business...."

He crossed his arms over his chest and regarded her. "As long as I show up every morning?" He didn't bother to hide the amusement in his voice.

"Well, yes...I mean no...." Jess suddenly noted his slow-growing smile. Oddly, she didn't mind. In fact, it seemed to have a reciprocal effect. "You're laughing at me," she accused, fighting back her own smile.

"Yes." There was a deep note of pleasure in his voice.

"Yes! So you admit it—"

"I mean yes, I am still staying in McMinnville. And yes, at the same motel." He smiled at her, and it occurred to Jess that she hadn't seen him smile very often.

"You really should do that more often," she chided gently.

"What?"

"Smile."

His smile widened.

"Haven't had much to smile about lately, huh?"

Brody's mind was on how untouched and pretty she looked. Untouched? Her skin looked as silky and soft as that of her infant son. But he was crazy if he thought he could make a little time with his boss—or rather, one of his bosses. Still, with Jessica Culver around, it was amazingly easy for a man to get sidetracked.

"Could be," he murmured, only half aware of what she'd just said.

"The same goes for me," Jess agreed lightly. Suddenly the problem with the tractor didn't seem half as pressing as it had earlier. The disturbing exchange in the barn was forgotten, as well. For a few moments, she'd allowed her doubts about him to fester. Perhaps she was still paranoid after Maggie's phone call several days ago.

Still, it was clear that Brody possessed a tough, uncompromising masculinity, perhaps even an underlying hardness. Yet even though she sensed he might be hiding something—something in his past, perhaps—she also sensed he wasn't deceitful. But when he smiled, it was as if years of experience with a harsh and bitter world had suddenly fallen away.

"Excuse me," Brody said, and Jess turned slightly so that he could step through the doorway. She watched as he crossed the few steps to the table.

There he paused, one hand on the jacket he'd dropped over the chair. "Have you eaten yet?"

He knew by her expression that the question had surprised her. Quickly, before she had a chance to refuse, he added, "I was just thinking maybe we could go out and grab something. I'm not especially fond of eating alone." That wasn't true. He hadn't minded eating alone until now. But the thought of going back to the motel with only the four walls for company was suddenly abhorrent.

But who was he trying to kid? It was Jessica. He didn't want to leave her.

His eyes held hers questioningly.

She was biting her lip, obviously considering. "I hate eating alone, too," she confessed. She eased the baby into the crook of her arm and saw that he'd drifted off to sleep. There was a slight twinge of guilt in her voice as she began, "But I've never left Nathan before, and—"

"We can take him," Brody interrupted. His eyes softened as they moved to the child. "From what I've seen around town, we don't have to worry about fine dining. The only restaurant I've noticed is that drive-in across from the gas station."

"If I ever had the chance to get organized, I'd have had dinner already fixed by now. Unfortunately, with a baby in the house..." Jess's gaze drifted meaningfully to her son's face, but her own was radiant with love. Her forefinger traced his bow-shaped mouth. They both smiled when Nathan blew out a bubbly sigh.

"Of course there's the Barnyard Inn," she added. "It's on the highway south of here. They've got the best fried chicken you've ever tasted. But it's really just a tavern where they've set up a few more tables and decided to add a menu.''

"Afraid you'll corrupt me, Mrs. Culver?" Brody couldn't resist teasing her. "I'll have you know I *have* seen the inside of a bar before."

Jess was reminded of her earlier scrutiny. She doubted his past was lily-white. "And probably sooner than you should have, too!"

She gasped when she realized she'd voiced the thought aloud. Her horrified gaze connected with his, but she found he was smiling.

"You're right," he agreed. "But that doesn't solve the problem of tonight's menu."

Jess sighed. "We'd probably never get in on a Saturday night, anyway." The clock on the wall showed five o'clock. By the time they got there it would be nearly five-thirty. "Even this early," she added.

"Too bad." Brody was genuinely disappointed.

"But they do take orders to go. We could bring it back here." Her eyes had begun to dance. "I can call ahead and order. Then it'll be ready."

Burdened as Jess was with the baby, it was Brody who made the call to the Barnyard Inn. He hung up the wall phone next to the refrigerator and turned to face her. "You'll come along, won't you? I'll need directions."

"Directions?" She wrinkled her nose at him. "Why, Mr. Alexander, I thought it was my company you wanted."

"That, too."

Brody's quiet tone brought her gaze rushing to his in a flash. Their eyes locked. In that split second, something dangerous, almost reckless, passed between them.

Neither seemed to care.

"I SEE NATHAN'S decided he likes his pacifier now."

"Sometimes." Jess turned her gaze from the scenery speeding by and peeked cautiously at the baby in her arms. She had taken the time to change Nathan's diaper and bundle him into a warm flannel bunting before they left, but he seemed restless. He'd awakened from his all-too-brief nap, and the motion of the car was not lulling him back to sleep. "I'm afraid he's temperamental about it," she murmured. "Like his—"

She stopped abruptly. Brody's eyes swung sharply to her. He sensed she'd caught herself just in time. Like whom? His father? Eric Culver? Or some other man? Who, he wanted to demand, was his father?

"Like his mother," she finished quietly.

She sounded almost listless, but a furtive glance to the side revealed nothing. The profile she presented as she gazed out the window was stark and emotionless. It was a look Brody was very familiar with. It came from a painstaking effort to hide what was really inside.

He wasn't fooled. She wore her pride and loneliness like an invisible cloak around her. Brody was stunned to discover he wanted to reach out and fling it away. He wanted her to talk about her divorce. And to hell with Eric Culver.

"That's funny." He purposely injected a light note into his voice. "You don't look like the type to rant and rave."

And Eric had never looked like the type to... But no. No! She tried to shove the remembrance into the past where it belonged, but her mind refused to obey. Her thoughts ran wild for one more instant. No one had ever guessed. No one even suspected. After all, he had a wife, and he made certain that everyone knew it.... He had fooled them all. Especially her.

She heaved a quiet sigh. "Neither do you," she commented dryly.

Brody neither agreed nor disagreed.

They drove on in silence for a few more minutes until Brody spotted a long, low-slung building near the next intersection. "That must be the place," he remarked.

Jess pretended to frown. "Were you holding out on me, after all? I thought you didn't know about it."

"I didn't," he said dryly. "But obviously someone does."

The Barnyard Inn was certainly no landmark; the one-story building was drab and painted a dull beige. But there were dozens of cars crammed into the small gravel parking lot.

Brody considered himself lucky to find the one remaining parking space. With his hands still resting on the gearshift between them, his eyes moved slowly around the lot and back to the building. "You sure the chicken here is the only draw?" He shook his head disbelievingly. "This looks like the local hangout to me."

She chuckled. "If I say it is, does that mean we don't get to eat tonight?"

Brody's gaze drifted over her. He resisted the impulse to linger, glad that Jess's attention was claimed by the baby. Nathan had spit out the pacifier. Jess was trying to ease it back into his mouth. "I suppose it wouldn't be wise to leave you stranded out here," he said with a slow grin. "You look like a lady who could use a little fattening up."

He was still smiling as he shut the car door. Jess decided to stay in the car and wait, since Nathan was starting to squirm a little. She still wasn't entirely comfortable in public with the baby. Fussy babies in a grocery store or restaurant had never bothered her before, but they weren't hers. She sighed. Was she trying to be too perfect a mother? Or simply hoping for too perfect a baby?

Ten minutes later Jess was convinced she and Nathan had both lost out forever. She frantically checked her watch.

She'd fed him less than three hours ago, but Nathan was apparently convinced it was more like thirty.

"I should have known better, sweetheart. But I thought you'd last another hour." Jess tried desperately to soothe him. He continued to squirm and root frantically against her breast. "Please, Nathan," she begged. "If you can just hold out for a few more minutes, just till we get home." She sneaked the pacifier into his mouth. He spit it out impatiently. Jess was convinced his frustrated screams would shatter the windows of Brody's car. And where was Brody? Had he decided to leave her stranded, after all? It certainly looked like it. Probably for someone who didn't need fattening up!

Another minute passed, then another. "Oh, damn." She moaned aloud. She couldn't nurse Nathan here. She'd fed the baby with Lucas coming in and out of the room, but everything was neat and in place and all covered up—and now she hadn't even brought a blanket. Oh, why hadn't she thought of this when she'd agreed to come with Brody in the first place? And why was she worrying about being the perfect mother? She was the world's worst mother!

It was Nathan who finally made the choice for her. Jess could take his heartbreaking wailing no longer. Her mind made up, she raised her sweater and fumbled for the catch on her bra.

She breathed a sigh of relief when Nathan hungrily found her nipple. His wails ceased, and Jess assured herself that no one would even notice. Brody had parked at the very end of a long row of cars. And soon it would be dark.

Just then, the car door was yanked open. "Sorry I took so long." Brody leaned across the seat and dropped a bag into the back, then eased into the driver's seat. "There was a mix-up in the orders. And you'll never guess who I saw on the way out—"

His voice dropped off abruptly. It was completely by accident that his gaze slipped down. His eyes jerked up immediately to confront Jess's startled expression—which he was sure mirrored his own.

But more surprising to Brody was how moved he was by the sight before him.

CHAPTER SEVEN

THE ENSUING SILENCE was terrible.

Brody pulled the door shut and stared straight ahead.

Totally unperturbed, Nathan continued to avidly suck and swallow. The tiny sounds of contented gratification he made seemed overly loud in the cramped confines of the car.

The easy familiarity between them had vanished. Brody wasn't sure who was more embarrassed, he or Jess.

Jess was doing her best to feed her child as inconspicuously as possible, but her other breast was more than half bared. She wasn't sure whether to laugh or cry.

Brody was having a hard time ridding his thoughts of anything but the creamy, supple ribbon of flesh he'd just glimpsed. His reaction to the sight was wholly male and very physical. He wanted to reach out and touch. She had such touchable skin; he could almost feel the velvety smoothness of her breast under his hands.

Yet at the same time, this natural exchange between mother and child filled him with wonder and triggered an emotional response he'd been unprepared for.

It was Jess who finally broke the awkward silence, her voice painfully low. "I'm sorry. I should have brought a receiving blanket with me, but I didn't think we'd be gone long. And I—I thought Nathan would wait."

Her voice sounded curiously strangled. Brody's head whipped around. He saw that she had confined her attention to her son, her hand lightly cradling his head. She possessed a purity that was rare these days, a purity that unnerved him as much as it puzzled him. But a trace of pink colored her cheeks, and Brody suddenly knew without a doubt that Jess wasn't a woman who could nurse in public without thinking twice about it. She would want to preserve her modesty at all costs.

All at once he was consumed by the urge to lean over and smooth the faint lines between her brows. He felt suddenly protective of her, maybe even a little possessive.

These were feelings that had no part in his mission here. Brody was well aware of that, but it didn't stop him from fumbling in his pocket. "I've got a handkerchief here somewhere. It's clean and it should do the trick." He shook out the handkerchief and passed it to her.

Jess accepted it wordlessly. Even when she'd covered herself and Nathan with the clean white linen, she still felt awkward and exposed.

Brody glanced at her from the corner of his eye, careful to keep his gaze level with hers. "Do you want me to wait until he's finished?"

She shook her head. "It's all right if you go ahead," she told him. "He'll be finished soon, anyway."

"I can wait. It's no problem."

She was touched by his concern. "No," she said again. "We'll manage. Really."

The smile she flashed made Brody's gut tighten all over again. What, he wondered grimly, was he even doing with Jessica Culver? It wouldn't be wise to risk getting involved with her—not that she'd indicated she wanted any part of him, Brody reminded himself fiercely. He had a lot riding on this case. Culver's fee was too good to pass up. It could finally give him the chance to start over, and he sure as hell didn't want to blow it because he'd gotten soft over a woman. Sure, Jess was liable to get hurt. But it wasn't his problem, was it?

All the same, it flashed through Brody's mind that he was being pulled into deeper and deeper waters by a force he had no control over, and that notion wasn't a particularly welcome one.

It irritated him even more when he realized he was driving extra cautiously, carefully avoiding any bumps or potholes that might jostle the pair next to him. But he was powerless to sit by and deliberately ignore her predicament when they stopped in her driveway.

Nathan, content and satiated now that his tummy was full, was fast asleep. The confined space in the bucket seat made movement difficult, and Jess hadn't yet had time to adjust her clothing. The color in her cheeks was even more noticeable than before.

Brody had already come around and swung open the door for her. Seeing the spot she was in, he positioned himself next to her. Their eyes met briefly before he averted his gaze. God, he thought disgustedly. How noble. Why was he even bothering?

He hesitated, then held out his arms. "Here, I'll take him."

When Jess passed the baby to him, Brody eased him over his shoulder, one big hand supporting the back of Nathan's head, the way he'd seen Jess do. Brody had never held such a tiny infant before, and for a moment he felt totally inadequate, as awkward as Jess had been earlier. Nathan was so small—so tiny. Yet he nestled his downy head against Brody's shoulder and slept on trustingly.

To his amazement, he was glad when Jess made no effort to retrieve the child once she was standing beside him. Instead, she pulled the sack containing their dinner from the back seat and led the way into the house. "Hold on, little fella," he murmured. "We'll have you tucked in tight as a drum in just a minute."

Brody followed behind her. His eyes sharpened when he came to a halt behind Jessica on the back porch. It had escaped his notice until now, but he noted the shiny brass of a new dead bolt on the back door, just above the old one. A niggling little suspicion nudged its way up his spine, but another part of him scoffed. There was nothing so unusual about installing new locks in a house recently vacated ... or was there?

He nodded at the dead bolt while she fished in her purse for her keys. "Looks like a new one," he said casually. "I suppose all the rain Oregon is so famous for tends to make a lock a little temperamental sometimes."

Jess looked up, her keys in hand. "Oh, the old one works fine," she began. "I just thought it might be a good idea to have dead bolts installed on all the exterior doors after I moved in." She gave a short laugh. "One can't be too careful these days, even in a town as small as Amity." She shoved the key into the lock and swung open the door.

Brody's expression was both disturbed and speculative as he once again trailed behind her. He didn't totally buy her reason for changing the locks. He strongly suspected her ex-husband had been the prime motivation. Someone else might not have caught it, but for a fleeting instant, he'd glimpsed a hint of some emotion that he couldn't quite define. Fear? Panic? But that made no sense. When she and Culver had divorced, she'd had nothing to fear. Because of the election, she had been the one to hold all the aces.

But Brody didn't like the thought that Eric Culver might be responsible for that look in Jessica's eyes. He didn't like it at all.

Jess disappeared in front of him. He heard a thump and a low mutter before a lamp flared in the corner of the living room. "Watch your step in here," she warned.

Brody hadn't been beyond her kitchen and utility room these past few days, and now his eyes widened at the sight of the boxes and crates scattered across the floor. All the furniture had been crammed into one corner. There was no time for any further reaction, and Brody followed at her heels as she weaved her way through the litter toward the stairway.

The baby's room, on the other hand, could have been featured in a TV commercial or a magazine ad. The walls were papered with elephants and Mother Goose characters. A huge teddy bear grinned at him from a gay yellow hammock trussed up in the corner and filled with fluffy stuffed animals.

Jess stood at the crib. "I'm afraid he'll wake up if I take him out of his bunting," she whispered. Her glance traveled from the slumbering baby to Brody's face. "Can you lay him down? Or do you want me to?"

The question was moot. Nathan had already been placed gently on his tummy. Jess's eyes bestowed a silent thank-you as she drew a lightweight blanket over the baby.

Once they were downstairs and in the kitchen, Brody folded his arms across his chest. "How long did you say you've lived here?"

Jess was just about to reach into the cupboard for plates and cups. "Here in this house?" she asked distractedly. "Or here in Amity?"

"Here," Brody stated very deliberately, "in this house."

She glanced back to find his expression one of mild reproof. For a moment she stared at him uncomprehendingly. His gaze slid meaningfully toward her living room. "Oh," she said in a small voice. "Almost six weeks." She set two plates on the counter, her smile rather sheepish. "I know it's a sight. I'm embarrassed to have anyone inside. But starting the nursery has had to come first, and I just haven't had the time to do anything about it, what with—"

"I know," he interrupted. "Planting Christmas trees, right?"

"Right." A faint humor laced her voice. "And having babies."

Brody studied her quietly. Despite the impish spark of amusement on her face, she looked tired. He didn't like the faint smudges under her eyes, and he couldn't help but think she was clearly a woman who had taken on too much. The move, the baby, starting a business...

She was going to interfere with his true purpose here.

He didn't care.

He moved to take the plates from the cupboard and transfer them to the table. Jess had already laid out silverware and glasses. She glanced at him questioningly when she filled hers with milk, then flushed when Brody shook his head. "I'll leave that to the nursing mother in the house," he said dryly.

The chicken was just as good as Jess had promised—sweet and juicy inside, with a crispy coating outside. They were halfway through the meal when Brody looked across at her. "You're a very independent lady, aren't you?"

She paused, her fork poised in the air. To his surprise, a look of distress flitted her features before she shook her head.

"No?"

"No," she repeated firmly, and found herself on the receiving end of a long, searching look.

"I don't know many women who would buy a house, start a business and have a baby all at the same time."

"Does sound like Superwoman, doesn't it? Unfortunately, it wasn't by choice that it happened that way."

Her sigh was wistful, almost sad. Because she'd left a lover behind in California? At the thought, a twinge of guilt stabbed at him.

"To tell you the truth—" this time her smile was strained "—this is really the first time I've been on my own in my entire life. Sounds crazy in this day and age, doesn't it? Especially for a woman who'll be thirty soon."

"You mentioned the day you hired me that you were divorced. Were you young when you married?" His observation was deliberately offhand. He already knew the answer; he was far more interested in what he didn't know.

"Not really." She hesitated. "I was twenty-two."

Twenty-two. At that age, Brody had felt he'd lived a lifetime. He suspected Jess couldn't make the same claim.

She didn't.

"I'd just finished college," she went on. "But I was still very immature and unworldly. I suppose part of it was growing up in such a small town—"

"Here in Amity?"

Jess nodded. "My parents had a farm a few miles north of here. Farming doesn't leave much time for recreation, I'm afraid. There wasn't time for anything but work in the spring and summer, and in the winter I was in school. My dad's brother lived in southern Oregon and I used to visit them every summer." Her tone filled with fond amusement. "My cousin Maggie is four years older than I am. She's the complete antithesis of me, I'm afraid. Bold and daring and not afraid of anything or anyone. I was always so shy, and my parents were rather protective.... I guess I grew up rather sheltered." A faraway expression entered her eyes. "I always wanted to be more like her." There was a small silence. "Maggie thought I should wait until after Nathan was born before starting the nursery."

Brody's eyes never left her face as he reached for a roll. "Why didn't you?"

Her thoughts seemed to turn inward. Her response took a long time coming. "Because I needed to do this for me." Despite her quiet tone, there was no denying her resolution. "I've always had someone taking care of me, you see. Someone watching to make sure I never took the wrong step. First my parents, and then my husband. And now *I* have someone to take care of. I want to do this for me and for Nathan. I've never had the chance to prove myself. But it's a scary feeling, because what happens if I fail? It's not just me. Now I have Nathan to think of, too."

"If Lucas has anything to say about it, I don't think you'll fail." His voice carried a trace of dry humor.

Jess smiled. "True," she agreed.

"What about your parents? Did they want you to come and live with them?"

"My father died quite some time ago," she explained. "My mother sold the farm last year. She has a sister in Reno, and she moved there so they could be closer. She remarried just last month."

Brody found he couldn't look at her. Instead, he confined his attention to buttering his roll. "Can I ask you something?"

"Sure."

"Starting the nursery. Was it something you and your husband had planned?" He risked a glance at her. If he could just find a clue as to how she felt about Eric, he might come closer to understanding this entire situation. He didn't quite trust Eric; he couldn't afford to trust Jess, either, but he had to ask.

Those beautiful blue eyes turned as cold as frost. "No," she denied flatly. Her back was rigid as she picked up her plate and carried it to the sink.

That one word carried a wealth of meaning; Brody got more than he'd bargained for. Was it possible Jess's ambition had driven her from Eric? Something had happened to precipitate her break from Eric. Why, Brody couldn't have said. But he felt it with every instinct he possessed.

"And Lucas? Somehow I had the impression he was your partner." He didn't know why he was even bothering. He was hinting at a relationship that didn't exist. He'd known it from the start. Still, he couldn't abandon or forget his true purpose for being there.

For just an instant, he felt her gaze bore into him. Brody met it with a blandly innocent look of his own. But a voice inside warned him it might be wise to back off for the moment. If he asked many more questions, Jess might realize what he was up to.

"No," she said finally. "Lucas is a friend. A very dear friend."

"I'm glad," Brody responded softly. "I think the two of you need each other." He paused. "You've known him a long time, haven't you?"

She sat down at the table again. Brody's gaze lingered on her slow smile, that sweet, warm smile that lit up her eyes like the summer sun. "Lucas is like a father to me. I can remember Lucas as far back as I can remember my own parents."

She went on to tell how Lucas had owned the farm next to her parents'; how her family was really the only family the old man had. Brody sat very still, aware of a bittersweet twinge of envy. He thought himself beyond such an emotion and despised himself for it. Listening to Jess talk about Lucas called to mind too many painful reminders of his own empty life. He remembered the drunk who had fathered him. He remembered his mother, whom he hadn't thought of in years.

It wasn't like him to be self-pitying. It wasn't like him to be sentimental. But strangely, Brody understood Jess's desire to stand on her own two feet. He'd discovered that same need at a very early age, only his instinct for survival was borne out of necessity. There had been no one who cared—until Murphy.

Murphy. There was an unexpected twist in his heart. Murphy had been gone for two years now, but there were times when it seemed like yesterday.

It was Murphy who had taught him that everyone needed someone at some point in their life. No one could be totally self-sufficient and independent.

But Murphy was gone. And once again, no one cared.

Impatiently he shook off the dark mood that had claimed him. He was vaguely aware that Jess had stopped talking. "I should be going," he muttered. Making a production of consulting his watch, he stood up. He then made the mistake of glancing at her.

She was standing as well, her fingertips resting lightly on the tabletop. Eyes that were impossibly wide and questioning settled on his face. Brody silently cursed, knowing that he'd startled her with his abruptness.

The light from the ceiling was stark and glaring. His form was a harsh outline looming in front of her, big and powerful. Strong hands gripped the back of the chair. The plane of his jaw was harsh and unyielding. Condemning? She'd said something wrong, but what? Jess stared at him, wondering at her reaction, wondering at his.

There had been a few times, times like now, when Jess had glimpsed a kind of coldness in Brody Alexander. There was a subtle hardness in the slant of his mouth. It was as if

there were something raw, almost wild in him that he kept
under tight control. Oddly, it was this restraint that caused
a flurry of awareness in her. Eric had always been so cool,
so precise. Brody was cool, too, but in an entirely different
way.

Was it because he was so unlike Eric that she was attracted to him? Jess wouldn't lie to herself. She was attracted to Brody, and who he was and where he came from
didn't really matter.

It was Brody who tore his gaze away first. He reached for
his jacket and thrust his arms into the sleeves.

"I'll walk you out," Jess said quickly.

"Sure." Brody's tone was curt as he started toward the
back door.

Jess flipped on the light and followed him onto the porch.
The night air was cool and faintly damp. She shivered as the
breeze swirled around her slender figure.

He turned when she was on the last step. "There's no need
to come all the way out. I really don't need an escort." His
voice was pitched low. This time the words lacked his earlier brusqueness.

Whatever mood had overtaken him seemed to have fallen
away. Jess had the strangest sensation that he wanted to
apologize but didn't know how. She hugged her arms
around herself and nodded. "Thanks for the dinner," she
said quietly. "And the company."

Her lashes lowered. All she could see was how his shoulders stretched to fit the worn leather of his jacket. The shiver
that ran up her spine had nothing to do with the chill of the
night. It was not quite fear, not quite excitement. Brody
looked bigger, tougher than ever. So much a man. Oh,
Lord. So much a man....

A hollow emptiness welled up inside her. To her horror,
there was a huge lump in her throat. "I miss having some-

one to talk to in the evening," she whispered. "It—it was nice."

The confession seemed to surprise her as much as it did Brody. He wanted desperately to echo her words, but he knew she'd never believe him. His rudeness was unforgivable.

He saw her shiver and yanked off his coat and quickly pulled it around her shoulders. "Here. You shouldn't be out here without a coat." His voice was gruff, but there was a huskiness to it that took away the edge.

Her hands clutched at the sleeves hanging past her hips. The warmth from his body was still trapped within the folds. A faint spicy scent swirled around her. She stared at him mutely, conscious only of Brody and a warm feeling of excitement that slid down her spine.

"Jess." He hesitated, then everything tumbled out in a rush. "Jess, I want to help you—with all the stuff piled in your living room...."

"When?"

Was that breathless, eager voice really hers? Jess felt herself flush. She hadn't meant to be so forward. It simply wasn't like her to be impulsive. Once, with Eric, she'd been impulsive. Falling in love with him had been impulsive and carefree and all those things she'd thought she wasn't. But she'd have sworn that six years of marriage to Eric had stifled that impulsiveness forever. Dear God, it should have.

That it hadn't was something she didn't quite see as a blessing. It only reminded her of Eric . . . and how little she knew of men.

She could feel Brody's eyes on her face. "Whenever you like." His gaze held hers questioningly. "Tomorrow's Sunday. How about then?"

She gestured vaguely with one hand. "You don't have to," she began.

"I want to." He moved a step closer, his tone low but intense. "Really, Jess." His voice dropped further. "I want to."

All at once the air of tension was rekindled. But this time it was a different kind of tension. No, that wasn't right, Jess thought hazily. It was more an awareness, a mutual awareness so acute it was almost painful. Brody's mouth was no more than a breath away. He wasn't smiling, but his mouth no longer looked hard. Indeed, the firm contour of his lips was harshly sensual. Jess held herself very still, aware of two different and conflicting sensations warring inside her.

Instinct told her Brody Alexander was a dangerous man. Dangerous where women were concerned and certainly dangerous to her painstaking quest for peace of mind. But when had instinct ever served her well? It certainly hadn't with Eric. She wasn't scared of Brody, though. Just a little wary. She knew what it was like to be tossed aside. And after the trauma of the past year, men were the last thing on her mind—even a man like Brody.

But at the same time, she was drawn to him like a moth to a flame. She wanted to reach out and touch his lips, learn their shape and texture with her fingertips; and that tiny cleft in his chin, the only vulnerable spot in such a stern, masculine face.

Their faces were only inches apart. They stared into each other's eyes. Jess's heart seemed to have forgotten how to beat.

The sound of a car horn carried through the clear night air.

Brody stepped back; the spell was broken. "Tomorrow?" His eyes echoed the question.

"I...yes." God, yes. Her gaze met his hesitantly. "As long as it's no trouble."

"It's not." The words were as decisive as they were brief. He took another step back, stopped and gave her another long, intent look that made her pulse hammer wildly within her.

She'd thought he was going to kiss her. Would she have welcomed it? Jess still wasn't sure. But as she turned to walk back into the house, she decided it was a good sign that she'd even considered letting him kiss her. It only proved that while Eric might have dented her faith in herself as a woman, he hadn't completely destroyed it.

And welcome or not, she had the feeling that Brody Alexander was the kind of man who, when he kissed a woman, made darn sure she enjoyed it.

CHAPTER EIGHT

JESS LAID NATHAN BACK in his crib in the early hours of the morning. She tenderly smoothed his cheek. He was such a miracle, this child of hers, this child she had thought would never be. She had loved him fiercely before he was born, even more fiercely after. Having her son more than made up for the nightmare of the past year.

It still filled her with a burning resentment that Eric had wanted her to terminate the pregnancy. His life was as he wanted it and children would only be a burden, he'd always told her. He'd been furious when he found out she was pregnant. A chill ran through her as she remembered the angry fight that had followed. Jess had known what to expect. Eric was always taunting, always accusing, always criticizing. She should have been used to it, but she wasn't. Her parents had never fought the way she and Eric had. No one had ever been deliberately cruel to her—until Eric.

How naive she had been. How stupidly and unbelievably blind. Normal couples didn't fight as they did. Normal couples laughed and talked together. They shared a bedroom—and a bed.

He had accused her of deliberately getting pregnant. Dear God, what a laugh that was. She had wanted a child very badly, and Eric had used that as an excuse—among other things—for staying out of her bed. But that wasn't why she'd stopped using birth control. Without the need, why bother? She and Eric had rarely slept together.

But now that she had Nathan, Jess felt she had a sense of purpose in life. She was finally living her own life, free to make her own choices, make her own mistakes.

Quietly closing the door to Nathan's room, Jess slipped back down the hall. Once inside her room, she sighed ruefully. In spite of the purple paint, it was a nice bedroom, or at least she hoped it would be eventually. It was spacious and airy, with high ceilings and warm pine paneling covering one wall. But right now the window was bare, and an assortment of cardboard boxes was crammed along one side. She'd managed to wash and press the lacy white curtains she'd bought. Unfortunately they didn't look half as nice draped over the wooden chair in the corner as they'd have looked at the window.

That avenue of thought brought her right back to Brody. She sat down on the rumpled bed, not bothering to remove her robe. She was too keyed up to go back to sleep. The truth was, she'd spent a goodly portion of the night thinking about his insistent offer of help. She had entertained the notion that the offer was merely a token one, then dismissed it just as quickly. She sensed that Brody wasn't the kind of man to go back on his word.

And he had to come back for his jacket.

A smile appeared from nowhere. She lifted a hand to tuck an errant strand of hair behind her ear, but the movement was suddenly arrested in midair. Slowly she lowered her hand to join its mate on her thighs, her expression becoming thoughtful as she studied both hands.

Her fingers were long and slim, but whereas once they had always been carefully manicured, her nails were now clipped short and bare of any polish whatsoever. She'd spent several hours in the barn planting cuttings yesterday; there was still a trace of dirt under her left thumbnail. Eric would have been horrified. She seldom wore any makeup, and she hadn't worn her hair up in months. She almost wished he could see her now!

Lucas and Brody didn't seem to mind her appearance. Jess wasn't sure what elusive trait she possessed that made the two men so determined to watch out for her. She could understand Lucas's protective instinct, but last night she had sensed that same instinct in Brody, as well. Certainly Eric had never attempted to shield her. To him she was merely a prize, a possession to be flaunted.

"You're really one heck of an independent woman," she chided herself ruefully. Here she was, supposedly trying to prove her own sufficiency and self-reliance, and all the while relying quite heavily upon two men.

On that note her gaze traveled to the window. Tiny silver droplets glistened against the outside pane of glass, the residue of an earlier shower. The morning was a gloomy one, with the threat of more rain almost certain. Ominous clouds crowded the sky in every direction.

Jess thought anxiously of her newly planted cuttings. Brody had finished the last of the protective coverings for the seed beds just yesterday. She hoped they did the trick, since a torrential downpour would likely wash away the top layer of soil.

With a sigh, she rose and began to straighten the bed, wishing she dared crawl back in to sleep for another hour. Whether Brody showed up or not, she intended to make a little headway inside the house today—if only to keep Lucas quiet, she decided with a twitch of her lips.

SHE NEEDN'T HAVE WORRIED that Brody wouldn't show.

Brody was awake at dawn. He lay there for the longest time, his hands linked behind his head, listening to the gentle wash of the rain outside.

He couldn't get her out of his mind. His emotions had run the gamut from amusement to a seething resentment. He kept remembering the way she had looked last night—her embarrassment at being caught nursing the baby, her faint look of confused hurt when he'd left so abruptly. Once again Brody cursed himself soundly, angry at her for having such a reaction in the first place, and even more furious at himself for caring that he might have hurt her.

It shouldn't have bothered him. He shouldn't have given a second thought to her feelings. He'd been accused before of being thoughtless and insensitive—even selfish. But life had taught him to reach out and snatch whatever he could, because chances were good that it wouldn't be his for long. Certainly no one had ever accused him of being a Good Samaritan. Nor was he particularly stalwart where temptation was concerned. Why now?

The answer had nothing at all to do with him...and everything to do with Jessica Culver.

Why hadn't he kissed her? The question tormented him throughout the night. The inherent impulse for survival had honed his instincts to a fine edge. She had looked so lovely, so ethereal and tempting with the moon spilling down its gauzy veil of silver. He hadn't mistaken the surprised awareness in Jess's eyes. She had wanted him. Oh, not in a blatant, provocative way, but in a much more subtle, innocent way, so subtle that perhaps she wasn't even aware of it.

But there was that word again—*innocent*. Totally guileless. Culver had painted her as a first-class witch. But such an image didn't reconcile with the woman he had seen last night. Yet, for just an instant last night, when Jess had talked of her newfound independence and fear of failure, he'd glimpsed a hint of torment. He had the strangest sensation that her innocence wasn't lost, just buried deep inside her.

Slowly Brody let out his breath. No, he hadn't kissed her. He hadn't dared give in to the desire churning in his gut. Because he was the one who was afraid?

Brody didn't have an answer. And all of a sudden, he didn't want an answer.

He drove over to Jess's after a long, cold shower. Waiting for her to answer his knock, he noticed the layers of white paint peeling on the door frame and absently decided her house could use a paint job.

Jess experienced a curious jolt of pleasure as she opened the door. Brody's faded, worn jeans clung to his thighs, outlining every sinew and hard line beneath. His faded denim shirt accentuated the firm definition of his arms and shoulders. The rugged, earthy aura that surrounded him caused Jess to marvel that she had ever mistaken him for Eric that first day.

Their blondness was the only similarity, and Brody's hair was thicker, streaked with a dozen different shades between tawny and pale gold. The damp smell of wind and rain and some faint, spicy scent followed him as he stepped inside.

"Hi." Brody absorbed the flare in her eyes, unable to stop his own from mirroring the pleasure he saw there. His gaze quickly took in her dark slacks and pale blue shirt. Her hair fell lightly over her shoulders—just the way he liked it.

"Want some coffee?" Jess sent him an inquisitive glance and started automatically for the cupboard.

"Not unless you're having some."

Brody stopped near the table and turned to face her. She was standing on the other side of the kitchen. Her feet were bare. He noticed they were long and slender, like the rest of her.

At his look, Jess paused, one hand still on the cabinet door. "Actually, I . . . I'm afraid I don't drink much coffee these days."

Brody frowned. He seemed to be waiting for her to go on. At the expectant silence, Jess cleared her throat, wishing she could be more blasé about the whole affair. Oh, to be a free, uninhibited woman! *Uninhibited*. The word made her wince.

She pressed her lips together nervously. "I don't care for decaffeinated, you see, and the caffeine...can go through to the baby." This last comment was unnecessary. He'd apparently gleaned her meaning. Jess felt herself redden as his eyes dropped to her breasts.

"I see." Brody crossed his arms over his chest, his smile totally unrepentant. His gaze lingered frankly on her breasts, then finally pulled away and traveled the length of her. Even her toes looked pink. He wondered if she blushed all over. The possibility was intriguing.

Just then the heavens decided to let loose their burden. Rain poured from the clouds in drenching sheets. Jess rushed to the window, her hands splayed on the pane like a child's. Except her eyes watched not in wide-eyed wonder, but in worried distress.

The driving, pelting rhythm could be heard against the rooftop. Brody came up behind her. "What is it?"

"My cuttings," she muttered. "Oh, damn. If they're ruined, I don't know what I'll do."

Brody glanced from her face to the dreary gray landscape outside and back again. "You didn't take off the coverings already, did you?"

"No. No, of course not."

"Then what's the problem? They're protected from the elements. 'Everything but a hurricane,' wasn't it?"

"Everything but a torrential Oregon downpour," Jess said glumly. "I was hoping for a gentle April shower. This is ridiculous."

"It'll be fine, Jess." He gestured at the ominous clouds. "See, it's letting up already. Besides," he added dryly, "those coverings aren't going anywhere, and I have the battle scars to prove it."

Jess turned away from the window to find him grimacing at his hands. She peeked over his shoulder. What she saw made her gasp.

"My God, Brody! How on earth have you been able to work like this?" Her eyes flashed accusingly up to his. "Why didn't you tell me? I'm sure we could have found you a pair of gloves somewhere."

She had already seized one of his hands and claimed it in her own. For an instant he stood paralyzed, acutely conscious of her closeness. "It doesn't matter," he murmured.

Her lips tightened. "It does," she said briefly.

Brody said nothing. Instead he stared down at her, his mind on her striking coloring. Her hair was so dark it was almost black, and was lustrous and shiny. But her complexion was so fair it was nearly translucent; he'd never seen such beautiful skin.

"You should have told me," she repeated.

Before he knew what she was doing, she had pushed him into a chair and whirled away. Seconds later, she knelt in front of him with a small first-aid kit on the floor beside her. "Bottoms up," she ordered.

Brody wordlessly complied as she examined first one hand and then the other. His left wasn't bad. The fleshy area below his fingers had already seen several blisters come and go. His right hand was a mess. Blister had formed over blister, leaving several areas raw and chafed.

She carefully massaged a healing cream into his left palm, then applied herself studiously to his right. Brody nearly groaned, but it wasn't with the physical pain that she sought to ease.

Her touch was sweet agony. Brody battled an awful feeling of helplessness. He didn't like being beholden to anyone. He didn't want to be beholden to *her*. He wanted desperately to push her away, but something totally foreign held him there. He was caught between that horrible vulnerability and the very human need to be comforted.

It didn't matter that the hurt was so small it was inconsequential. Brody couldn't remember the last time anyone had fussed over him, exhibited such tender concern. His mother once had, but it had been so long ago the memory no longer existed. Certainly his father had never cared. And with Murphy he'd been beyond the age of bumps and scrapes. But Jessica's touch was infinitely gentle, almost caressing. It was as if she had the power to heal the ragged edges of his blackened soul, as well.

Along with that feeling was another one just as potent, just as devastating. The longer he sat there, the more Brody found himself consumed by a desire unlike anything he'd ever experienced. There was a painful gnawing in his gut, a tingling sensation where her hand cradled his. Her head was bent over his hand. He wanted to plunge his fingers into her hair, tilt her head back and claim her mouth for his own. He ached with the need to feel his lips against hers, to discover for himself if the full, tempting curve of her mouth tasted as sweet as it looked.

Instead he sat there, as still and silent as a statue, hating himself for his weakness, hating Jessica for causing it.

Her eyes were very wide and very blue when she finally looked up at him. "I'm sorry," she said quietly. "I really should have thought to tell you you'd need gloves."

It was suddenly important that she not blame herself. "It's not your fault," he protested, then surprised them both with a smile. He glanced at his right hand, where Jess had nearly covered his palm with Band-Aids. "I feel like a patchwork quilt."

Her eyes danced. "I can just hear Lucas when he sees you."

"He'll probably think I'm trying to get off easy."

"So you're onto him already, huh? If he gives you a bad time, just remind him it proves you know one end of a hammer, after all." A laugh threatened to bubble over his blank look, but suddenly she bit her lip. "You know," she said slowly. "Maybe you'd better not come in tomorrow."

"Because of this?" He lifted his hand. "Or Lucas?" Either reason appeared to astonish him.

"Your hand, silly." Her tone was light, but her eyes were concerned as they rested fleetingly on his bandaged hand. She began to load items back into the first-aid kit.

Brody was on his feet now and towering above her. "You know," he remarked conversationally, "not only do I feel like a patchwork quilt, but I think I know a woman who's determined to get in all the practice she can get for when her bouncing baby boy decides to get into some trouble."

Jess stood as well. "Meaning I'm overdoing the motherly routine?" She let out her breath in a sigh. Hadn't Lucas accused her of the same thing?

"Maybe just a little." Brody glanced wryly at his hand.

"Nevertheless," she began—and this time the light in her eyes was a militant one. "I really think that you—"

"Don't," he interrupted. "I know what you're going to say."

"Oh?" In spite of herself, her tone was wrapped in laughter.

"That you've decided to reconsider my generous offer of help today. Believe me, you won't get off so easy." He couldn't resist teasing her. Nor could Brody explain his sudden good humor. All he knew was that he didn't want to leave.

"You've really got me pegged, haven't you?" A slender brow winged upward, giving her an elfish look. "I suppose you're a man who has tons of experience figuring out the female mind, eh?"

Strangely, the thought of Brody Alexander with another woman roused a pang of jealousy. Yet Jess was curious at the same time. What kind of woman would a man like Brody be attracted to? A sexy, sophisticated vamp? Sexy, yes. Sophisticated? Maybe. The all-American cheerleader type? Jess didn't think so. More than likely he'd want a woman who possessed the same raw kind of sensuality that he did. One thing was certain: no man in his right mind would be attracted to a woman with a one-month-old baby and dirt under her fingernails. Especially one who needed fattening up.

Brody watched the fleeting expressions chase across her face, his laugh uneasy. Probing minds was his job; after his years in the army, it was almost second nature. The one thing he'd learned above all was that things were rarely as they seemed. Unfortunately Jess had the most amazing knack for making him forget that, and it was but one more reason to be wary of her.

But none of that mattered right now. "As for Lucas," he went on, thoroughly enjoying the view as Jess bent over to retrieve the first-aid kit from the floor, "if he happens to accuse me of being lazy, I'll just return the favor by giving him a bad time about his lady friend."

Jess straightened slowly. It took a minute to digest what he'd just said. When she did, her mouth dropped open. "His what?"

"His lady friend." He eyed her quizzically. "The one he was out with last night."

"Lucas was with a woman last night?"

"Yes," he repeated patiently. "At the Barnyard Inn. I saw them at a table in the back. I'd say she was a little younger than Lucas. Short dark hair, not much gray."

Betty. Lucas had been with Betty! Why, he'd been holding out on her, the sly old devil.

"I'm sure I told you," Brody continued. Suddenly he stopped. A slow, suggestive grin edged his mouth. His gaze flickered to her breasts. "Maybe I'd better rephrase that. I *started* to tell you—"

"I remember." Hot color flooded her cheeks as the memory rushed into her mind. Smiling weakly, she went off to replace the first-aid kit in the medicine cabinet, wishing he hadn't been quite so delighted at her incriminating blush.

She found Brody in the living room, hands on his hips as he looked around.

"It's a mess, isn't it?" Her gaze rested on the cardboard boxes piled in the corner. "I've got cartons upstairs that belong down here and vice versa. I got all this from my mother, so I had no idea what in any of the boxes. I told the movers to put things wherever they could find room. Boy, was that a mistake," she said with a half laugh. "I'm beginning to think getting this mess straightened out is hopeless."

"Only for a helpless new mother." His tone was teasing, but his eyes reflected only concern as he met her gaze.

Jess's heart did a curious little somersault. The last thing she wanted was his pity—anyone's pity, for that matter—but knowing that Brody cared was like a balm to her wounded ego. Marriage to Eric hadn't done wonders for her pride.

"There's no denying I'm a new mother," she said, wrinkling her nose at him, "but helpless?"

Brody shifted his gaze to look out the window to the neat rows of tiny Christmas trees in the distance. "That," he observed dryly, "has already been established."

And it seemed that Jess was determined to prove it yet again. Brody waited patiently while she decided where she wanted her furniture placed. It took a full twenty minutes before she finally made up her mind and he was able to remove the boxes piled on the sofa, which had found a temporary home in her dining room. He had no sooner stepped up to one end of the sofa than he found Jess firmly stationed at the other. "No way, little lady," he said mildly. "This is why I'm here, remember?"

"You expect me to just sit around and watch?" Those big baby blues were round and incredulous. Her totally innocuous expression didn't fool Brody. She wasn't budging an inch.

"You'll dent my male pride if you don't." He grinned at her, but the light in his eyes conveyed an equal determination. She stood her ground for a moment, then surprised the hell out of him by moving away.

Brody was feeling rather smug at the easy victory. He bent to his task, then glanced over his shoulder, not at all prepared for the sight of that shapely little derriere swinging in the air as she wrestled with an overstuffed chair. He straightened with a roar. "Jess!"

From across the room he heard her sigh. "What?"

He pointed to the chair. "Sit."

Jess sat. If the fiercely determined look on his face was any indication, she didn't doubt he'd tie her down if she didn't. "You sound like a drill sergeant," she accused without heat.

When Brody returned to his task, she leaned back and let her leg dangle over the arm of the chair. If Brody was so determined to make her lazy, she might as well be comfortable. "As long as we're on the subject," she added, thinking of her comment about drill sergeants, "was your stint in the army a career? Or was it just for a few years?"

He bent down and butted his shoulder against the sofa, a derisive smile on his lips. "It was a career," he confirmed.

Jess watched as he began the slow-going process of moving the cumbersome sofa through the wide, arched doorway between the two rooms. "Did you give it up?" she asked curiously.

He gave what he thought was a mighty heave. The sofa barely moved an inch. "I resigned my commission," he confirmed, deciding this would be a good time to change the subject. "What," he grunted, "is in this thing? It feels like you've got half the gold from Fort Knox inside here."

Her leg immediately swung over the arm of the chair.

"No!" he barked out. "You just stay right where you are."

Jess started to murmur an "I told you so," then hastily reconsidered when she glimpsed his fierce scowl. "Actually," she said lightly, "it's a Hide-A-Bed."

"A what?"

"A Hide-A-Bed," she explained patiently. "You know, a sofa with a mattress inside that unfolds when you pull it out."

One look at her and Brody wished he hadn't asked. The subject of beds was definitely not a safe one. Jess stood watching him with her hands on her hips, a posture that stretched her blouse across her breasts and outlined their fullness a little too keenly for his peace of mind. Much as his body wished otherwise, beds and new mothers definitely didn't mix. He dragged his eyes away reluctantly.

Still, he couldn't stop himself from wondering what Jess would say if she knew his thoughts. Would she be shocked? Dismayed?

He didn't realize that he was the one who might have been shocked. The thought kept running through Jess's mind that if she hadn't turned embarrassingly red before, she certainly should have now. Her appreciative gaze was trained on the masculine figure before her. She was held spellbound as he bent, shifted and twisted. Beneath the fabric of his jeans and thin cotton shirt, muscles flexed, knotted and grew taut with strain.

Deep inside, a budding warmth unfolded. The feeling caught hold and flamed through her veins. Brody Alexander possessed a raw virility that both disturbed and fascinated her. Jess couldn't think when she'd been so acutely aware of any man.

There was a dull thud as the sofa slid into place. Brody glanced back at her. "Did you want to hang that now?" He pointed to the oak-framed mirror propped under the window.

Jess nodded. "Yes. Over the sofa." She went to search out a hammer and picture hangers.

Five minutes later, Brody stepped back to survey his handiwork, his feet braced apart, his hands resting carelessly at his hips. Jess, who had resumed her place in the chair, found her attention momentarily diverted. Dimly she noticed that he had rolled up the sleeves of his shirt, displaying strong muscular forearms coated with silky-looking hair much darker than that on his head. His hands were big and strong looking, the fingers lean and not the least bit fleshy. Her throat grew dry. What kind of magic could those hands make on a woman's body?

"How's that?"

The question startled her. Jess tore her gaze from his hands almost guiltily, only to find that she'd been discovered. Brody had turned and now watched her, one side of his mouth curving up in a slight, almost mocking smile.

He knows! she thought in desperation. Avoiding the glint in his eyes, she muttered, "It looks fine."

The smile widened. "Fine?" he repeated. "Does that mean I'm going to have to move it? The mirror, I mean. Please, not the sofa."

That earned a reluctant smile and a shake of her head. Still, Jess wished her awareness of this man weren't quite so disturbing. Her mind sped on. Was it because of Eric? she wondered fleetingly. She hadn't meant to feel such longing. The thought dismayed her as much as it alarmed her, but she couldn't deny that she wanted him to touch her. She wanted him to kiss her, and caress her and . . .

There was a small, mewling cry from upstairs. "I think," Brody said lightly, "you're being paged."

Jess nodded. It was almost a relief to leave his disturbing presence behind as she sprinted up the stairs and turned her attention to her son. Brody was forgotten as she slid her hands under Nathan's tiny body and lifted him to the quilted change table.

"Hush, sweetheart," she soothed automatically.

Nathan continued to fret, impatient as always to be fed immediately upon waking. "You're certainly determined not to miss a meal, aren't you? Well, Mama's here and I'm all ready for you." Jess laughed, her face reflecting the joy she got from her son. With brisk efficiency she unsnapped his sleeper and changed his diaper, pausing occasionally to press a kiss on his rounded tummy. When she was done, she lifted Nathan to her chest, pulled a blanket from the padded crib railing and turned.

A tall, starkly male form filled the doorway. How long Brody had been watching her, Jess had no idea. He continued to watch her as she started across the room, his expression enigmatic. For an instant, she felt a prickle of unease.

Nathan squirmed against her chest, his cries growing louder. "He's hungry," she clarified unnecessarily. She cast a slightly embarrassed look at Brody from the corner of her eye.

Brody smiled faintly and stepped aside.

Jess made her way downstairs, all her senses quiveringly aware of the man directly behind her. There was a sharp, painful tingling in her nipples, signaling that her milk was coming in. It wasn't the first time Jess had wished there was room for a rocker in Nathan's bedroom. She sat in the chair she'd recently vacated. Behind her, Brody stepped to the window. She sensed he knew of her unspoken wish for privacy.

Her hurried movements made her fingers awkward. She fumbled with the bottom buttons of her blouse, then finally gave up. Yanking the material up hastily, she offered Nathan her breast. He searched blindly, then latched on to her nipple fiercely. Jess breathed a sigh of relief at the peaceful silence, dropping the lightweight blanket loosely in place over herself and the baby until only the top of his head was visible. Her face was soft with contentment as she closed her eyes and leaned her head back.

In the mirror, a searing golden gaze absorbed her every move.

"Were you alone when Nathan was born?"

Jess's eyes flicked open. She looked up in surprise. His tone wasn't rough, but there was an edge to it that puzzled her. She hesitated, not certain what he wanted. "My mother was on her honeymoon—she still is," she said slowly. "But my cousin Maggie drove up from Medford to stay with me the first few days I was home."

"Not then." The pitch of his voice was very low. "At the hospital. During labor."

She sensed rather than heard him move closer. Their eyes collided. Hers were questioning, his were shadowed and unreadable. There was a sudden tension in the air.

Jess nodded and was the first to look away. "Maggie and I thought we had it all worked out. I was going to call her at the first sign I might be in labor. But Nathan came earlier than the doctor ever expected. Maggie had taken one of the lodge's boats over to the coast for some repairs." Her smile was pitifully brave. "Wouldn't you know that's when Nathan decided it was now or never. By the time she got the message, he was already here. And Lucas was... Well, let's just say he doesn't have much of a stomach for childbirth."

A mist of fiery red swam before Brody's eyes. His hands balled into fists. What was it that Jess had told him last night? That she was on her own for the first time in her life. On her own, pregnant... and scared.

Damn him. God damn Eric Culver. No matter what she had done, she didn't deserve to be alone at such a time. Someone should have been with her... *someone.*

Slowly he unclenched his fists. He wasn't even aware of moving; the next thing he knew, he was crouched down beside her. "I'm sorry, Jess."

Her eyes looked directly into his, calm and accepting. "It doesn't matter." Her tone was quiet, almost whimsical. "Nathan and I are just fine now." Her gaze lowered. Her free hand crept around to gently cradle the dark down of her son's head.

Her mouth was smiling, but Brody sensed an elusive hurt hidden away behind the carefully courageous facade.

"I wish I'd been here." Again there was that deep, rough catch in his tone. Brody didn't understand it himself. The words seemed to come from some part of himself he hadn't known he possessed. He knew only that they had to be spoken. "You shouldn't have had to go through it alone." His voice lowered further. "I wish I'd been here for you," he said again.

With his golden eyes and tawny head of hair, he reminded her of a hotheaded Viking warrior. But the fierce undertone in his voice was at complete odds with the compassionate understanding in his face. Jess felt something melt inside her.

His shoulder barely brushed hers. It was the only point of contact between them, yet in some strange, curious way, she had never felt as intimate with any other human being. She managed to edge closer to him without disturbing Nathan.

She leaned forward to kiss the raspy hardness of his cheek.

"Thank you," she said softly. "It's nice to know that someone cares." Their eyes held a moment longer, then she shifted her attention to the baby at her breast. "When he's done," she suggested lightly, "why don't we finish rearranging the furniture in here. After that, how about some lunch?"

CHAPTER NINE

BRODY COULDN'T HAVE CARED less about lunch. But he'd gone through the motions, anyway.

What he'd wanted was Jess—her body beneath his, her face alight with passion, her soft, rich curves molded against his hardness, her arms clinging wildly to him....

The thought had brought him up short. Culver had called Jess a clinging vine. *She's a charmer, and a deadly one.* By Culver's own account, she'd practically blackmailed him into giving up custody of Nathan, and the proof was that she was here, minus a husband, minus a father to her son. It was Culver who had been wronged. And if the baby wasn't his there could be no doubt she'd been a faithless wife.

But he'd been unable to stop watching Jess all day, unable to stop his overactive mind, unable to stop vacillating first one way and then the other. And that had just compounded his frustration.

He'd hoped the day would prove enlightening. Instead, he'd grown more and more confused. He'd expected a spoiled, selfish coldhearted witch, not a homespun farm girl who'd clearly been sheltered and protected all her life. And the photos Culver had provided showed a side of her he had yet to see—the stunning, sophisticated wife of Justice Eric Culver.

Could she possibly know who he was, why he was here? Could that be the reason behind her front of utter guile?

If it was a front, it was a damned good one, Brody reflected grimly. Whenever Nathan had been in the room, again and again her eyes had strayed to him—possessively, protectively, fiercely loving.

Throughout the day, he had waited for her to talk about Culver and her divorce, probing gently, paving the way. But she had divulged nothing about her marriage, and he knew an unreasoning disappointment. Was it because there was simply nothing to tell, or because she had as many secrets as he?

Clinging vine . . . or fallen angel?

One thing was certain: he was starting to care a hell of a lot more than he should have. He had so many questions—*too* many questions. And the answers shouldn't have mattered, but they did. Damn, but they did.

He felt like a heel. It was like watching one part of himself throw poison darts at her, while the other found an irrational pleasure in being with her. She had seemed to enjoy his company as much as he did hers. She'd puttered around, laughing and talking, unpacking the hodgepodge of boxes, clearly pleased that her house was finally beginning to look like a home.

But his desire had made him feel ashamed, and for the life of him, Brody didn't understand his reaction. Was it lust? He wished he could say it was, but every instinct inside him cried out differently. He was even beginning to feel protective of her baby.

Oh, there had been women in his life—casual encounters. He scarcely remembered his first; he certainly didn't remember the last. Only once had he ever fancied himself in love, and he'd been just a kid then. But Brody was well aware that women seemed to like his harsh masculinity, and more often than not, he'd used that knowledge to his advantage.

But Jess was different. Damn, but he shouldn't have looked at her earlier. The bare breast he'd glimpsed had his insides twisted in knots. It had looked deliciously round and firm, its swelling curves tipped by a dusky pink nipple.

Later that afternoon she'd nursed the baby again, looking every inch a Madonna, so chaste and pure it should have made him sick. But mockery directed at either one of them was the last thing on Brody's mind. The minute she'd sat down, her fingers at her buttons, the fantasies that filled his mind had taken his breath away.

They'd also made him feel like a wide-eyed ten-year-old trying to sneak a peek at a girlie magazine. Jess was no sultry-eyed package specially prepared to entice and tease, but no woman on earth could have been more provocative. He'd wanted to rip the flimsy blanket from her shoulder, open her shirt, spread it wide and look his fill. God forbid that he should fancy himself a saint. He'd finally gone outside and checked to make certain the torrential downpour hadn't damaged her precious cuttings.

The cold rain still falling from the April sky had dampened his hair and clothing. It did nothing for his urges.

When he came back inside, she'd asked him to stay for supper. His mind said no, but his lips said yes.

He had a devil of a time sitting across from her and keeping his hands on the table . . . and *off* her.

When the dishes were done she took his hand and pulled him from the kitchen. When they were standing in the dining room, she stopped. "What do you think?" she asked softly, tipping her head to indicate the adjoining living room. Her gaze took in the end result of the day's work. The room looked warm and inviting with its plush, overstuffed furniture. A collection of leafy green plants grouped in the corner added a splash of brightness. Not a single cardboard box littered the floor.

"*I* think we make a pretty good team," Jess said.

She had relinquished possession of his hand. Brody experienced a twinge of regret, then he noticed her frown. "What is it?"

"It'll be nice not having to tackle my way through here," she said wistfully. "But look at the color of these walls. I thought they were horrid before. Just look at them now."

Glancing at the dismal dark green of the walls, he decided the previous owners must have been color-blind. He amended his previous opinion that the outside of the house needed a coat of paint. It looked as if the inside needed one, too.

"It makes it so dark in here," she murmured. "It wouldn't be so bad if this was the only room that needed painting. But did you notice my bedroom?"

Brody had helped switch boxes from room to room and put up the drapery rod, but he'd been far too conscious of the bedroom's occupant to pay much attention to anything else. It took him a moment to recall.

"Purple, right?" He cast her a sidelong glance.

Jess chuckled. "It reminds me of one of the paintings you sometimes see of the Old West—"

"Don't tell me," he broke in dryly. "The room above the saloon, right?"

"Exactly. Can you imagine waking up to that every morning?"

Brody was already imagining the unspeakable. His mind was having a field day at the idea of waking up in that room—with her—and he reluctantly focused on her, only to notice how her laughter sparked tiny lights in her eyes. He wanted to close his eyes and shut out the sight of her loveliness. How could she be both natural and fresh and so earthily sensual at the same time? Brody felt he'd been hit by a lightning bolt. He wanted to pull her into his arms and satisfy the desire that had been burning inside him since they'd met. Another part of him wanted nothing more than to hear that lilting, carefree laugh again.

Jess looked up and caught the almost hungry expression on his face. It had an unexpectedly sobering effect. Her smile vanished. Her heartbeat quickened.

She noticed suddenly how tall Brody was—half a head taller than she. A shiver touched her spine, but it was a shiver of pleasure. She stood at eye level with many men. But next to Brody she felt small . . . feminine.

Was this feeling right? Or wrong? Jess didn't know, and she didn't care.

Brody's shirt was open at the throat, baring tanned skin covered by a dense patch of curly dark hairs. Eric's chest was smooth, completely void of hair. She focused on that wiry nest of curls with rapt absorption.

Something was happening between them. Something dangerous, almost frightening. Something wonderful.

"I really should be going." It was Brody who broke the hushed silence. She didn't want him to go. She wanted him to stay and—what? She didn't dare pursue the prospect any further.

He lifted a hand. She thought he intended to touch her, but he dropped it abruptly.

His eyes were suddenly dark and unreadable. Jess slowly released her pent-up breath, silently speculating at the slight hardening of his facial muscles. This tingling feeling of awareness wasn't one-sided. She hadn't mistaken the smoky desire in Brody's gaze. But there was a sizzling sort of tension in the air that warned her he was fighting it. Why? All at once she was filled with a mute despair and uncertainty, wholly unsure of herself and her femininity. It was a feeling she was only too familiar with.

What man in his right mind would want a woman with shadows under her eyes, a stomach like quicksand and breasts too big for the rest of her?

"I'll get your coat." Her tone was quiet, almost resigned.

Their fingers brushed when she handed it to him. Jess stood awkwardly while he shrugged into it. Brody glanced up and met her uncertain gaze. "Where's yours?"

She frowned blankly.

"Your coat. I refuse to let you go outside two nights in a row without a coat." When Jess merely stood there, hands locked together in front of her, his brows rose a fraction. "Aren't you walking me out tonight?"

Her wide blue eyes flashed up to his. He watched as surprised pleasure chased the shadows from her face. "Oh," she said in a small voice, then smiled. "I didn't offer to because last night you said you didn't need an escort."

Brody studied her for a moment. More and more, he didn't want to hurt her. If he was smart, he'd walk away now, as far and as fast as he could. But something inside told him he wasn't going to be smart about this—not smart at all. "Let's just say I want one now."

There was a mysterious quality to his voice she couldn't quite identify, a kind of reluctant resignation. But his eyes were warmer than she'd seen them thus far. Jess felt the look clear to her toes, and practically ran to the closet. She'd propped Nathan in the baby swing after dinner; he was fast asleep. When she turned back to Brody, his golden gaze hadn't wavered from hers.

They walked outside together. The night was chilly. The air still carried a hint of dampness, but the dreary cloud cover of the day had moved to the east.

Brody's eyes were drawn to the sky. It was filled with a hundred tiny starbursts of light. "I don't believe it," he mused aloud. "I've never seen so many stars in my life. And after all the rain there was today."

"I know," Jess said softly. "The weather can change so quickly here. It's just one of the things I love about living here. I half expected the rain today, though. I saw some sea gulls late yesterday. That's a pretty good sign there's a storm on the coast. Much as I love Oregon, I don't think I'd care to live out there."

"Why not?" Brody ducked to avoid a gnarled, outstretched branch of the huge oak tree.

"It rains too much."

"It rains too much?" Disbelief punctuated the question. "You can say that after a day like today?"

Jess chuckled. "Believe me, they get more rain than we do here in the valley. Of course, you're all right as long as you have a survival kit made expressly for western Oregonians."

"A survival kit," he repeated. She sounded so deadpan he knew he was about to fall into something. "What, exactly, is in this survival kit?"

"Why, what else?" Her tone was innocence itself. "An umbrella and a hooded jacket."

"Neither of which I have." Brody made a face. "I think you're in league with Lucas. Is this a subtle way of telling me that Californians aren't welcome here?"

"I hired you, didn't I?" Jess's tone was light, but her heart set up a rapid tattoo. "Besides, I'm not in a much better position myself since I spent most of the last seven years there."

Brody had the feeling that this admission was a reluctant one. "You did? Where?" He injected just the right note of curiosity into his voice, grateful for the darkness. It hid the guilt creeping through him.

There was a slight pause. "Sacramento." Another pause. "I—I spent my last year of college there. And that's where I lived while I was married." They stopped near where his car was parked. Her voice was almost too bright as she resumed. "Were we neighbors?"

Brody silently bemoaned his fate. The conversation was going from bad to worse. His deceit was heavy on his mind. Why couldn't he just admit it?

But he couldn't give this case up. Dammit, he couldn't! There was too much to lose.

"Close but not that close. I'm from San Francisco. Though I haven't spent all that much time there the last twenty years." He tried reassuring himself that it wasn't an out-and-out lie. Even as the thought flitted through his brain, he wondered why he even cared. He shouldn't have. Dammit, if it were anybody but Jess, he wouldn't have.

"No," she murmured. "I don't suppose you have." She slipped her hands into the pockets of her coat. "Can I ask you something?"

"Sure." He stiffened instinctively.

"Why did you give up your military career?"

It wasn't as bad as he'd thought. By her own words, Jess had been sheltered by her parents most of her life. And he had no doubt she'd led a pampered life as Eric Culver's wife. Still, they were so different. He had lived his life in the shadows, while Jess had lived hers in a world full of sunshine. She had never known hatred, while he had never known love—at least her kind of love.

"Politics, I guess. A difference of opinion." A hazy circle of light shone down from the barn. Brody stared broodingly into the shadows beyond. "Or maybe I was running."

"You?" In spite of herself, she smiled. Brody was so strong. He didn't seem like a man who would run from anything.

He glanced at her and caught the look. "Believe it, Jess. If I was running, it was from a life that no longer had any meaning for me." His laughter was harsh. "Coming from me, that's quite an admission. I'm hardly the philosophical type."

His statement didn't surprise Jess. Brody struck her as a realist, a pragmatist who went straight for the jugular. She, too, had left a life that had ceased to have meaning. It was Eric—always Eric. She had never counted. Her only regret was that she had waited so long to finally own up to it.

"Tell me what happened," she said softly.

For an instant she thought he would refuse. Then, crossing his arms, he eased down on the hood of his car. "I was stationed in Georgia at the time," he began slowly. "We got a tip that there was some funny business going on in the finance department. Someone juggling the books and depositing funds into a bogus account.

"It was a touchy operation. The head of the finance department, a full-bird colonel, was the prime suspect. I was the officer in charge, and since it was so sensitive, I handled the investigation myself. It took a while to establish credibility, but eventually I got the proof I needed that the colonel *was* embezzling. But because of his rank, protocol dictated the matter be taken to the base commander first, before formal charges were filed."

In the moonlight, she could see the taut line of his jaw.

"The colonel was a staff officer and a friend of the general's. I was told in no uncertain terms that the matter would be handled internally. The general would see to it that the colonel made restitution. Absolutely no charges were to be filed."

Her lips parted. "But why?"

"The publicity. Having a staff officer accused of embezzlement would cause too much embarrassment, too much public scrutiny. Supposedly it would create more problems than it would solve." There was a hard glint in Brody's eyes. "I was further told that as long as I cooperated, the general would call in a few favors and make certain that my name was on the next promotion list to major."

Her eyes widened. "A bribe?"

"It wasn't the first time I'd seen it happen. The fact that the guilty party was an officer, and not an enlisted man, made all the difference in the world. I'd had it with the big guys pulling rank. I was tired of all the petty politics and bureaucratic maneuvering." It hadn't helped that six months earlier, Murphy had been given his walking papers only weeks before he'd have been eligible to retire from the police force. He, too, had stepped on the wrong toes. This, though, Brody kept to himself.

"Right after I enlisted, I made the mistake of getting involved with a brigadier general's daughter." His lips curled. "I found myself on my way to Vietnam so fast I didn't know what hit me."

Involved with a brigadier general's daughter. A pang of jealousy swept through Jess, and for a fraction of a second she heard nothing else. It hurt to think of Brody with another woman, even though he must have been very young. Jess swallowed and pushed the disquieting feeling aside. "That's when you resigned—when the general offered to assure your promotion?"

He nodded. "But not before I told the dear general what he could do with his offer. When he found himself flat on his back I didn't have much choice."

Jess gasped. "You *hit* him?"

There was a grim smile of satisfaction on his lips. "I was lucky I didn't find myself in Leavenworth. Only the fact that I had an ace in my hand kept me out. That's something I've never quite been able to reconcile."

Jess searched his face. The upper half of his body was plunged in shadow. His expression was a mystery, but his voice was fraught with self-contempt. "Why?" she asked simply.

His gaze slid away. "I still could have blown the whistle, Jess." When he spoke again, his voice was very low. "Even after I was discharged, I could have called the newspapers, TV stations. The media would have loved to sink their teeth into a story like that." His jaw hardened. "Instead I just walked away—and did nothing."

He had shifted slightly as he spoke. She discovered that his face was closed and expressionless, but Jess wasn't fooled. Brody might have put the incident out of his mind, but he still carried a burden of guilt.

She gazed at him steadily. "You must have had your reasons," she said evenly.

"Oh, I did. By then, I just didn't care. I just didn't give a damn. I still don't."

There was no mistaking the weary cynicism in his tone. His features were closed more tightly than she'd ever seen them. His eyes were cold and empty. In spite of everything, Jess knew instinctively that he wasn't as hard-hearted as he thought.

Her lips pressed together firmly. "I don't believe that."

"I was never a model officer, Jess. Especially before I was commissioned. I stayed in because the money wasn't bad and the benefits were good," he stated flatly. "It was easier to stay in than tackle civilian life all over again."

"But you worked your way up through the ranks, all the way to captain," she protested. "I may not know much about military life, but I know you must have had something or you couldn't have stayed in it that long."

Oh, he had something, all right. Brody's thoughts were caustic. He was a risk taker, a thrill seeker. Undercover jobs and masquerades were his forte. It hadn't taken long for his superiors to discover his knack for duplicity. He was good at carefully laying the bait and sinking the hook; good at lying, at deceiving. . . .

But this was one act that left a bitter taste in his mouth. His deceit cut into him like a knife. "I'd finally learned that playing by the rules had its rewards, Jess. Once I decided to play, the rest came easy."

His implication was clear, but Jess no longer cared. He was a renegade, the worst kind of rogue. But it really didn't matter. So what if he hadn't walked the straight and narrow? In the end, Brody had stood up for what he believed in, for what he wanted. She hadn't, and it had cost her her marriage. But who was she trying to kid? Her marriage had been nothing but a mockery, in name and deed, from start to finish. She just had been too blind to realize it.

The bleak acceptance in Brody's eyes sliced her to the quick. There was a long, drawn-out silence while she stared at him intently. "So you believe that you're the kind of man who doesn't give a damn about anyone or anything." It was a statement, not a question.

Brody said nothing.

"You know what I think?" She moved a step closer.

He gave a short, harsh burst of laughter. "I have the feeling you're going to tell me anyway."

Brody still sat with one hip propped against the car hood, his eyes lowered. He wouldn't look at her, and suddenly she knew why. Brody was a man, just as human as any other, as vulnerable and as capable of being hurt as she. It wasn't like Lucas to show his emotions for the world to see; perhaps Brody was the same. Or maybe his vulnerability was buried so deeply inside him, he didn't even recognize it.

But Jess knew, and at the realization, something twisted inside her. A wave of melting protectiveness poured through her. She wanted to wrap her arms around him and lure him out of the shadows and into the sunlight. Motherly instincts again? The thought provoked a smile. Not this time, she promised him silently.

She edged so close to him their legs touched. At the contact, Brody's eyes swerved to her sharply.

"I think you're being too hard on yourself," she said softly. "I think that if you were really as heartless as you think you are, you wouldn't be here right now." She placed her hands on his shoulders and kept them there even though she felt him stiffen. "And I think if you let yourself believe otherwise, then you're a fool, Brody Alexander."

She leaned forward very deliberately, her eyes never wavering from his. It was Brody who groaned silently and squeezed his lids shut. She was reaching clear into his soul and beyond, seeing what no one else had ever seen, and he couldn't take it.

With a start he felt her lips touch his. It was a kiss so fleeting, so featherlight, that it was scarcely a kiss at all.

"Good night, Brody."

When he opened his eyes, she was gone.

Tonight he was the one left with a hammering pulse, and with it, the feeling of her mouth burned forever into his.

IT WAS A NIGHT with too much to think about. Hours later, Brody lay on the bed in his motel room, the cheap polyester spread twisted beneath him. Hands tucked under his head, he stared at the eerie patterns dancing on the ceiling. He knew there'd be no sleep for him tonight. He'd known that the minute he left Jess's place.

She might as well have been here in this room with him. Her presence was a tangible force in and around him. All he could see was her face, fresh and natural and lovelier than anything he'd seen in years. Oh, yes, she was here, reminding him of things he didn't want to think about, arousing emotions he no longer thought he had. He should have been running, running as far and as fast as he could. .

The last thing he needed was a call from Eric Culver.

He knew who it was the minute the phone began to ring. He almost didn't answer it. Finally he leaned over and dragged the receiver to his ear.

"I tried to call earlier," Culver said calmly. "Where were you?"

"I was with Jess," he answered shortly.

"So it's Jess now, is it?" The soft laughter echoing in his ear grated on him. Brody gritted his teeth. "I take it things are going well?"

"Well enough." His response was guarded. Brody sat up on the edge of the bed and switched on the light.

"Any new developments?"

"No."

There was silence on the other end. Brody sensed Culver's disapproval. He could have told him about Lucas and Jess. It would have been so easy to link the two of them together. If nothing else, it might pacify Culver. Why was he suddenly finding scruples he hadn't known existed?

"I told you this wouldn't happen overnight," he reminded the other man tersely. "If you want this done right, you're going to have to trust me."

"I'm just…impatient to get hold of the baby." There was an underlying hardness in Culver's voice; it occurred to Brody it was the first time he'd heard it. An odd chill snaked up his spine.

"Of course," he said slowly. "So you can check on his paternity."

"Naturally."

Every nerve inside Brody went suddenly tense. God, he sounded smooth. And he kept calling Nathan "the baby."

Now that he thought about it, Culver rarely mentioned that the child might be his.

Damn. *Damn!* Did Culver know something he wasn't telling? Yet more and more, Brody was having a difficult time believing that Jess had cheated on her husband.

Clinging vine...or fallen angel?

"I should have known Jessica wouldn't make this easy. Tell me, is she the perfect little mother?"

For an instant Culver's mockery made Brody see red. "If you're thinking you might be able to prove negligence on her part, I'd say the chances of proving it are mighty slim. She's very protective of her son."

"Then you'll have to come up with something else, won't you?"

Culver had an amazing knack for infuriating him. "I told you from the start I wouldn't be involved in a kidnapping." He thought of those few moments yesterday when he'd held Nathan. To even think of stealing that small bundle of innocence away from his mother sickened him.

The tension seemed to vibrate between them. Brody wasn't sure he liked the crackling silence on the other end of the line.

"If you're so familiar with Jessica already," Culver said finally, "why don't you capitalize on that?"

"Meaning?" Brody stiffened as if he'd been jabbed in the back with a gun.

"Meaning I shouldn't have to tell you how to do your job, Alexander." Culver's voice was harsh. "You say there's no evidence I can use against her. I'm leaving it up to you to see that there is."

Brody's stomach was churning. "I can't believe what I'm hearing. Are you suggesting that she and I—"

"Exactly." Culver sounded bored.

Brody's grip on the receiver tightened. "Don't push me," he warned.

"I'm not pushing," Culver said coldly. "I'm merely reminding you that you're there to do a job for me."

"You're asking me to have a cheap little affair with your ex-wife." Brody was torn between disbelief and fury. "What kind of man are you?"

"A desperate one, Mr. Alexander. I suggest you remember that." Culver's tone took on the sleek quality that Brody despised. "After all, what kind of mother will Jessica make if her son never knows what man he'll find in her bed *this* time?" There was a significant pause. "Or am I wrong in thinking you find her...desirable?"

"That's not the point." The edge in Brody's voice revealed his frustration.

"Isn't it? She's an attractive woman, Alexander. It's the obvious solution, I'd say. Remember, you're not the only private investigator in this town. I intend to see this through, and I'm sure I'd have no trouble finding someone willing to take your place—especially once they see Jessica."

"You said you'd give me plenty of time," he reminded him hotly.

"And I find I'm growing impatient," Culver snapped. "Now, are you in on this or not?"

Brody muttered a low obscenity under his breath. Culver had him by the throat and he knew it. If he balked, Culver would just hire another private detective.

He might not trust Jess, but he sure as hell didn't trust Eric Culver, either. The man was proving too damned unpredictable. And he couldn't deny that the thought of another man with Jess filled him with an irrational fury.

"I'm in." The words were bitten off curtly.

"Good." Culver's voice reflected his satisfaction. "Just remember, Jessica may give the impression of being above

reproach, but it shouldn't be too hard to wear her down."
Culver gave a low laugh. "Believe me, she's dying for it.
Just don't let yourself be taken in by that sweet angelic face.
And keep in mind, there's a bonus in this if you pull it off."
There was a click and the line went dead.

A bonus. As if he could forget, Brody thought caustically. How could Culver suggest so casually that Brody seduce the woman who had once been his wife?

Yet Brody couldn't deny that the idea *had* occurred to him. Good Lord, when Jess was around he could think of little else. But Culver made it sound so dirty and sordid.

He shoved his hand through his hair, his mind in chaos, his emotions in a state that was no better.

He was no longer sure why he was here; no longer sure he could stay.

But he couldn't leave. Not yet.

His mind drifted to the kiss he and Jess had shared. That wonderful, impossible kiss that had been scarcely a kiss at all.

Christ! What had he gotten himself into?

CHAPTER TEN

LUCAS ARRIVED bright and early Monday morning. The minute he walked through the back door, Jess knew something was different. His blue eyes were lively and snapping, and he was whistling. Jess had never heard him whistle in her life.

From her post near the kitchen sink, she murmured a good-morning. "Well, well," she teased. "Sounds like you must have had a good weekend."

"Not a bad one." He took a cup from the cupboard and helped himself to coffee.

Jess hid a secretive smile. So this was how it was going to be. If she wanted to hear about Betty, she was going to have to pry it out of him. Well, that was fine.

"All the rain yesterday must have had you climbing the walls."

The whistling abruptly ceased. A look of utter confusion crept into his eyes. "Uh . . . not really."

"Not really?" Jess assumed a look of wide-eyed innocence. "Why, Lucas, I know how you hate to be cooped up inside once the weather starts to dry out. Why not?"

He cleared his throat. "Actually, I was . . . busy."

"Oh? Doing what?" Jess wiped her hands on a dish towel and turned to face him.

He shifted from one booted foot to the other, reminding Jess of a child caught doing something he shouldn't have been. "I . . . ah, took in a movie in McMinnville."

"A movie," she exclaimed. "I wish you'd told me. I've been dying to see that new spy thriller. Is that the one you went to see?"

There was complete and utter silence.

"Is that the one, Lucas?" Jess couldn't remember when she'd enjoyed anything so much.

He scratched his head. "Fact is, Jessie, I don't remember the name of it."

"Oh." She turned away so he wouldn't see her satisfaction. Jess had the feeling his eyes hadn't been on the screen at all, and nothing could have pleased her more. "Did you go alone?"

Again there was a pregnant silence. Jess glanced over her shoulder and saw the dawning comprehension on his face. "Suppose you tell me." His shaggy brows lifted. He crossed his arms over his chest expectantly.

Jess grinned. "You were with Betty, weren't you?"

Lucas scowled. "You were there," he accused.

"I never left the house yesterday." Her expression was impish. "But you'd better watch out—I have spies everywhere," she warned, lowering her voice to a conspiratorial whisper. When he continued to glare at her, she sighed. "All right. I honestly didn't leave home at all yesterday, but Brody saw you Saturday night at the Barnyard Inn."

"He did, did he?" Lucas's eyes narrowed. "And just how do you know that, since Brody isn't even here yet?"

It was Jess's turn to fidget uneasily. She really wasn't sure how Lucas would react when he learned that she'd spent her Sunday—and Saturday evening—with Brody.

"He stayed for dinner Saturday." Her voice was breathless. "And he was here yesterday, too."

"Oh? Doing what?" She could tell by his tone he was deriving a great deal of pleasure from turning the tables on her.

Jess pointed toward her living room. Lucas walked to the doorway, then stopped short in amazement. "You did all this yesterday?"

She nodded, her eyes reflecting her pleasure. "The upstairs, too. With Brody's help," she clarified. "In fact, Brody did most of it." She watched the old man closely. "Well? Are you going to admit it's not so bad having him around, after all?"

"I never said I didn't want him here—" Lucas pushed back his hat, a rare grin lighting his grizzled features "—but I'll admit having that boy around is proving to be rather handy."

Jess smiled, and a warm glow spread through her. That was, after all, why she'd hired Brody. And knowing she had Lucas's approval only made the victory that much sweeter.

IT WAS A DIFFERENT STORY later that morning, however. Lucas's friend Ray stopped by promptly at ten to check on her tractor. Jess stood by nervously as he prodded and probed, twisted and turned. But the dratted piece of machinery refused to start. He tried again, to no avail. Ray muttered and shook his head all the while, and her anxiety grew.

Finally the stocky redhead straightened. "You want an honest opinion?"

Jess nodded, stilling her apprehension. "Yes."

He hooked his pudgy fingers under his belt. "Junk it," he said succinctly.

Her fingers twisted before her. Damn, she thought wildly. Oh, damn.

Her thoughts must have showed in her expression. Ray peered at her closely. "You didn't pay much for it, did you?"

"It was thrown in along with the house," she said faintly.

"I can see why," Ray observed. "Nobody would ever part with outright cash for such a poor excuse of a machine." His voice turned kinder. "You could pick up a good one down at the co-op. They've got a real little beaut there, just the right size for an operation like this. It's a nice piece of machinery, and a bargain, too, since the price comes in right around twenty thousand."

"Twenty thou—" Quickly she bit back her cry of despair. The figure was even more than she'd expected. "That's for a new one?"

Ray squinted his eyes. "That's a fair guess, I'd say. And the implements, too. A rake and a disk and maybe a loader."

"And what about for a used one?" she asked earnestly.

Ray looked skeptical. "They're hard to come by," he admitted. "At least a good, reliable one. Peter Rasmussen—he bought your folks' place—picked one up at an auction yard near Portland last spring. Didn't last but a month." He hesitated. "You just don't know what you're getting, Jess. I'd stick with a new one if I were you."

Numbly Jess summoned a smile and thanked him, then walked with him to the wide double doors that led from the barn.

Twenty thousand... A sick feeling rose up inside her. Lord, it might as well have been a hundred and twenty thousand. And here she thought she'd budgeted so carefully and so wisely. She simply hadn't counted on having to replace the tractor—she thought she'd had one. The realtor had told her he was under the impression the tractor might need only a few minor adjustments at the most, and she'd never given it another thought.

That had proven to be a foolish mistake—and a costly one.

You're learning the nuts and bolts of being on your own, all right, she chided herself harshly. *The hard way.*

She was still standing where Ray had left her, one shoulder leaning against the barn door, when Lucas and Brody walked into the barn five minutes later.

"Didn't Ray come?" Lucas glanced around in surprise when he saw no sign of his friend.

Jess grimaced. "Come and gone." Her voice low, she quickly relayed Ray's disturbing verdict. "Please don't say I told you so," she finished. The half laugh she attempted fell miserably flat.

"You know better than that," Lucas chastised firmly.

"That's exactly right," she agreed glumly. "I *should* know better. A barn full of machinery... I thought it was a great deal."

Lucas shook his head. "It was still a good deal, Jess. You said yourself this soil is perfect for a nursery."

"I know." She sighed. "That's really all I was thinking about. And I was so determined to handle everything myself." Inwardly she winced.

The old man's eyes were troubled. He understood her motives. He was guilty as hell of being just as proud of his own independence. "Jess," he said quietly. "How is this going to affect you?" He hesitated. "I don't want to pry, but can you come up with that kind of—"

"No." She cut him off with a shake of her head, knowing instinctively what he was asking. A mirthless smile curled her mouth. "Do you think I'd look like this if I had an extra twenty thousand dollars lying around?" The smile faded. Her eyes grew bleak. Dimly she noted that Brody had moved deeper into the rear of the barn. "Two years," she murmured. "If only I didn't have to wait two years before I see a profit. And if only I didn't have to get along in the meantime."

Her eyes were drawn to the house. Lucas knew intuitively she was thinking of Nathan. The old man cursed roundly. If he had the money, he'd gladly turn it over to her. But he'd had a bad few years before he sold his farm, and now all he had to his name was the house he lived in.

"I'll have to see about a business loan," Jess decided quietly. Her gaze sought the old man's. She was aware of his feelings about borrowing money, for any reason. As a young man, just starting out, he'd nearly lost his home and land during the Depression. It was only by a hair that he'd managed to eke out a living. Since then, Lucas had believed that if a person couldn't pay cash, then the purchase would simply have to wait.

Lucas nodded slowly. He pulled his cap from his head, his eyes on Jess as he followed her progress toward the house. Her posture was proud and determined, but his heart ached at the bleakness he sensed she felt inside.

His own step was just as determined as he turned and walked into the barn. He found the man he sought deep in the shadows near the far wall. "You heard?" he asked.

Brody nodded slowly.

Lucas jammed his cap on his head. "I asked you once if you thought you could fix this old antique." His faded blue eyes gazed directly into Brody's. "Now I'm asking you again, son."

Son. Something knotted and squeezed around Brody's heart. Lucas and Jess . . . and Murphy. One was lost to him forever. And the other two were looking to him as a source of faith and hope.

Don't do this to me! he wanted to shout, frustration and fear heaving violently within him. He had already failed once. Murphy might still be alive if he had come home only six months sooner. Brody was no child of God to work miracles. And after losing Murphy, there was nothing left in him. He had no heart left to give; his soul was empty. It wasn't like him to be noble. Once, perhaps; but not now.

The knot pulled tighter. An acrid taste rose in his throat. What would they say, Lucas and Jess, if they knew the real reason he was here? That he'd been hired for a little mud-slinging?

If only he knew whom to believe—Jess or Eric. Where Jess was concerned, he was torn in two. He couldn't deny the facts. Jess had left Eric, knowing what it would do to his career—and pregnant, yet! Brody felt he'd given her every opportunity yesterday to talk about Eric, about her marriage. She was hiding something. Gut instinct told him so, and that same instinct told him Eric was just a little too cunning for comfort.

Before Ray had come this morning, Jess had rushed out to buy him a pair of gloves. He wanted to trust Jess, he realized. But did he dare? He didn't know. Dammit, he didn't know.

Lucas reached out and placed a hand on his shoulder. "What do you say, Brody? I've got a garage that's seen about thirty years' worth of junk. Might even be a part or two you could use on this here brute." There was a brief pause. "You wanna give it a whirl?"

Lucas hadn't yet moved his hand. Brody was tempted to wrench away, but instead he held himself very still.

"I'll try" was all he said. He turned away before Lucas could see the gut-twisting guilt and bitterness showing in his eyes.

Lucas squeezed Brody's shoulder, then his hand fell away. "Try hard, son. Try real hard."

THREE O'CLOCK Tuesday afternoon found Jess sitting in front of the loan officer at the savings and loan in Amity. She was dressed in a tasteful navy sheath and matching pumps. Her silky hair had been twisted into a simple top-knot. She looked cool and elegant, every inch a successful businesswoman. Her appearance had pleased her when she'd left home and, Betty had even commented on it when Jess had dropped Nathan off at her house.

But inside, Jess was a bundle of nerves, and the loan officer wasn't helping matters. She counted herself lucky that she at least had a five-year business plan to show him. Still, he hadn't been overly optimistic at the prospect of her obtaining a loan, and she'd sensed something was wrong the moment he began assessing her application. He asked a few questions. Every so often a faint frown etched its way between his eyebrows.

Finally he looked up at her. "Can I be frank, Mrs. Culver?"

Judging from his expression, he had little to say that boded well for her. "Of course," she returned quietly.

He gathered the sheaf of papers and taped them to the desktop. "You've put together a very complete package. However..."

Here it comes, Jess thought dismally.

"I think I'd better caution you not to get your hopes up."

She met his gaze steadily. "Why is that?" she asked evenly. "I have my home and land as collateral. My mortgage is with your institution, and I have several certificates of deposit here as well. In fact, my mortgage is my only debt."

"That's true," he admitted. "But the mortgage is a new one so your credit history is practically nil. You have no steady source of income. You have no previous experience operating a nursery—no profit or loss statements to show—no business experience, period."

"Of course I have no business experience," she cried, torn between anger and a debilitating helplessness. "I'm just starting out."

The man across from her shook his head. "I sympathize with you, Mrs. Culver. But there are a lot of variables to consider here. What if we had a drought, or unseasonably heavy rainfall? Either one could deal you a very heavy blow financially. It might even wipe you out." He cleared his throat. "And what if some personal crisis should occur. If you had some unexpected medical expense you hadn't counted on?"

Jess thought of Nathan. "I have insurance," she said tightly. Inwardly she quaked. She did have insurance, but it was only the bare minimum. The cost for a full-service plan was outrageous.

There was an awkward pause. "There are still many variables to consider."

"You're turning down the request, then?" Her lips barely moved.

Both his expression and voice were carefully neutral. "I'll put it before the board, Mrs. Culver. But as I said, please don't get your hopes up."

Jess left even more frustrated and disappointed than when she'd entered. Yet she knew instinctively what the loan officer had seen: a woman without a husband; a woman whose ambition stretched too far. Was he right? Had she bitten off more than she could chew? For the first time, Jess felt her resolve begin to waver.

The past year had been hell. She shuddered to think of all the weeks she'd spent with Maggie, helplessly adrift until her divorce was final and her ties to Eric were severed forever. All the time spent trying to regain her self-esteem and rebuild her self-image after that shattering night when she'd discovered Eric's infidelity; the months of uncertainty and fear that followed as she prayed he hadn't meant what he'd said: *I'll get even with you, Jessica. Someday I'll get even.*

Had she survived all that only to stumble and fall once more?

Her mood was somber on the drive to Betty's. Betty's house was small but charming. The sidewalk leading to the door was lined with dozens of richly colored tulips.

Jess had barely removed her finger from the doorbell when Betty opened the door. She motioned Jess inside, a finger to her lips.

"He's sleeping?" Jess asked softly.

Betty nodded. "Can you stay for a few minutes?" she whispered.

Jess hesitated only a second. The chance to talk to another woman—and get her mind off her loan—was a welcome one. "I'd like that." She followed Betty down the hall.

In the kitchen, Betty turned bright eyes on her. "Do you like hot chocolate?"

Jess seated herself at the small maple table in the corner. "My one weakness," she said with a chuckle.

Betty pulled out a pan and turned on the stove. "I was really glad when you asked me to watch Nathan this afternoon." She stole a look at the younger woman. "I've been wanting to talk to you about Lucas."

"Oh-oh." Jess raised her eyebrows. "Is he giving you problems, too?"

"Problems?" Betty laughed and pulled a carton of milk from the refrigerator. "My dear, I'd have been chasing that man years ago if I'd thought I could get anywhere with him. The truth is, he never looked twice at me before I started working at the farm store." She poured the milk into the pan and set it on the stove, then folded her arms across her ample bosom.

Jess stifled a smile when Betty turned back to the stove. She had the feeling Betty was wrong there. "From what I've seen, those days are over."

"Well..." Betty peeked back over her shoulder, her expression both cautious and hopeful. "He did ask me out for dinner Saturday night. But I was the one who suggested going to a movie yesterday afternoon." She began stirring cocoa into the milk. "And he's coming over again tonight for supper. But sometimes I have the feeling he's holding back."

Jess frowned. "'Holding back'?"

Betty poured the hot liquid into two cups and carried them over to the table. "I'm not sure I know how to say this," she admitted sheepishly. "This is all rather new to me, you know."

Jess smiled encouragingly.

Betty ran the tip of her finger around the rim of her cup. "I want him to be with me because it's where he wants to be. Not because it's something he can't help."

"Not because it's something he can't help," Jess repeated. She tipped her head to the side. "You think he's fighting it?"

"Sometimes," the older woman confided. "It's like he's—holding back."

"That sounds like Lucas, all right," Jess observed dryly. Her eyes softened when she spied Betty's anxious expression. "I wouldn't worry too much about it just yet. I love Lucas, and I know he loves me; but those feelings seem to come out in deeds rather than words."

"I suppose you're right." Betty sighed, then quirked a dark eyebrow. "Speaking of worrying, I understand you've been doing a bit of that."

Jess laughed. "Has he been playing on your sympathy, telling you how mean ol' Jess keeps hounding him to see a doctor? He actually thinks I'm babying him, but that's not it at all.''

Betty laughed. "Oh, yes, I've heard about your mothering instinct. I understand it far better than Lucas, though. I've never had children or grandchildren, but I did have the children in my classes to take care of and watch over. Some women never lose that instinct to want to take care of someone.'' Her smile told more clearly than words that it was Lucas she was thinking of. "It certainly won't hurt for him to see a doctor," she added. "But I really don't think there's any great hurry. Lucas does seem very healthy for a man his age. I'll be glad to put in a good word for you—" Betty's eyes twinkled "—as long as you do the same for me.''

"Done," Jess said, glancing at her watch and rising from the table. "Maybe you won't need to, though. Lucas was due at Dr. Olsen's office ten minutes ago—his last appointment of the day."

That conversation was still in her mind when Jess drove by Dr. Olsen's office a short while later. It took a concerted effort to resist the temptation to scan the cars in the parking lot; at the last second she succumbed.

Lucas's battered old pickup wasn't there.

Jess gnawed her lip uncertainly. Lucas wouldn't have come in for his appointment early, at least not early enough to be done with the exam so quickly. Had he even shown up at all? Battling a twinge of guilt, she decided to stop and check.

Minutes later she returned to the car, plunked Nathan in his seat and shoved the keys into the ignition. She couldn't remember when she'd been so angry.

When she reached home, she jumped from the car. "Lucas," she yelled. "Lucas!''

Just then, Lucas ambled from the work shed. "There you are," he called out. "How'd it go at the bank?"

Jess was too distraught to think before she spoke. "Exactly the way I expected," she snapped. "I doubt I'll get the loan, and it didn't make me feel any better when I noticed your pickup wasn't at Dr. Olsen's office." Her back was ramrod stiff, the light of battle shining in her eyes. "I reminded you of that appointment just this afternoon. Why didn't you go?" she demanded.

A faint sheepishness passed across his weathered features. "Now, Jess," he began.

"Don't 'now, Jess' me! Dammit, Lucas, you promised me you'd go." Jess was walking a perilously fine line between anger and hurt, and managing neither. The day had been too full of disappointment and frustration. She was hanging on to her composure, but only by a thread.

Lucas shoved back his hat. Jess recognized the look on his face only too well. "Didn't go because I don't need to," he insisted stubbornly. "There's too much work to be done here."

"That's my problem, not yours."

"Seems to me you said that before," he grunted. "And I still think you spent too damn much time with your cousin Maggie. You're just as stubborn and headstrong as she is."

Stubborn? Good Lord, this man had invented the word. But his stubbornness had crystallized into downright bullheadedness. "You promised me you'd see Dr. Olsen." She glared at him accusingly. "You promised, Lucas."

His eyes avoided hers. "That has nothing to do with it. I'm not going to stand around and let you worry yourself sick about all the work when there's something I can do to help."

Jess stifled a hysterical laugh. Worry herself sick? She'd passed that point long ago. "If it's going to drive you into the ground, then I don't want you here!" she cried.

"Is that a fact?"

She gave him back stare for stare. "It is!"

Without a word, Lucas whirled and stomped off toward his pickup. Jess was just furious enough to let him go. It wasn't until he'd backed out, leaving her behind in a cloud of dust, that reaction set in, and she realized what she'd done.

BRODY HAD WATCHED the scene, or most of it, with growing amusement. There was Jess, shrilling like a banshee, and Lucas digging in his heels. Lucas could talk about her cousin Maggie all he wanted, but Brody had already decided he and Jess were cut from the same mold.

Then to his shock, Jess burst into tears.

It seemed to happen all at once—Lucas hightailing it off in his pickup, leaving a stunned Jess staring after him. Throughout the day, the sun had tried to pierce through the ominous, low-hanging clouds. But now the wind whipped to a frenzy, and big fat raindrops started to fall from the sky. Brody wasn't even aware of moving, but he'd scarcely reached her side before Nathan, still inside her car, began to wail.

He stopped, a hand at her elbow, one foot poised in the direction of the car. Brody swore softly, caught both literally and figuratively between mother and son. One look at Jess's stricken face was like being punched in the stomach. He wanted nothing more than to draw her into the safety of his arms, but Nathan's cries had reached an ear-shattering pitch.

His attempt to rescue Nathan from the car reminded him a little of the first time he'd seen Jess up close, but by now he was scarcely amused. His big fingers were awkward as he unbuckled the belt around Nathan's car seat, his hands unsure as he lifted the baby to his chest. The rain pelting his neck and back felt like stinging needles of ice as he eased carefully backward. He thwacked his head on the doorframe and dropped the diaper bag onto the ground, narrowly missing a mud puddle.

And all the while, tears continued to run unchecked down Jess's cheeks, mingling with the driving rain.

Brody grabbed her hand and began to move quickly toward the house. She stumbled along beside him until she gained her footing. Together they pounded up the backporch steps. The screen door slammed behind him. He collapsed against the doorframe and closed his eyes in relief.

It wasn't until he felt the tickle of hair against his chin that he realized he still had Jess crushed against him in a one-armed death grip. He wondered if she had any idea of the fierce battle being waged between his mind and body. He didn't let her go completely, though. A part of him was loath to do so. Instead he eased the pressure of his arm. His hand dropped to rest on the slender curve of her hip, with his fingers very near her spine.

Jess didn't move. Against him, he felt her take a deep, tremulous breath. Then slowly she raised her head and looked at him. "Brody?"

His heart wrenched at the tiny break in her voice. "Yes?"

"Don't leave me."

Her husky plea went straight to his heart. There was no force on earth that could have made him leave. He'd gotten quite a shock when she'd come out of the house this afternoon, so cool and elegant and sleek. It was like seeing a stranger, the stranger who had once been Eric Culver's wife, the woman he had yet to discover.

It no longer mattered whether Culver was right—that maybe, just maybe, she was a barracuda, a witch. She might be the most dangerous woman on this earth, and Brody was well aware he was asking for trouble. But what the hell— he'd been in trouble much of his life, anyway.

"I won't."

"Thank you." Her lips parted in a tiny, quivering smile that was both forlorn and hopeful, a smile that tore right into his heart.

"You don't have to thank me." The rain glittered like tiny black diamonds in her hair, which was in danger of coming loose. A few tugs and he could have it twined around his fingers. Slowly, as if testing her reaction, Brody reached up and guided a dark curl behind her ear. God knew he'd never been good when it came to self-denial. He fought an urge to linger . . . and lost.

There was a heated rush of silence. Neither of them moved. Neither spoke.

Her lips were parted, her incredibly blue eyes wide and faintly questioning as they lifted to his. Brody took in the delicate slope of tear-dampened cheeks and fragile jawline. Her mouth reminded him of cherry blossoms in the rain: pink and smooth and dewy. He wanted to memorize every inch of her with his fingertips, taste and learn her warmth and sweetness, absorb her into himself.

His hand slid into her hair. His long fingers curled gently around her nape, then tightened imperceptibly.

Inside his brain a warning bell went off. He pulled her head back slowly, as if he were trying very hard to stop himself.

As indeed he was. Eric Culver be damned. He was about to do the impossible, the unthinkable. He didn't care. *He didn't care.* Nor was it happening the way he expected, the way he would have chosen. And he knew it was all wrong....

But nothing had ever felt so right. He was leaning closer, head lowering, drawing her near.... He almost groaned as his mouth met hers. She tasted of rain and wind and the salty tang of tears. She smelled of all things pure and innocent—spring and flowers and the elusive but ever-present scent of baby powder.

The kiss was far from light and impersonal. Even if he'd wanted it that way, fate had decreed otherwise. The soft mouth clinging to his was shyly eager. Her lips melded to his with a sweet, beguiling sorcery of their own. Brody made a sound deep in his throat and crushed her to him.

Between them, a tiny fist against his chest thumped its disapproval. Brody released Jess and glanced down, almost in surprise. Stormy blue eyes blinked up at him. He'd completely forgotten that Nathan was wedged between them.

He laughed shakily. Jess's laughter was no better. She stepped back and held out her arms. "I'll take him now." She brushed the soft down on the baby's head. "Thank goodness you're not as wet as I am," she murmured. "But I think you probably need to be changed. And so," she added ruefully, "do I."

Brody noted that she had yet to look at him. There was a soft bloom on her cheeks. Was she embarrassed because she'd asked him to stay? Maybe, he decided. He also detected a hint of uncertainty in her flushed features. The realization was oddly pleasing.

"Jess." She'd started to turn away. His voice stopped her. "You mind if I rummage around in the kitchen and see if I can find something to eat while you change?"

Her smile was warmer than the brightest of suns. "Not at all," she said softly.

Upstairs, Jess showered quickly and changed into an old jersey sweatshirt and pants. By the time she'd fed Nathan and laid him in his crib, there was a mouth-watering aroma drifting from the kitchen.

Brody was at the stove, efficiently wielding a pancake turnover in one hand and just as efficiently transferring crisp slices of bacon onto a plate with the other. The somber depression that had surrounded Jess since yesterday disappeared, as if a curtain had suddenly been lifted from her shoulders. Pancakes and bacon in the evening. She took a perverse delight in the knowledge that Eric would have hated it.

But Jess was much more content with focusing her attention on the man before her. His shoulders stretched the thin cotton of his shirt, and his hips seemed incredibly narrow in comparison. The mere act of observing Brody made her shiver. He'd never looked more male; she'd never felt more female. Perhaps it had something to do with just having had a baby. Since Nathan's birth, every part of her was alive with a sensitivity that had never existed before. In spite of everything—the hurt, the disappointment—she was still a woman, with the same wants and needs as every other woman.

Eric had never given her the chance to be a woman—not in the truest, purest sense of the word. But all that was in the past, she reminded herself. All in the past.

Brody turned then, and something in his eyes told her he knew she'd been watching him. Oddly, she didn't mind.

"Hi," he said with a slight smile. "Nathan in bed?"

She nodded.

His eyes delved deeper. "You okay now?"

Soft as the question was, there was an edge that warned Jess he would know if she was lying. "I think so." Her smile was wobbly. "Or at least I will be when I get things straightened out with Lucas." She pulled out a chair and sat down at the table.

"I know the last few days haven't been easy for you." He started across the room holding two plates heaped full of pancakes and bacon. Her glass was already filled with milk. Brody was, she decided, a most thorough and observant man.

"No." Their eyes met over the plate he handed her. "You heard?" she asked quietly.

He smiled. "It was hard not to." He and Lucas had spent the day assembling the greenhouse frame in the area just south of the house. There'd been no chance to work on the tractor until shortly before Jess arrived home. "You want to talk about what happened?"

She grimaced. "With the loan? Or Lucas?"

He passed her the butter. "Both."

"The loan is easy," she stated flatly. "I was told not to get my hopes up since I have no track record when it comes to managing a successful business. As for Lucas—" she blew out a weary sigh "—I'm not sure what to say."

"I didn't hear everything, but I got the impression he missed an appointment. With the doctor?"

"Yes. I made the appointment for him myself, for this afternoon at four. He promised me he'd go, Brody. But he didn't." The prongs of her fork tapped against her plate. She looked and sounded more than a little indignant.

Brody hesitated. "He does seem healthy, Jess. He strikes me as the kind of man who isn't happy unless he's busy."

"But Lucas is sixty-eight years old and he hasn't seen a doctor in years." Lines of worry appeared between her slender brows. "He sold his farm because it was too much for him, but he's too independent and full of stubborn pride to admit it, at least to me. If something happens to him, it's going to be all my fault. And if I don't watch out for him, who will?"

A slow smile claimed his mouth. "How about Betty? They've got another hot date tonight, you know."

"I know. I was at Betty's before I came home." Jess's lips tightened. "Believe me, nothing would make me happier than to see Betty and Lucas have a lasting relationship. But no one knows better than I what can happen to a one-sided romance, and if Lucas doesn't start giving a little, Betty will set her cap for someone who will."

Before Brody could say a word, Jess pounded her fist on the table so hard the dishes rattled. "It also makes me madder than hell that none of what I know about the two of them has come from Lucas. Why, I wouldn't even know about tonight if it weren't for you and Betty. Why couldn't Lucas tell me?"

"Maybe because he's just as stubborn and independent as you." He studied her quietly. "And maybe because he just didn't have a chance."

There was no sting to the words, but Brody's gentle chastisement was the last straw. What was wrong with her? she agonized silently. Why was she always the last to know? First Eric, and now Lucas. Eric had rarely confided in her, but Lucas wasn't like Eric. The knowledge hurt, perhaps more than it should have, but suddenly all the hurt and pain and confusion of the last year rushed back with a vengeance.

She could neither speak to Brody nor look at him, and so she confined her attention to her plate, although her appetite was gone. An unaccustomed ache closed her throat. Foolishly—oh, so foolishly—she wanted to cry, which was ridiculous. She hadn't even cried when she'd found out about Eric's betrayal. Yet every nerve in her body tightened as she battled the urge with all her strength. Praying that Brody hadn't seen her silly action, she reached for her plate and whirled away from the table, but he was too fast for her.

He caught her around the shoulder and removed her plate and glass from her hands so quickly she was left feeling absurdly awkward and exposed.

"Hey," he said, stunned. "It's not as bad as all that. And I didn't mean to hurt you, Jess. I swear." He reacted without thinking, pulling her into his arms and wrapping them around her. Above her head, he spoke softly, soothingly. "Lucas will be back, Jess. Not tonight, obviously. But he won't stay mad. He'll come around before you know it. You'll see."

His teasing approach did little good. Every sweet, supple inch of her was as taut as a bowstring.

His hand at her back, Brody felt the deep, shuddering breath she took. "It's not just Lucas."

"The loan, then?" Brody thought of his nest egg hidden safely away in San Francisco. Dear God, it was hers, if only she would take it. Jess could talk about Lucas and his stubborn pride all she wanted, but he knew she wouldn't accept it.

"No." Her voice was muffled. Her mouth was pressed against the warm skin of his throat.

"Then what?" He decided to vary his approach. "Do you have some deep, dark secret hidden in your past that you're afraid someone will discover?"

"No." But she was running, Jess thought, running from a past she couldn't evade forever, as she was just beginning to discover.

His hands slid around to gently cup her shoulders. "Are you an escaped convict? A notorious jewel thief running from the authorities?"

Jess wanted to laugh. God, if only she could. But inside she felt like a fragile spring flower that had been plucked and crushed, then left to wither and die.

Eric had done that to her. She had been so eager, so willing, shamelessly yearning to share all the love that blossomed within her heart. But love was the one thing Eric had never wanted from her.

For so long now, Jess hadn't let herself think about her own needs—the need to be touched, to touch in return. Eric had always taunted her with her weakness, jabbing and poking with that steel-honed tongue of his until her heart was raw and bleeding. She had been starved for closeness, but eventually she had learned to bear the pain of that loss. It wasn't wrong to need someone else, was it? To want to be held and comforted, as Brody was comforting her now.

But he was asking too much. She didn't want to talk about Eric. She didn't want to think about him.

Her hands came up to Brody's chest. Her fingers clenched and unclenched. "Brody, please..."

He shook his head in wordless denial. Searching her eyes, he considered the self-doubt, the confusion and the fear he saw reflected there.

She was so scared, felt so desperately alone, and he knew damned well what lay behind those feelings—or rather, who. He also sensed she needed to talk as much as he needed to hear her side of the story. Brody was suddenly sure it would be vastly different from Eric Culver's. He also knew he was taking unfair advantage, but the need pounding away inside him was deep and driving—and it had nothing to do with Eric Culver and the real reason he was here.

All pretense at lightness vanished. "All along I've thought you were a woman with too much to handle, too much to think about here—" he touched his forehead, then his heart "—and here."

Her gaze flew up to his. The truth was starkly written there, in those beautiful blue eyes that reflected an instant's panic.

"No, don't pull away," he said firmly. His hands tightened just enough to remind her she wasn't free. "You're a woman with secrets, Jess. I've known almost from the start. Oh, you hide it well—maybe too well." Soft as his voice was, his gaze speared into hers. "And I can't help but wonder why such a pretty lady with so much going for her has such shadows in her eyes." He paused for the space of a heartbeat. "And I think that reason is your ex-husband."

CHAPTER ELEVEN

"How did you know?" Jess willed her voice not to tremble.

"It wasn't hard to figure out—the move here, everything in such chaos. And you said you were alone when Nathan was born. It's unusual." He hesitated. "I know sometimes if a marriage is in trouble, couples believe a baby will bring them together—"

"Instead of tearing them apart?" The shrill, high-pitched sound might have belonged to someone else.

His hands slid down to grip hers. "Is that what happened?"

No! Yes! Oh, God, don't do this to me. I just want to forget!

Time was suspended in an agony of silence. Jess could only stare at Brody, at the chiseled squareness of his jaw, the set of his beautifully shaped mouth that was sometimes almost harsh. But there was nothing harsh about him right now. His features reflected only a silent plea that she couldn't ignore.

"Tell me, Jess. Tell me." His eyes implored her. "Please."

Please... Memories crowded in, memories she was powerless to resist. In all the years she'd been married to Eric, had he ever once said that to her? No. Instead it was she who'd always said it.

Please touch me, Eric. Please hold me.... Don't you want me? Please, Eric. I need you, I need you to show me that you care.... *Please make love to me.*

"Talk to me, Jess. Please talk to me."

The voice jarred her back to the present. Abruptly all her resistance drained from her. What did it matter if Brody knew? There was no reason to hide her marriage to Eric. Except the last, final, irrevocable straw.... Yes, she thought tiredly. She would tell Brody of her marriage—most of it.

But not everything.

She scarcely realized he was guiding her from the kitchen until she felt the back of the sofa at her knees. Brody pushed her gently down, then immediately deserted her. A second later he returned and sat down next to her, the cup of coffee he'd had at dinner in his hand.

There was an awkward silence. Jess opened her mouth a dozen times, only to change her mind. It seemed that her newfound courage, like her nursery business, was off to a shaky start.

Brody sighed. It wasn't a sound of impatience or even regret. It was more an expression of tolerant indulgence, of understanding. "This is difficult for you, isn't it?"

Her eyes met his squarely. "I wish it weren't," she said honestly.

His lips smiled; his eyes didn't. "So do I," he said softly. "You think it would make it easier if I asked the questions?"

"And if I don't like what you ask?"

"Then don't answer."

The response brought her head around. Her eyes widened. Brody appeared utterly serious. "Are you telling me you'll be satisfied?"

This time his smile filtered through to his eyes. "Probably not."

That made Jess smile at a time when she very much needed that release. At least he was honest.

For just an instant, a faint cloudiness darkened her eyes. She wanted to believe that Brody cared. But she had wanted to believe that Eric cared, too. She'd wanted it so desperately, she had almost fooled herself into believing it.

Her gaze returned to Brody. He was holding out his coffee cup. Jess accepted it unthinkingly, took a sip and then handed it back. Brody lifted it to his lips again, finding the spot so recently vacated by hers. It was a strangely intimate gesture, but curiously it seemed to release some of the pent-up tension inside her.

"You mentioned that you lived in Sacramento while you were married. That's where you met your husband?"

Jess nodded and leaned back against the cushions. "I took a part-time job with the state supreme court during my senior year in college." She paused. "The girls in the dorm thought it was hilarious—me falling for a supreme court justice. No one, including me, really believed it could go anywhere."

"He was a supreme court justice?" Just the right amount of surprise was reflected in his voice. Brody mockingly applauded, the self-disgust in his mouth tasting like ashes. He should have been on the stage.

A fleeting smile touched her lips. "I know," she said softly. Her eyes traveled fleetingly downward, taking in her faded jersey sweatshirt and pants. "Unbelievable, isn't it?" Her smile dissolved. *Unbelievable.* The word characterized every stage of her marriage from first to last. "His name is Eric Culver." She turned her head slightly. Should she tell him Eric was no longer on the bench? This was painful enough, without adding that ugliness to it. She felt her way carefully. "Have you heard of him?"

Brody shook his head. "I've spent a lot of years away from California, remember." He tried telling himself it wasn't an out-and-out lie, but it grated nonetheless.

Relieved, Jess went on, "The newspaper's society pages were always printing some little tidbit about him—where he'd been and who he'd been seen with. He was Sacramento's most eligible bachelor." Lord, what a laugh that was. "I was flattered by his attention, charmed by his worldliness. I married him less than six months after we began seeing each other. Right from the start, the press loved it and made the most of it. Eric is twenty years older than I, but that made no difference. One reporter even likened it to a fairy tale."

Brody had a very clear picture of what had transpired. He had no trouble envisioning the suave, sophisticated Eric Culver sweeping a young innocent like Jess off her feet.

A faint distress crept into her features. Seeing it, Brody reached out and laced her fingers through his. His grip was warm and strong as he drew her hand to his thigh, letting their clasped hands rest there. The gesture was comfortably familiar. It gave Jess the courage to go on.

"Eric has a kind of—charisma, I guess you could say. He can talk a person into just about anything, and make it all seem perfectly natural. It suited me fine to simply be part of the background and give him the role of shining star. He didn't want me to work, and so I didn't. Instead I learned to be the perfect wife, the perfect hostess he demanded."

Demanded? Beside her, Brody went very still inside. It was a strong word, one he wasn't sure he liked. Yet he sensed Jess wouldn't use it lightly.

But suddenly a wholly unexpected cynicism entered her voice. "It's true that ignorance is kind. It took a while—far longer than it should have—for me to realize that I didn't feel needed. I was a prize to be flaunted and shown off to his colleagues and associates." It was really nothing but a ploy so that no one would ever suspect Eric's secret, but Jess didn't say so.

Brody's eyes met hers. "A role?" he asked softly. "Window dressing?"

"Exactly." Her voice was flat. "And somewhere along the way, I began to feel I'd lost my own identity. I wasn't Jess Ryan anymore, or even Jessica Ryan Culver; I was Justice Culver's wife—no more, no less. Eric's career was everything; I no longer mattered. I never did. I wanted to get a job; he refused. He said it was demeaning for his wife to work outside the home." Her laugh was bitter. "I never worked inside his home. Eric had a cook and a housekeeper long before he ever married me. I felt like an outsider in my own home."

She took a deep, serrated breath. Brody had the distinct sensation she was fighting some fierce inner battle.

"But the hell of it is, I could have settled for that. I was stupid—and foolish enough—to have settled for that. Eric was not—" she faltered slightly "—a terribly demonstrative man. He could be so cold and unfeeling sometimes. I wanted so much to please him, but when we were alone together, he rarely looked at me—only enough to keep me hoping and praying that maybe I was wrong. And what he said always sounded so reasonable, so damned convincing: he was under a lot of stress, or the docket was extremely heavy. There was always an excuse. Our marriage was so completely one-sided in every way. I did all the giving, and he did all the taking." Her voice caught painfully. "I saw a side of Eric Culver that no one else even suspected he had."

A slow burn began to spread through Brody's veins. All along, Culver had led him to believe Jess was the guilty party, that he was only the victim, the defenseless pawn, in her scheming machinations.

But that wasn't Jess. That wasn't the woman he had come to know. "And so you left him?" The question fell into a hushed void.

"Yes." He watched her swallow deeply, struggling for control. "After six years, I was tired of living a lie, tired of pretending."

His fingers were immeasurably gentle as they combed through her hair. "Six years," he murmured, then hesitated. "You can tell me this is none of my business," he began slowly. "But if you were so unhappy, why did you—"

"Why did I stick it out for so long?" A bitter smile touched her lips. "Because I was a fool. I kept hoping things would change, that he would begin to think about my needs, for once. And every so often, he'd do something so terribly sweet I'd fool myself into thinking it could really happen. It didn't occur to me until it was too late that he was treating me like a child, that he was only trying to pacify me. And then it was like throwing a starving dog a bone once a year." She drew a deep, tremulous breath. "But most of all, I was scared."

His hand tightened around hers. "Of being alone? On your own?"

"Partly." Her tone was very low. "A lot of it had to do with my own self-image. Confidence has never been my strong suit; I suppose part of it was the way I grew up. And when I married Eric, he managed to strip away what little I had."

Brody muttered something under his breath.

Jess swallowed deeply before she could go on. "Nothing I did was right—my hair, my clothes, little everyday things in the household, like meal planning. I felt as if every decision I made was the wrong one. I was afraid to make any kind of decision. I knew my marriage was a failure, and it was just one more example. If I left Eric, what was to stop me from failing again?'' Her tone was one of quiet resignation. "I was afraid to trust my own judgment."

And I'm the last man you should trust. That bitter thought invaded Brody's mind, even as a dozen other nameless emotions spilled through his body. But he didn't want to think about it all. Damn, but he didn't.

Their clasped hands were strangely reluctant to part. Brody took advantage and curled his arm around her waist, pulling her up against him so that her back rested flush with his chest. She looked so lonely and forlorn, he felt a deep-seated need to comfort her. He didn't question that need. He knew only that to deny it was to deny his very self.

There was no resistance on her part. She responded by linking her fingers even more tightly with his and settling against him.

"Jess." His voice was scratchy. There was a strange quality to it she couldn't quite identify. "You said you saw a side of him that no one else saw. What did you mean by that? Did he—did he hurt you?"

She was quiet for a long time. "No," she said finally. "At least not physically."

"How, then?"

The words were ground out. Jess twisted slightly, her eyes flying to his face. He looked almost haunted, as haunted as she suddenly felt.

She was silent for a moment. "Little things, mostly. So often, Eric was careless and thoughtless. He came from a fairly well-to-do San Francisco family, but I had no experience in that kind of world. He was harsh and critical, so cold and taunting. And he wasn't a very forgiving man." She plucked at the fold in her pants. "It took me a while to learn how to fight back."

Her gaze fell. "I was in a car accident once," she added, her voice very low. "I was lucky. I only had a few bruises and scratches, but I didn't realize how bad it was until I saw the damage to the car. I was still scared and shaken up when I called Eric from the hospital. He was at a—a friend's. They were working on a case, and he refused to come get me. He didn't say it, but it was as if he just didn't want to be bothered with me. I ended up taking a cab home. I know it sounds silly, and weak, but I was so hurt that he—''

"Shh." Her tortured voice tore straight into Brody's heart. He didn't think she was even aware she was clutching the front of his shirt. "I don't think you're silly, Jess." He gathered her more closely into his arms. "And I definitely don't think you're weak."

Her eyes cleaved to his; her expression was both searching and wondering. "You don't?"

"No." He kissed the tip of her nose. The incredulity on her face made him smile, even while the betrayingly moist sheen in her eyes made him ache inside.

His smile slowly faded. "Did Eric know you were pregnant when you left him?"

Every muscle in her body tightened. The lamp burned dimly in the corner. The shadows all around were friendly ones; the time was just right for telling secrets. But Jess was suddenly cold, so cold she felt the sun would never find its way into her body again.

She started to draw away, but Brody wouldn't let her. "Did he?" His arms tightened. "Tell me, Jess. Please." Silently he prayed that she wouldn't question his insistence.

She didn't. "He knew," she said briefly. "He was furious, naturally."

Brody's blood froze cold as ice. " 'Naturally'?"

"Eric never wanted children." The statement was flat and emotionless.

Brody deliberately made his voice as casual as possible. "And custody of Nathan—"

"Is solely mine." Her laugh was harsh. "Why would Eric want custody when he never wanted a child in the first place?" A fiercely possessive light flashed in her eyes. "Nathan is my responsibility and that's the way it's going to stay."

"He has no visitation rights?"

"No. He had his chance when the divorce settlement was being discussed. He never requested either custody or visitation rights, and I certainly never offered. It's better that way since I wanted no child support, either. Besides, even if he'd fought for custody, he'd never have gotten it." She suppressed a shiver. Even now, *especially* now that she had Nathan, she was still afraid that someday Eric would make good his threat of revenge.

Had he been standing, Brody had no doubt that statement would have set him back on his heels. His mind traveled swiftly back to his first introduction to Eric Culver. Bits and pieces of conversation flashed through.

I want to know for certain whether Jessica's child is mine. This could be the only chance I'll ever have to be a father.

And then later...

She's a very physical person...a clinging vine.... It shouldn't take her long to find someone to keep her warm at night.

And now Culver wanted that someone to be him...*him*!

Jess shifted slightly in his arms. Brody's eyes were drawn to her. "Is that all?" he asked quietly.

It wasn't. But what remained would stay locked inside her forever. It was too humiliating, too shameful and still much, much too painful.

Brody felt her slump in his arms. "Isn't that enough?" she asked tiredly.

For a moment Brody stared sightlessly over her head, both mind and body in chaos. Why hadn't Jess told him she'd filed for divorce at such a crucial time—just months before the election? She must have known the publicity would rip Eric apart at the polls. Had that been her intention all along? What was it she'd said? That she hadn't yet learned to fight back.

Was that her way of getting back at Eric? Her way of getting even for all the shattered vows and broken promises? Or was it something else?

His eyes squeezed shut. "Jess." Her name had a guttural sound. She was going to hate him; he knew it, yet he had to ask. "Jess, who is Nathan's father?"

She was silent for so long he thought she hadn't heard. When Brody finally opened his eyes, he found her expression totally bewildered.

Her lips parted. "Weren't you listening? I just told you..." Oh, no. *No!* Brody thought she had... She would have laughed at the irony of his assumption, if she weren't dying a little inside with every tortured breath.

Then again she heard his voice. "I'm not condemning you, Jess, I swear. After what you've just told me, I can understand why you might seek out someone else—"

But Jess scarcely heard. Her mind seized only on his first words, and something inside her came apart. Suddenly she was shaking, glaring at him through eyes that burned like fire.

Her voice cut across his. "You're not *condemning* me? Damn you, Brody, I may have been lonely. I may have been scared. But I was married!" she spat at him. "Nathan is the only good thing that came out of my marriage. Eric is Nathan's father, do you hear? Eric!" She pushed against his chest, sprang to her feet and whirled around, angrier than she could ever remember.

She didn't see Brody flinch; she didn't see the helpless despair that twisted his features as he jumped up and caught her, wrapping her tightly against him while she struggled to be free. For Jess, it only added to her rage to be so easily caught, so easily subdued.

Brody had one fleeting glimpse of the anguish in her eyes, and a wrenching pain tore through him. She was trembling, he realized. Tangling his fingers in her hair, he pressed her head against his chest.

"I'm sorry," he whispered. "I'm sorry, Jess. I had no right to question you."

He felt the deep, shuddering breath she took. "How could you think that?" Her voice was muffled against his chest. "How could you think that I would be unfaithful?"

His heart contracted. A hot, moist bead of warmth slid into the hollow of his throat; then another and another. Tears of pride, he realized. Tears of angry despair.

"Oh, God, Jess, I don't know what I thought." He muttered into the dark cloud of her hair. "I've been so damn confused since I met you. But I didn't mean to hurt you, I swear."

Slowly she raised her head to gaze at him with glistening blue eyes. "You believe me, don't you?"

His breath caught at the break in her voice. His fingers skimmed the curve of her cheek, wiping away the moisture. "I believe you," he said, and knew it for the truth.

She drew back slightly. Her hand came up to cover his, as if she couldn't stand for him to leave her. "Really?" Her gaze clung to his.

"Really," he said firmly. "I also think Eric Culver didn't deserve a woman like you. I think he was a fool for not realizing just how much of a woman he really had." *And I think I'm going insane with wanting you.*

The words were like diamonds and gold, a healing balm to her wounded heart. There was a peculiar tightness in her stomach. She was twenty-nine, Jess thought hazily. A woman, the mother of a child. She was a virgin no more, no longer an innocent. But what did she know about loving a man? Eric had never wanted that from her. He had turned her need for him into something shameful. When he had chosen to come to her bed, the act was over almost before it began, and always in the dark. *Always in the dark*.

But Brody could teach her. He could teach her all she wanted to know, and more.

If only he would kiss her again, she thought yearningly. Kiss her so that she didn't have to think.

All at once, something changed. The air was suddenly charged with their physical awareness of each other. She stared at his mouth.

He stared at hers.

After what seemed like an eternity, Brody swallowed dryly. "Jess." Her name carried a subtle warning. "Jess, don't look at me like that."

"Why not?" The tip of her tongue darted out to moisten her lips. At the unconsciously provocative gesture, Brody wanted to squeeze his eyes shut.

"Because you and me—" there was a fractional hesitation "—it just isn't a good idea."

Her eyes searched his. "I'm not sure what you mean," she said slowly.

Brody couldn't remember when he'd felt so helpless. "This is happening for all the wrong reasons." There was a quiet urgency in his voice. "Think of what you just told me, Jess. You've been alone. You've been hurt and neglected."

"That has nothing to do with it." She sounded as certain as Brody was confused.

"Doesn't it?" His voice was low, his control deceiving. "You don't understand, Jess. You're finally in charge of your life, but I'm not." That, at least, was the truth. "I don't even know where I'm going when I leave here."

She stared at him as if she were trying to reach clear inside him. She was calm, almost serene, so damned accepting. Would she be as forgiving when she learned the truth?

"I know that," she said finally. The quaver in her voice stabbed into his chest. "And much as I wish I could say it didn't matter, it does. But I also trust you, Brody. I trust you not to hurt me. I trust you enough to believe that you care, even though you're afraid to show it."

It was all so unfair. How could he do this to her? He cried out silently, his mind full of tortured desire. How could she do this to him? "Jess..." He tried desperately to defend himself against her sweetness.

"Shh." Her arms slid around his neck. Her lips hovered temptingly beneath his. She no longer cared if she was giving away too much of what was better left hidden. "Don't say anymore. Please, just hold me." She held her breath as a flicker of fear went through her. Would Brody think her wanton and bold, as Eric had? She was shrinking inside, but determined to draw on this newfound well of courage. Drawing back, she searched Brody's face for the familiar, icy disdain she'd always found in Eric.

But Brody's hard face reflected only longing, a confused kind of longing, perhaps. But it was enough to send her heart into a wild frenzy. "Please," she whispered. "Will you please just hold me? And kiss me.... Kiss me just once?"

Her eyes held an appeal he couldn't look away from. Brody was trapped in a web from which there was no escape. His hands dug into her waist. He was suspended in an agony of doubt, knowing he should push her away but finding himself unable to.

Her lips were parted. Waiting. Wanting. She was trembling...and so was he.

His head dipped, its movement slow and uncertain. Brody kept his eyes open as his lips barely grazed hers, watching as desire chased the lingering shadows from her face.

And he knew that one kiss would never be enough. He'd meant to end it quickly, but the vibrant promise of her body against his was suddenly too much. Desire so strong he could scarcely think cut through him. For an instant he felt totally out of control. His lips took hers with fierce hunger until he remembered how only moments before, this tempting creature in his arms had spoken of shattered dreams and broken promises.

There was a subtle softening of his lips on hers. The kiss was longer, infinitely sweeter and intimately knowing, his tongue stroking and seeking.

There was nothing tentative in the caress of his mouth on hers, but Jess reveled in the wonder of being held full and tight against a hard male body. She had one glimpse of his face, and the dark intensity she saw there made her heart skip a beat and then run wild.

Both mind and body were a wild tangle of pure sensation. Her hands clutched his shoulders. Her fingers thrilled to the feel of muscle and bone and warm male flesh. He was intensely male to the lonely female starving within her. Every nerve ending in her body screamed with life.

It felt so good to be held in a man's strong, secure embrace. Jess felt that deficiency like a thousand tiny needles, the sensations sharper, stronger than they'd ever been before. This breathless feeling of closeness, this richness of touching, was what she had always wanted, what she had needed...what Eric had never given her. With lips and eyes sealed, she could pretend the nightmare of the past year had never happened. Her tongue touched his hesitantly. The muffled groan of pleasure he gave echoed in her mouth. It excited her beyond anything she had ever known.

And he wanted her. *Brody wanted her.* She could feel the heat and fullness of that need swelling taut against her thighs. She clung to him, fearful of losing the almost painful delight she felt.

Brody touched her as if he owned her. Jess needed no urging, no sweet persuasion to keep her mouth where they both wanted it, feeding their mutual need and fanning an even deeper craving. He wanted to hold her, to pull her down next to him, and lose himself inside her forever.

His hand slid beneath the soft fleece of her sweatshirt. He splayed his fingers over her naked back, lingering for long, uninterrupted seconds before sliding around to explore her ribs.

It was exquisite torture for them both when his palm strayed slowly upward. His callused fingertips encountered a lacy barrier, and then he covered her softness with his rough palm. Her breast was full and ripe and supple, her skin warm and almost unbearably soft. He shaped and plundered and stroked, achingly aware of the velvety peak straining against his fingers. It was enough to drive him into sweet oblivion.

Slowly, reluctantly, Brody broke off the kiss. He wanted Jess so much he was shaking with it, and if he didn't stop now, he wouldn't be able to.

Jess whimpered, a sound of protest. Her eyes were smoky and dazed as they drifted open and looked into his; her lips were damp and swollen from his kisses.

"Brody?" Her arms tightened around him.

His hand stroked her hair. "Tell me, Jess," he whispered. "Is this right or wrong?"

She gave a little shake of her head. "If it's wrong, why does it feel so right?"

She arched against him and he was lost. His mouth had reached for hers again when suddenly he pulled back. With gentle precision, he eased her away from him.

Eyes cloudy and questioning, Jess watched as he stood.

"You're leaving?" Disappointment pierced her voice.

Slowly, reluctantly, Brody bent and lightly kissed her lips. "I think I'd better," he murmured, "before something happens we'd both regret."

Regrets? There would have been none. But Jess remained silent. Something in Brody's proud posture warned her that arguing was pointless.

She didn't realize that walking away just then was the hardest thing he'd ever done in his life.

ANGER MARKED every line of Brody's lean frame as he threw open the door of his motel room. The golden glitter of his eyes was hard and deadly as he stalked to the phone and stabbed out Eric Culver's home number in San Francisco.

He wasted no time with preliminaries when Culver finally answered. "You lied to me," he accused harshly.

There was a stunned silence. "Mr. Alexander? Is that you?"

Brody shoved his fingers through his hair and swore hotly. "Don't play innocent with me, Culver. I want to know what the hell you're up to."

"Mr. Alexander—" Eric's voice was patience itself "—I'm afraid you've lost me. Perhaps you're the one who should explain."

Brody silently applauded Culver's aplomb. He was so cool, so convincing, exactly as Jess had said. But the reason he wanted Nathan was crystal clear, and Brody was through deluding himself about Eric Culver.

"Explain?" His voice was deceptively calm. "It's funny you should say that, because I just got quite an earful from Jess about you. From what I hear, you weren't exactly a model husband."

"So she's confided in you, eh?" There was an edge to Culver's soft laughter that turned Brody's stomach. He could almost see Culver's thin-lipped smile, and he suddenly had the unerring conviction that Eric Culver was a human power broker—that he could be a one-man wrecking crew if he chose.

"You led me to believe she was involved with another man." Brody's voice was harsh and accusing. "There was never any other man and you know it."

"She told you that?"

"Yes. And I was a fool for not realizing it long before I did."

"Good Lord, man, you're a fool for believing her." The amusement that surfaced in his voice was quickly replaced by something else. "I warned you, didn't I? I told you how sweet and innocent and eager she was—"

"Just admit it, will you?" Brody's voice, low and taut, sliced across his. "Nathan is your son, your own flesh and blood, for God's sake! Jess never betrayed you."

"All right. So what if the boy is mine? Jessica *did* betray me; not with another man, but she sure as hell betrayed me when she left me. I hired you to do a job for me, Alexander, and I hired you because you're a man who wouldn't let his emotions get in the way. I want that baby, Alexander. Do you hear? I want him, and I don't care what you have to do to get him."

"Then maybe you hired the wrong man, after all," Brody said softly. "Because this is wrong, Culver. And it's over. Don't you see that?"

"It's justice, do you hear? She stabbed me in the back. She robbed me of my career—my life. And that's something I'll never forget!"

"She's paid the price, Culver. Believe me."

"She hasn't!" Culver practically screamed. "We won't be even until I have the one thing in the world that matters to her—her son."

"Your son, too," he reminded him harshly.

But if Culver heard, he gave no sign of it. Brody heard nothing but cold, relentless implacability. "What are you saying, Alexander? That you want out? You're forgetting I've already made a substantial down payment—"

"Consider the check in the mail." Brody's jaw was bunched. "I can't... No, I won't do this to Jess. The way I feel right now, I'd pay to be rid of you."

There was an instant of crackling silence. "Dammit, Alexander, don't you realize how foolish you're being?"

"On the contrary," Brody said tightly. "I finally got smart. You want to get back at Jess, but you know as well as I that you wouldn't have a prayer in a custody suit. Especially if I testified about our little deal. Somehow I don't think the judge would be particularly sympathetic to your motive. Revenge and fatherhood don't exactly go hand in hand—and we all know that's the only reason you want Nathan."

"Is that a threat?" Culver demanded.

Brody's tone was ripe with satisfaction. "Damn right," he said, and severed the connection.

CHAPTER TWELVE

THE PORCH STEPS CREAKED a noisy protest as Brody climbed them toward Lucas's front door. He asked himself for the hundredth time that morning just what the hell he was doing. What business of his was it if Jess and Lucas were at each other's throats? What did it matter to him if those two never saw each other again, never spoke for the rest of their lives? It was none of his damned affair what they did or didn't do.

He should have left. He could still leave, for that matter. If he had any sense, he would. After all, he'd broken his ties with Eric Culver; there was no reason to stay, nothing to keep him here in Oregon.

But here he was, having been awake since dawn, wondering how to get Lucas and Jess back together and trying to figure out a way to keep Jess safe from Eric.

He shouldn't have cared. He wished like hell that he didn't. But he did, and he might as well learn to live with it.

The door opened. Lucas stood there, fully dressed though it was barely six in the morning, the ever-present blue denim cap jammed on his head.

"Might as well come in and have some coffee, son." He grinned. "Got some of the real stuff here, not that watered-down excuse like Jessie makes."

Brody stepped inside. He had the damnedest feeling Lucas had been expecting him. In the big, cluttered kitchen,

Lucas shoved aside the newspaper scattered across the table and plunked a steaming cup of coffee before him.

Brody reached for it automatically, but he made no move to drink it. Instead, his keen eyes followed the old man's progress toward the white enamel stove in the corner and back again. Now that he was here, what could he possibly say to Lucas that wouldn't make him sound like the interloper he was?

But it was Lucas who spoke first. "I expect you're here about yesterday."

Brody nodded slowly.

The other man scraped back a chair and sat across from him. "Might as well say what's on your mind."

"All right, then." Agreeing was easy. Saying it was not. Why was it so difficult for him to talk about emotions, even ones that weren't his own? Because he'd never cared enough? Or because no one had ever cared enough about him to let him know how they felt? Murphy had cared, and *he* had cared, yet grown men didn't go around confessing such things to each other. Oddly, Brody wished he had...just once.

Now it was too late.

He cleared his throat, willing away the demons of the past. He raised his head and looked straight at Lucas. "Jess cares about you, Lucas. She didn't mean what she said yesterday. She's had a lot to deal with lately and I don't think you should hold it against her."

Lucas appeared to consider. "I know that," he said finally.

"Well?" It was Brody's turn to be blunt. "What do you intend to do about it?"

Lucas paused, his cup halfway to his lips. Slowly he lowered it. "I don't intend to do anything about it," he said with a shrug. "As far as I'm concerned, it's forgotten."

Brody folded his arms across his chest. "And the appointment with the doctor?"

The old man gave an exasperated sigh. "You're as pushy as she is, you know that?"

Brody merely raised his eyebrows. There was a laugh trying to escape deep in his chest, but he held it in, knowing he didn't dare give an inch or Lucas would take a mile. He contented himself with a lazy half smile.

"All right." Lucas relented grudgingly. "You can tell her I'll go."

The smile faded. "I think," Brody remarked quietly, "Jess would appreciate it if you'd tell her yourself."

"I suppose she would, at that," he murmured, almost to himself. He slowly raised his faded blue eyes to meet the younger man's gaze. Brody was surprised to see a flash of dry humor there. "I wonder," Lucas said with a quirk of his mouth, "if Jessie knows how lucky she is to have you on her side."

The statement went through Brody like the tip of an arrow. The breath he'd just taken turned to burning pain in his lungs. He was glad Lucas had turned away, muttering something about breakfast.

"Lucas." Brody had never felt comfortable enough with Lucas before, but inside he knew the time was right. It was now or never. "Lucas, can I ask you something?"

"Don't know why not." The cheerful voice was accompanied by cupboard doors opening and closing.

"Did you know Jess's ex-husband?"

For long, drawn-out seconds there was an all-encompassing silence. Then a black iron skillet was thumped on the stove top. "He was only here with her once." There was a harshness in Lucas's voice that was foreign to Brody. "The two of them came to visit the first Christmas they were married. Supposed to stay a week, they were. He left her in tears after a day and a half. Never told Jessie, but I was glad to be rid of him." He snorted. "Damned pompous ass!"

That, Brody reflected with a hint of dry wit, was being kind. He sobered abruptly. "How did he treat her?" he asked quietly. "Do you know?"

Lucas shook his head. "That's something only Jessie knows. She's never said a word against him, yet I've never been able to rid myself of the feeling that he made her miserable. I don't think Eric cared—" his eyes met Brody's "—not like you do. She should have met you years ago. You're a hundred times the man Eric Culver is."

There was a small silence, during which Brody sat disbelievingly, thinking that Lucas was nobody's fool. Then the old man cleared his throat. "Now," he said, turning back to the stove, "how about some breakfast. Then we'll scrounge around in the garage and see if we can't dig up a few spare engine parts for Jessie's tractor before we head out there. She always did say I was an old pack rat."

Brody scarcely heard. His throat was humbly tight, but he had the craziest urge to reach down and pick up his heart from the floor. If he hadn't felt guilty before, he did now. He was consumed with it, consumed by the fires of hell, for surely that was where he was headed.

He suddenly knew why he hadn't been able to leave. For the first time he finally admitted he was half in love with Jess. But he was hopelessly caught in the current of events both past and future. How could he ever tell her who he was and what had really brought him here?

But Lucas was wrong, and the taste of self-disgust was like acid in Brody's mouth. He cared, yes—dear God, he more than cared. But he was no better than Eric Culver. He was worse. Much, much worse.

When Jess found out the truth, he had no doubt she would agree.

SHORTLY AFTER EIGHT, Jess got a call from Lucas informing her that he and Brody were going to Salem to try to track down a part for the tractor and probably wouldn't be back before noon. The conversation was brief. Jess scarcely had time to murmur an "Okay" before Lucas had hung up.

Nevertheless Jess was smiling when she turned away from the phone. So Brody had been right, after all. Lucas had forgotten all about yesterday's harsh exchange. Could her luck possibly be changing? She hoped so.

She lifted Nathan from his infant seat and held him out before her. "Well, my little man, looks like it's just the two of us this morning," she announced cheerfully.

She had just begun to lower him toward the seat again when a firm knock sounded at the back door. "It's just us," a voice sang out. "The Three Stooges."

Jess's eyes widened. Maggie! She opened the door and Maggie, Tony and Anna filed into her kitchen.

"You're the last ones I expected to see here," Jess exclaimed, giving Maggie a quick hug. Maggie chuckled at her surprise. Tony grinned, and Anna smiled shyly.

Jess ruffled Tony's blond waves. "And you two! It's Wednesday. Are you playing hooky from school?" She glanced over at Anna in time to see a look pass between mother and daughter, that she didn't quite understand. Oh-oh, Jess thought. So Maggie was still having trouble with Anna.

All of a sudden Maggie's smile seemed a little forced. "The kids both have the day off," she offered. "The district is sending all the teachers to training workshops for the day."

"So you thought you'd come up and spend the day with me?" Jess smiled. "That's sweet of you."

Maggie sighed. "I wish we could," she said regretfully. "But we're on our way to Portland to pick up a new grill and rotisserie for the lodge kitchen.'' She rolled her eyes. ''You wouldn't believe the shipping charges. But I knew you'd never forgive me if we were this close and didn't stop.''

''And you brought Anna and Tony along to keep them out of trouble, hmm?'' Jess intended the comment to be a teasing one, but she realized her mistake when that same look kindled between Anna and Maggie.

Jess stepped quickly between them. ''Would you like to hold Nathan?'' she asked Anna. She cast a laughing remark over her shoulder at Maggie. ''If your mother gets him first, we'll have to pry him away from her.''

To Jess's relief, Maggie chuckled. ''The truth comes out. I suppose you'll never let me hold him.'' Her eyes softened as they turned to Nathan. ''I can't believe how much he's grown.''

Anna hesitated, but her expression was shyly eager. She glanced toward the door going into the living room. ''I think I'd feel better if I were sitting down,'' she confided. ''I'm afraid I'll drop him.''

Jess chuckled. She was relieved to hear Maggie's laughter join hers. In the living room, she pointed Anna toward the rocking chair. From the corner of her eye, she saw Maggie surveying the room with her hands on her hips.

Her lips twitched when she caught Jess's glance. ''This is certainly a change from the last time I was here. You *have* been busy, haven't you?''

Jess eased Nathan into the crook of Anna's arm. ''Actually,'' she murmured, ''Brody did most of this.''

''Brody?''

Jess straightened. She could feel Maggie's eyes boring into her back. Slowly she turned. ''Brody Alexander. The man I hired to help with the nursery.''

''Oh, yes. The handyman. He's working out okay?''

"Fine." Her reply was brief. Why she suddenly felt so ill at ease, she couldn't be sure. Perhaps it was because she sensed Maggie had never approved of her hiring Brody in the first place.

Maggie picked up a vase on the mantle. "Do we get to meet him?"

Jess's gaze flew to hers. She could have sworn there was a slight edge in Maggie's tone, but Maggie's expression reflected only a frank curiosity.

She forced herself to relax. "I don't know," she said honestly. "He and Lucas went to Salem to find a part for my tractor. They probably won't be back till noon."

"We won't be able to stay that long. Too bad." Maggie pulled a face and added teasingly, "I was looking forward to giving Lucas a bad time. Nothing like a few fireworks to wake everybody up."

Jess shook her head. "He does enough of that on his own, thank you." She felt a tug on her sleeve and looked down into Tony's freckled face. "Jess, can I go out and look around outside? In the barn, too?"

"Sure, Tony." She watched as he dashed from the room. His eyes, as green as his mother's and full of the same deviltry and mischief, had lit up at her reply.

Apparently Maggie's mind was following the same vein. "There's nothing he can get into, is there?"

"He'll be okay," she assured her cousin. "There's no ladder to the loft, and I doubt he could do anything to the equipment that hasn't been done before. He certainly isn't going to drive my tractor out of there!"

Maggie looked at Anna. "Maybe you'd better go with him."

Anna handed Nathan to her mother and went off after her brother.

"So that's it," Jess indicated Nathan now snugly ensconced in Maggie's arms. "What a schemer you are, Maggie Howard!"

Maggie settled back in the chair. "You always did see right through me." She wrinkled her nose at Jess, but the next moment her expression was serious. "What's wrong with your tractor?"

Jess dropped down on the couch. "It's more like what isn't wrong with it," she said gloomily. She went on to tell Maggie the details and about the loan she'd been forced to seek.

Maggie's expression was troubled when she finished. "I know you're not going to appreciate this, but I wish you had stayed with me a while longer, if only to give yourself time to recover from the divorce."

Jess shook her head. "This is the best medicine for me, Maggie. It's something I had to do, what I've always wanted to do." She hesitated. "When Steve died, you still went ahead with your plans for the lodge. In a way, it's not much different from your situation then."

Maggie eased Nathan over her shoulder. He'd started to doze, so she spoke very quietly. "That's what scares me. Starting a business—any business—is risky. One bad year can be devastating. No one knows that more than I. Remember three summers ago when we had so many forest fires in the southern part of the state?"

Jess shivered in remembrance. One of those fires had come perilously close to Silver Creek and Maggie's lodge.

"Tourists were afraid to come into the area. Luckily we had a wet fall or I'd have been forced to get a second mortgage on the lodge just to get through the rest of the year. Running a business is so much responsibility." Her hand cupped the back of Nathan's head. "Plus there's Nathan to think about."

"You had two children to consider," Jess reminded her, then smiled. "And you know I gave this a lot of thought before I decided to go through with it. Besides, at this point, it's sink or swim."

"True," Maggie admitted. "But what about Brody?"

Jess started. "What about him?"

"Hey, don't go all defensive on me." For a second there was a gleam in Maggie's green eyes, but it faded just as quickly. "I just have a feeling there's something going on between you two." She watched her cousin closely. "Is there?"

Jess focused on her hands. Just the mention of Brody's name caused her heart to jump. "Yes . . . and no."

"Good answer, Jess. You sound just like Tony when I ask him why he hasn't cleaned his room. Only his standard reply is 'Because.'"

A faint smile curved her lips. Jess glanced up to find that Maggie had laid Nathan across her lap. He was sound asleep. "All right," she said softly. "I know what you're going to say, Maggie. That it's too soon after Eric; that the last thing I need is another man to complicate my life." Her gaze met Maggie's almost defiantly. "I like the way he makes me feel."

Maggie gave her a long, searching look. "But is that enough, Jess? And what do you know about him? His home, where he comes from, his family?"

Jess hesitated. "I know some things." Up until now, she'd told herself she had no more right to delve around in his past than he did in hers. He had never been deliberately evasive, yet she'd sensed he was reluctant to talk about himself. Why? Was there something dark and mysterious in his past that he didn't want her to know about?

"What about the job you offered him? It's temporary, right?"

Jess nodded slowly.

"So he'll be gone in . . . what? A few weeks? Where is h
going from here?"

Jess thought of the rapt enchantment she'd known i
Brody's arms last night. She'd had no thought of stoppin
with just a kiss. If it hadn't been for Brody, there was n
telling what might have happened. She'd really had n
thoughts of anything but how alive and wonderful he mad
her feel.

"Yes," she said finally, her voice very low. "A month a
the most. And I don't know where he's going from here."
She released a long, pent-up breath. Maybe Maggie wa
right. Maybe she was deliberately blinding herself.

"Look," Maggie said tentatively. "I don't want to sa
anything against him, especially without having met th
man. But I know how awful it can be when you suddenl
find yourself alone. And one night of heaven isn't going t
last a lifetime."

"I know," Jess returned very quietly. Oh, yes, she knew
That was one lesson she'd learned from Eric.

She summoned a wan smile. "It's funny, isn't it? Her
you are, telling me to be careful. When we were kids, I wa
always the one telling you to look before you leap."

Maggie managed an answering smile, but her eyes wer
anxious. "To tell you the truth, I could still use a little ad
vice." Light as her tone was, it had an underlying note o
gravity.

Jess met her gaze. "Anna?"

Maggie nodded.

"Why don't you let me put Nathan upstairs?" she sug
gested. "Then we'll talk some more."

When Jess returned downstairs, Maggie was sitting Ir
dian-style on the floor. Jess joined her there, thinking it wa

just like the times they'd spent together in either Maggie's room or hers.

"You know," Jess murmured, "it's hard to believe Anna has turned into a problem child." When she stayed with Maggie this winter, she'd often thought what a fine job Maggie was doing of bringing up her children without a father. Tony was as rowdy and lively as any eleven-year-old. Anna was more like her father: quiet and watchful.

Maggie's mouth turned down. "Believe it, Jess."

"Boy trouble?"

"I wish." Maggie wrapped her arms around her knees. "You wouldn't believe the grades she brought home this term."

Jess smiled. "I seem to remember your mother saying that about yours once or twice, and complaining that the only thing you were interested in was Steve."

"I know, I know. This sounds like the old double standard here, but Jess, she had three D's and two C's."

Jess's jaw dropped. "Anna? Why, she's always been an honor student."

"Tell me about it." The sound Maggie gave was half laugh, half groan. "Right now I'd give anything to go back to the days when Anna was a baby. Don't wish for Nathan to grow up too soon, Jess. It won't be long before you're wondering if every decision you make is the wrong one."

Anna and Tony came back inside then, so the conversation was cut short. Jess laughed when Maggie chased a protesting Tony into the bathroom to wash before they left for Portland, but Jess was a little concerned. It wasn't like Maggie to sound so down. Was the problem with Anna more serious than she thought? Before they left, she elicited a promise from her to get away and spend a few days with her soon.

The house seemed empty when Jess went back inside. It was inevitable, perhaps, that her thoughts should turn to Brody and what had happened in this room last night.

Nor could she rid her mind of Maggie's warnings.

It was true that she loved the way Brody made her feel. With him, she felt like a woman—desired and desirable. That had happened so rarely with Eric.

But it was also true that she was no longer as naive and trusting as she'd once been with Eric. Still, she had told Brody just last night that she trusted him, and at that moment she had. With her, he was kind and gentle and careful. It was that tender concern for her—and her alone—which had prompted his withdrawal last night.

But he was every bit as much a victim of desire as she, and Jess sensed it would only take a spark to set the fire of passion ablaze.

Then there would be no turning back ... at least for her. It was a thought that scared her as much as it thrilled her. Maggie had said that one night of heaven wouldn't last a lifetime, and it was true. And in the long run, did she trust Brody enough not to hurt her?

All of a sudden, Jess wasn't sure.

CHAPTER THIRTEEN

MAGGIE AND HER FAMILY hadn't been gone long when the low rumble of an engine reached Jess's ears.

She glanced out the window to find Brody's car already stopped in the drive. Lucas had just pulled in behind him. Jess caught her breath. In spite of the phone call this morning, she wasn't sure what to expect from either one of them. There was a knot in her stomach the size of a fist. As if he sensed her gaze, Lucas glanced toward the house. He must have seen her hovering at the edge of the window, for he gave a tiny wave. Then he casually turned to Brody and slapped the other man on the shoulder as they headed for the barn.

She had no chance to speak to Lucas until he came into the kitchen an hour later to wash his hands. They were filthy from helping Brody with the tractor. Jess felt his eyes on her as she bent to place Nathan in the swing. She straightened and turned, stilling her expectancy.

Lucas confined his attention to drying his hands. "Jess, about yesterday—" he cleared his throat "—I thought I'd ask if you'd call Dr. Olsen's office and reschedule that appointment for me."

There was a protracted silence. "Is that what you want?" Her voice was very quiet.

Lucas shifted from one foot to the other. "It's not easy for me to admit I'm wrong," he began gruffly.

"I'm not asking you to admit any such thing," she interrupted firmly. "I only want what's best for you." Her eyes softened. "Don't you know that, Lucas?"

"I expect I do," he mumbled. "The truth is, I'm not used to having anyone make a fuss over me. But Betty thinks you've got a point, so you're probably right."

"I see." Her brows rose a fraction. "So Betty had a little say-so in this," she found herself teasing. "Something tells me you'd better get used to women making a fuss over you."

"Ain't that the truth." The familiar testiness in his voice was belied by the gleam of pleasure in his eyes.

Jess folded her arms. "Don't you think it's time you told me whether or not this thing between you and Betty is serious?"

He sighed. "Serious? You see, Jess, that's exactly why I've kept mum about it. I don't want you making more of this than what there is, because I know you. If nothing comes of it, you'll think it's your duty to go out and find someone else for me, when I'm not even sure I—"

"Why should I," she murmured, "when you already have Betty?"

"You see?" His hands on his thin hips, Lucas made the perfect picture of outrage. "That's exactly what I mean. The fact is, Jessie, much as I like Betty, she and I don't exactly have a lot in common—"

"Whoa! Explain that, please." Jess wasn't sure she liked the sound of that statement.

"There's the difference in our ages, for one thing." He seemed almost defiant.

"What!" Jess scoffed. "Maybe ten years? That's nothing, Lucas, and you know it."

He hesitated. "But then there's her job, too."

"Her job at the farm store?" Jess was bewildered.

"No." His voice was gruff.

She frowned. "The job she had as a schoolteacher?"

Lucas nodded. His eyes shied away from hers, and she sensed his embarrassment. "I'm not sure I understand, Lucas." Jess spoke very quietly.

Lucas shoved his hands into the pockets of his jeans and moved to stare out the window. "Think about it, Jess. I'm a farmer, the son and grandson of a farmer. That's all I know."

"And?" A vague comprehension began to dawn.

"And look at Betty. She's been to college. I barely finished eighth grade. She's traveled all over the country. She's been to places I've never seen, places I've never even heard of—"

"And she has a wealth of knowledge that far surpasses yours?" Jess's voice was sharp.

Lucas nodded, his expression resigned.

Jess marched over to him, and bodily turned him around, jabbing a finger at his chest. "Listen to me, Lucas Palmer," she told him, fiercely. "You're one of the best men I've ever known in my life, and you don't have to apologize to anyone for whatever education you do or don't have. The man you are comes from here—" her finger stabbed at his heart, then sailed upward to flick the bill of his cap "—not from here. I see nothing wrong with the two of you enjoying each other's company. If it doesn't bother Betty, it shouldn't bother you."

Lucas shook his head. "I wish it were that easy," he said slowly.

Jess laid a hand on his arm. "It's only as hard as you make it."

He said nothing for the longest time. The sad, almost wistful expression etched into his weathered face made Jess's heart twist. "Betty and I have both been alone for a long time, Jess."

Her tone was earnest. "But the important thing is that you don't have to be anymore."

A faint gleam entered his eyes. "You have an answer for everything, don't you?" he commented dryly. He began to move toward the door. "I'll think on it, Jessie. I can't promise any more."

It wasn't the response she would have hoped for, but Jess knew she'd have to be content. "Lucas." Her voice stopped him at the threshold. "When can I make that appointment with Dr. Olsen?"

His voice drifted back to her. "Whenever you want, Jessie. Any time's fine with me."

Jess was already reaching for the phone, her lips curved in a sheepish grin. It wasn't often that Lucas was in such an agreeable mood; she'd be wise to make the best of it.

JESS MANAGED TO GET LUCAS in to see Dr. Olsen that same afternoon. Lucas had even consented to letting her come into Dr. Olsen's office after the exam to hear the results. Jess knew the minute she spied Lucas's superior expression what the outcome was. She listened to his I-told-you-so's all the way home and didn't mind in the least.

Jess had little opportunity to talk to Brody over the next week and a half. She had the feeling he was avoiding her. After her disturbing conversation with Maggie, the suspicion that he was doing exactly that did little to ease her peace of mind. Had he decided she wasn't worth the time and trouble?

At least she felt her nursery was finally making some headway. Brody and Lucas had just finished the greenhouse yesterday, sliding in the last of the large, fiberglass panels on the south side. She had originally planned to install a heating and cooling system, as well, but she'd decided that would have to wait until her finances had improved. Still, she was delighted at the progress being made. Most of the roofing had been torn off the shed in preparation for turning it into a shade house to shelter young plants. The only dark cloud on the horizon was the idle state of her tractor.

The bank had phoned to tell her it would be another week or so before a decision could be made on her loan application. Battling the prospect of a crushing disappointment, Jess had made up her mind she would simply have to hire someone to bring in their own equipment and till the soil. Before the hot weather arrived, she needed to plant the bare-root trees and shrubs she'd ordered from the supplier.

She asked Lucas earlier in the week if he knew of anyone who might be willing to rent their time and equipment, but he asked her to hold off for a few days. Almost every night in the past week, he and Brody had worked on the tractor until well after ten. Brody sometimes stayed even later.

A part of her was immensely pleased, but she also felt guilty that the two men were so determined to accept the responsibility as theirs. But there was no arguing with either of them.

As for Brody, the few times they were alone, he was distant, almost aloof. The kiss they had shared might have been a far-off memory, a figment of her imagination. Jess was confused and hurt over his attitude. She couldn't forget the imprint of his mouth upon hers; it was like a brand burned into her lips. But what about Brody? Did he regret it?

That he might have had second thoughts caused a painful catch in the region of her heart. Was she wrong in thinking he felt the same? He aroused urges in her that were almost painfully sweet. She would die rather than suffer the humiliation of rejection yet again.

Every so often, she caught a glimpse of something so weary and cynical in Brody that she wanted to reach out,

take him in her arms and soothe and comfort him the way
she did her son. Yet whenever she was around, he was
guarded and tense. Jess didn't understand it. She didn't
understand him.

Nor did she understand herself. Was she falling in love
with him? Her heart rejoiced at the thought; her mind re-
belled. It was too soon, a voice inside cautioned. It was just
as Maggie had said: after Eric, she should have been leery
of jumping headfirst into any kind of relationship.

Still another voice whispered that that was exactly what
she needed. The woman inside her longed for fulfillment,
the tender touch of a lover to sweep her to paradise and the
blessed contentment of forgetfulness.

But she didn't want just any man. She wanted Brody, and
the attraction was more than physical. Much more. She had
known him less than three weeks, yet she couldn't deny there
was a curious—and very potent—feeling of rightness when
she was with him. Deep in her soul, she sensed that Brody
was a man who could heal her scars, erase them with a single, yearning caress.

Six o'clock Friday evening found Jess loading several
thick roast-beef sandwiches on a plate and filling a large
thermos with coffee. Betty had stopped by earlier that afternoon to see Nathan—and to ask Lucas over for dinner.
He'd left shortly after Betty. Nathan was napping, but Jess
tucked the portable monitor into her pocket in case he woke.

The barn door creaked as Jess carefully nudged it open
with her hip. The trouble light hanging from a hook in the
rafters cast a golden circle of illumination in the rear. Brody
and the tractor were in the center of it.

Brody had glanced up when the door opened. He saw the
plate she held in her hands. "What's this?" he asked in
surprise.

High noon and the last showdown, Jess was tempted to retort. She didn't. Instead she held up the plate and thermos. "I thought you might like a sandwich and some coffee."

He smiled. "Sounds great." His expression turned rueful when he withdrew his hands from the engine. "Oh-oh," he murmured. "Maybe I'd better—"

Jess wordlessly handed him the plastic bag containing a soapy washcloth and towel that she'd tucked under her arm.

"You think of everything, don't you?"

"I try," she assured him solemnly.

He merely laughed and sat down on a wide wooden box to eat.

They indulged in a few minutes of small talk while he ate, then Jess inclined her head toward the tractor. "You know," she stated quietly, "that this is above and beyond the call of duty."

Brody was in the act of lifting the sandwich to his mouth. His hand slowly lowered. "I know that, Jess." His voice was as quiet as hers. A half smile lifted the corner of his mouth. "Are you trying to get rid of me?" Beneath the teasing undertone there was an underlying seriousness.

"No." Jess shook her head. *God, no!* "Only..."

"Only what?"

His gaze was starkly demanding. Jess looked at the ceiling, the dirt-tracked floor, the rough, planked wall behind him—everywhere but at Brody.

A hard hand caught hers. He pulled her down beside him. A lean finger gently prodded her chin upward so that she was forced to look at him. "Only what?" he repeated.

Jess held his gaze as long as she could, feeling inexplicably awkward and shy. And oh, how inadequate! Her uncertainty brought home how little she knew about men. Her eyes lowered. It was the only way she could get the words out. "Only I've had the feeling you've been avoiding me the last few days," she whispered.

The statement was simple, honest and direct. So much like Jess that something twisted inside Brody. Jess was no scheming witch, no tempting seductress. All that she was, all that she had ever been, was here next to him. Close enough to touch. Close enough to hold.

Was it selfish to want her so much it hurt inside? Brody ached with the deep, driving need to pull her into his arms, fit the lush curves of her body under his and love the breath out of her until nothing else existed. But it wasn't that easy. Lord, if only it were.

The air left his lungs in a rush, a sound of mingled frustration and pain. Whatever his feelings for Jess, he had come here under false pretenses. Jess had said that she was afraid of the future, but his fear was even greater than hers. He knew what would happen if he divulged his part in Eric Culver's plot; it would hurt her as much as it would hurt him. Brody had no doubt about her reaction. She would hate him, and that was a very bitter pill for Brody to swallow.

And there were still so many secrets between them. His . . . and hers. He was unable to rid himself of the notion that she was holding something back from him.

He swallowed. "I haven't been avoiding you." His voice came out low and rusty.

Her lips parted; he thought he could see her tremble. "You haven't?"

Against all his better judgment, he shook his head.

Her eyes clung to his. "The other night when you kissed me," she began. "I—I thought you wanted me. Was I right or wrong?"

Brody sensed her self-doubt, but the truth was, he was holding a precarious balance between desire and caution. He knew of her longing, the longing she couldn't hide. He'd tasted it in the sweetness of her mouth. She could be his, if he hadn't discovered scruples in himself he'd thought no longer existed. He could kiss and love her into warm, willing submission. But her purity, that elusive sense of innocence unnerved him.

She deserved a much better man than he. But here she was, stripping away every single barrier he'd erected against her as if they were no more than tissue.

"This has nothing to do with right or wrong, Jess." He spoke very gently. "You're just starting to get your life back in order. I don't want to complicate things for you."

Her response was swift and vehement. "What makes you think you would?"

In his heart, Brody knew he should tell her. It would hurt her, yes, but she would never believe her pain would be any less than his. Brody couldn't face her scorn, her ridicule, the angry hurt he knew would follow. He wished he knew what—if anything—Eric planned, now that he was no longer pursuing the case. Damn! If only he'd been able to talk Eric into dropping the whole sordid scheme.

Deep inside, he nursed the silent hope that Jess need never know. But that wouldn't erase what he was, what he had been, and what he had done....

He reached up and brushed his knuckles against the sloping curve of her cheek. "You don't know me, Jess. I'm not the man you think I am."

"Then tell me," she challenged. "And tell me why you think you're not good enough for me, Brody Alexander."

Brody rose and began to pace around the barn. She didn't know what she was asking, he reflected bitterly. And she saw far more than he'd ever planned to reveal.

Jess's gaze never wavered from his tall form. She sensed that her observation had startled him. "That's it, isn't it?

You don't think you're good enough for me." She could scarcely believe it. First there was Lucas, thinking he wasn't good enough for Betty. And now Brody thought the same of her.

Slowly he turned to face her, his eyes hooded. He stood with his head held high, his feet braced firmly apart. There was something very proud in his stance, yet she sensed a curious vulnerability that was completely at odds with the stern and harsh-edged exterior of this contradictory man.

At his silence, Jess deliberately lightened her tone. "Do you have some deep dark secret hidden in *your* past that you're afraid someone will discover?"

If only it were that simple, he thought. If only...

"Are you an escaped convict? A notorious jewel thief running from the authorities?"

The merest glimmer of a smile appeared. Jess had borrowed the questions he'd fired at her, and dropped them back into his lap.

Brody's smile faded until all that was left was a bleak emptiness that reached clear to his soul. The look he fixed on her was long and penetrating. "What would you think," he asked very quietly, "if I told you I *had* seen the inside of a jail cell?"

If he had hoped to shock her, the ploy was an abject failure. Jess met his gaze levelly, her voice as quiet as his. "I would say you must have been very desperate."

Desperate. That he was, both then and now. He could deal with her anger or rejection, even pity. But this gentle caring was almost more than he could handle.

Jess looked at the man who stood before her, a swell of tenderness curling deep within her. Within Brody's carefully blank expression there was a world of hurt. Something caught in her chest, an elusive emotion that was part pain, part pleasure. It was as if she alone knew of his silent plea for understanding—for love. And she knew instinctively that Brody's childhood had been as empty as hers had been full.

"How old were you?" The question invaded the still, waiting silence.

"I don't want you to think—" his voice faltered "—badly of me, Jess."

Her heart twisted. "I won't," she promised. She patted the seat next to her.

He remained where he was. "You will."

"I won't. We've all done things we're not proud of." Jess thought of Eric, how ill-timed the divorce had been. Still, she'd had no other choice. She rose and pulled him down beside her on the box. "You told me before that you were from San Francisco. That's where you grew up?"

"Yes."

"What about your family? Are your parents still there?"

He sat with his hands braced on his thighs, his posture stiff. "My mother died when I was ten." He stared straight ahead while he spoke. "My father's an alcoholic, Jess. I don't remember seeing him without a drink in his hand or a bottle beside him. I haven't seen him for years."

"So your father wasn't exactly a model parent," she observed quietly.

Brody snorted. "He was never sober enough to know if I was or wasn't around."

She gave a half smile. "And most of the time you weren't?"

"I was on the street more than I was ever home," he stated bluntly. "Even before my mother died, I was always in trouble—getting in fights at school, that kind of thing. I was reckless and bold."

"And rebellious?" she guessed.

The corners of his mouth turned down. "That most of all."

Her fingers crept out and twined through his. "Something must have turned you around," she murmured.

A sad, wistful smile touched his lips. "Some*one*," he clarified, a rough thread of emotion giving his voice a slight edge. "His name was Murphy. Cullen Murphy. He was a tall, redheaded cop who worked for the San Francisco PD. I had run away from home more times than I could count, and one of those times, Murphy caught me shoplifting from a grocery store. I lied about my name and age, so I spent the night in jail."

Jess frowned. "How old were you?"

"Sixteen. But I was big, Jess. I looked older." He shook his head. "The next morning, Murphy paid my bail and took me home—*his* home. I was madder than hell when he told me he planned to petition the juvenile authorities for guardianship until I was eighteen. My father never even made it to the hearing, so all of a sudden I found myself under Murphy's wing. I didn't know what on earth his motive was, but I figured there had to be one. That he might care what happened to me was something I never even considered."

Jess lifted her brows. "Something tells me Murphy gave as good as he got."

"That he did. I was mouthy and hotheaded, but Murphy was just as tough as me. I'll never forget the time he washed out my mouth with soap."

Jess gasped. "He didn't."

The corner of Brody's mouth tilted. "He did, and believe me, I'd rather have had a belt taken to my backside. That was more a deterrent than anything else he could have done. I guess I knew then that he meant business."

"What happened then?" She gently encouraged him.

"Murphy wanted me to take a few college classes until I decided where the hell I was headed—he made me go to night school to get my diploma—but I'd had enough of books. He thought a little discipline might do me some good, though, and he managed to talk me into joining the army. I made it through basic training, but by then I'd decided there were too damn many rules and regulations. The first leave I was granted, I hightailed it back to Murphy. There was no way I was ever going back. But Murphy had other ideas. He told me in no uncertain terms that I'd better stick with it, or else. And he made sure I got back to the base by slapping a pair of handcuffs on me and hauling me there himself."

Jess struggled hard to keep from laughing. Brody caught the look in her eye. "I know," he said dryly. "I was madder than hell, but it was just what I needed. I was determined to show him that I could stick with it. By the time my first term was up, I'd learned to do what I was told—" he smiled crookedly "—most of the time, anyway. I'd also learned that rank has its privileges, so I reenlisted and managed to get accepted into officer candidate school. I could have stayed a second louie the rest of my career, and Murphy couldn't have been more proud."

There was a faraway look in his eyes. "Murphy had this dream," he said softly. "When he was growing up, his father was the crew foreman for a pretty big winery in California. Murphy planned to buy some land and try his hand as a grape grower when he retired from the police department."

Brody paused. There was a raspy undertone to his voice when he finally continued. "This time I was the one who was proud when he included me in that dream. I'd managed to put away some money, and the army has a plan where you can retire after twenty years, and I only had six years left to go. I really thought Murphy and I could buy that place in the sun he always wanted."

He stopped, and Jess's heart wrenched. The overly bright sheen in his eyes served as a warning. "What happened?" she asked quietly.

"Murphy was given his walking papers less than a year before the earliest date he could have retired. When that happened, it nullified the pension he'd always counted on." Brody's jaw hardened. "All the years he spent on the police force were just wiped away."

"But how?" Jess was bewildered. "How could that happen?"

Brody's voice was gritty. "Murphy was called in to a bar one night to remove a man—a member of the board of supervisors—who was drunk and causing trouble. It turned into quite a scuffle and the supervisor was arrested and booked into jail. Because of his position, though, he had a lot of firepower. He was determined to make heads roll, namely Murphy's."

Jess felt sick. "So he was fired," she murmured.

Brody's nod was terse. "A month later he was dead, the victim of a hit-and-run accident."

Something in his tone brought her eyes to his in a flash. "Wait a minute," she said slowly. "You don't think it was—"

"Suicide?" The harsh line of his mouth matched his voice. "It's occurred to me. Just like that—" he snapped his fingers "—everything he'd worked for, everything he believed in, everything he loved was gone, completely out of reach."

Jess couldn't look away from his face, from the self-condemnation reflected there. "You blame yourself," she said incredulously.

"I . . . sometimes I do," he admitted roughly. He got up and walked in a slow circle before her. "I was stationed in Georgia then. Out of the blue one day, I got a phone call telling me Murphy was dead. It wasn't until I came home for the funeral that I found out all of this had happened. If only he'd let me know, I could have done something to stop it," he muttered wearily. "But Murphy never said a word, Jess. The last letter I had from him everything sounded fine. Dammit, he never said a word!"

Comprehension was slow to dawn. "It all happened at once, didn't it?" she said slowly. "Murphy . . . and you resigning your commission because of the embezzlement."

Brody nodded, dragging a hand down his face. "Murphy was like a father to me, Jess. Hell, he *was* the only father I ever had, the only one who ever cared about me. Knowing he'd been maneuvered by the brass at the top of the ladder was hard for me to accept."

His voice was bitter. "I'd just wrapped up the embezzlement case when I left for Murphy's funeral. When I got back to the base, the general was waiting with his oh-so-generous offer, everything nice and neat and quiet." His jaw hardened. "Maybe Murphy's situation was the straw that broke the camel's back. But by then I knew I'd had it with being under someone else's thumb, so I just said to hell with it."

Jess rose wordlessly, laying a hand on his shoulder. At her touch, his muscles bunched and knotted, but she doggedly kept her fingers in place. "I'm sorry," she whispered. "I'm sorry about Murphy, and I'm sorry you had to grow up so alone. But everything that happened has made you the man you are today, and for that I'm glad." Her voice lowered huskily. "And I'm glad it's brought you here to me."

Brody turned slowly, aware of a strange, melting sensation inside him. Jess was so sweet, so guileless and so loving. For her sake—for his—he had to resist her. But he couldn't. Damn, but he couldn't.

"Come here," he said softly.

There was no need to ask again. Jess went willingly.

The instant her arms slid around his waist, he tipped her face to his. "I haven't scared you away?" He was serious, for all that the words were wrapped in laughter.

Jess laughed shakily. "I was beginning to think you'd robbed a bank or something." Her gaze sought his shyly. "If you were tough and you were hard, it was because you had to be. That's nothing to be ashamed of."

Eyes of golden fire searched her face, reaching deep inside her. Jess didn't flinch at the intensity of his gaze, but looked just as deeply into his soul. He kissed her then—not a kiss of passion, but one of gentle understanding, of acceptance.

When their lips finally parted, he rested his chin on her shining hair. "It would be so easy to fall in love with you," he said softly.

She inclined her head as if in thanks, her smile was both daring and impish. "The feeling is mutual," she murmured.

Brody smiled then, that rare, uninhibited smile that made her catch her breath. They stood for a while, arms around each other, both unwilling to break the peaceful intimacy.

Eventually Brody stepped back, releasing her reluctantly. "I should get back to work." One eyebrow lifted roguishly. "Otherwise my boss may fire me."

Jess merely laughed. Her eyes followed him to the tractor where he climbed up on the seat. "I was about to try this when you came in," he said. "I guess we'll see if I've still got the Midas touch."

He stuck the key into the ignition and turned it. The engine sputtered and coughed, then roared to life. Brody laughed at the startled wonder on Jess's face.

When he climbed down, she threw her arms around him. "This," she told him playfully, "calls for a celebration, King Midas. Why don't you come into the house and we'll discuss your reward?"

The kiss she pressed on his lips was reward enough, Brody thought giddily. "Give me a few minutes to clean up here and I'll be in," he promised.

Jess nodded and started back to the house. Her heart felt as if it had taken on a pair of wings. She felt dizzy and carefree and happier than she could ever remember. Whatever doubts, whatever fears she might have about Brody had no part in this moment in time. She didn't have to be alone anymore. And neither did Brody.

And right now, that was all that mattered.

CHAPTER FOURTEEN

THE PHONE WAS RINGING when Jess reached the back door. She ran into the kitchen, picked it up and gasped a breathless hello.

There was total silence. Jess stiffened instinctively. A prickle of fear raised the hair on her nape before she heard a smooth, masculine, thoroughly familiar voice murmur her name.

A soundless scream echoed in her mind over and over. No...*No!* It couldn't be him. *It couldn't!*

But it was.

Her legs were weak. Sheer willpower kept her on her feet.

"I know you're there, Jessica."

Jess gripped the phone more tightly, finally gaining hold of her runaway emotions. Anger lent her the courage and strength to confront him.

"What do you want, Eric?"

"What do I want? Why, I would think that would be obvious, especially to a doting mother like you. After all, I'm now a father, am I not?"

To someone else, perhaps, such a plea of aggrieved innocence might have been convincing. But not to Jess—she knew Eric far too well.

"Don't tell me you've had a change of heart." She dismissed the assumption curtly. "Don't bother, because I'm not buying it."

"No? Maybe you should, Jessica. Maybe you should."

His voice was smooth...yet deadly. She struggled to control the chills running up and down her spine. "Such touching concern," she said coldly. "Forgive me for being so skeptical, but I remember quite clearly that you wanted me to abort this baby."

"My mistake," he said softly. "And a costly one, I might add."

Raw fury shot through her. "And that's the whole point, isn't it? You measure everything in dollars and cents, prestige and power. You think I cost you your career, and you're not above using your own child as a weapon against me. I'm warning you, don't try it."

"Threats?" He seemed amused. "Why, you just said it yourself—dollars and cents, prestige and power. I may not be sitting on the bench anymore, but I still have all of those."

"Damn you, Eric!" She spat his name. "What do you want from me?

Macabre laughter echoed in her ears. "How are things with your new boyfriend? I hear the two of you are getting quite chummy, which brings me back to why I called in the first place. In light of your new relationship, maybe I should be taking more of an interest in my son's welfare. Especially knowing how his mother is prone to such wanton behavior."

Jess was stunned. "Eric!" she cried hoarsely. "How do you—"

The line went dead, but she could still hear his voice. *Maybe I should be taking more of an interest in my son's welfare.*

Eric knew about Nathan—he knew she'd had a boy. His disinterest in their child had been very clear, all along. That was why she'd never bothered to inform him of Nathan's birth.

A wave of icy fear swept through her. She had the feeling Eric was looking right over her shoulder. Was he here? He had no reason to come after her—except one. Revenge. But why now? Why had he waited so long?

Nathan.

And Eric also knew about Brody. How? her mind screamed. How could he possibly know anything about Brody unless...

Brody. Was there a connection between Brody and Eric? It would explain so much. Her mind raced on, filled with jagged thoughts and half-formed suspicions. Brody was from San Francisco. Close to Oakland. Close to Eric.

"Oh, no," she whispered. There was a horrible constriction in her throat; she couldn't breathe. Her knees gave way and she sagged against the wall. As if in slow motion, she slumped to the floor, clutching the phone with nerveless fingers.

That was how Brody found her. At a glance he took in her pinched, white features. He grabbed the phone but heard only the dull buzz of the dial tone.

He thrust the receiver back in its cradle and was down on his knees beside her in an instant. "Jess! Jess, what is it?" He tried to grab her hands, but she jerked them back as if she'd been burned.

She stared at him, her face filled with anguish. "He knows," she whispered, her voice raw. "He knows."

Again Brody reached for her. She scrambled away from him, cringing as if she couldn't stand the thought of him touching her.

His hands dropped to his sides. A single thought winged through his mind, but he refused to accept it.

"Jess." He deliberately spoke very calmly. "Tell me what's wrong. Tell me who was on the phone."

Her eyes were wide and glazed; the strangled laugh she gave sounded hysterical. "Surely you know."

He stilled the flare of panic that threatened to erupt. "Was it Eric? Did Eric call you, Jess?" When she said nothing, he lost his temper and hauled her into his arms. For a minute she fought him, legs and arms flailing wildly, until at last he wedged her body between the vise of his thighs and forced her arms down at her sides.

"Look at me!" he demanded.

Her movements stilled; her eyes met his. "Jess," he said more softly. "Jess, I want to help you, I swear. Please, sweetheart, let me help you. Now tell me... Was it Eric who called?"

She stared at him endlessly. Brody, feeling as if his whole life were suddenly teetering on the brink of destruction, remained quiet. He met her gaze silently, praying and willing her to see his tender concern.

At last he heard her whispered "Yes." All at once she collapsed against him. He felt the deep, shuddering breaths she took and sensed she was on the brink of tears. She was shivering, but she didn't cry. Brody held her shaking body until the tremors subsided.

He slid his fingers into her hair and tilted her head back. "Are you okay?"

She nodded. Her eyes looked clearer now. Brody pulled her to her feet and guided her into the living room. She sat on the sofa, and he dropped down beside her. "Tell me what he said, Jess."

Her gaze lowered. She didn't look at him as she spoke. "He knows about you. He knows that we—" she faltered "—he thinks we're involved."

Though Brody had prepared himself for something like that, he couldn't prevent the jolt of fear that ran through him. This was all his fault, he realized. Eric would never have called Jess if he hadn't withdrawn from the case. What next? he despaired inwardly.

Slowly Jess raised her head to look at him. "I don't understand how he could possibly know," she murmured. "Unless..."

"Unless he'd sent someone here to spy on you," he finished. He risked a glance at her. Her expression was a strange mixture of uncertainty and hope. He knew Jess suspected him. He also knew he couldn't stand to see her hurt anymore.

He cursed himself silently. He'd never hated himself as he did at this moment. "He could have, you know."

Her eyes were fixed on his face. "Who?"

He gestured vaguely. "A private detective maybe.... These things are done all the time." Luckily she didn't notice his hesitation. Holding his breath, he reached for her hand. This time she didn't try to pull away. "What else did he say, Jess?"

She began to tremble all over again. "He said he was a father now, and the reason he called should be obvious. I told him I wasn't buying it, and he said maybe I should. Then he asked how my new boyfriend was, and in light of that, maybe he should be taking more of an interest in his son's welfare." Her vision clouded with hot, scalding tears. "He's after Nathan," she choked out. "I know he is, Brody. I know it."

At the wild panic that flared in her eyes, a pain ripped through Brody. Unthinkingly he pulled Jess into his arms. She was stiff with fear. Over and over, he stroked the rigid lines of her back, soothing her as if she were a child.

"You have sole custody," he reminded her. "And he has no visitation rights."

"But he's smart and cunning. My God, Brody, he was a judge. He knows all the ins and outs of the legal system." The words were practically hurled at him, and Brody felt the thrust of each one like the deadly tip of a rapier.

"Jess." He hesitated. "Nathan is his son. Surely he wouldn't do anything to harm him." Brody's voice was taut and strained. He was trying to reassure himself as much as Jess.

Her hair sprayed back and forth over her shoulders as she shook her head. "You don't understand." Her breath came jerkily. "He never wanted a child in the first place. And it's not Nathan he wants now—it's just a way to get back at me."

Suddenly all the fight seemed to drain from her. She slumped against his chest. "Oh, God," she whispered, and the pain in her heart brought agony to her voice. "What have I done? I should have known it wasn't just an idle threat. I should have known."

An eerie chill crept up his spine. With gentle insistence, Brody tipped her face up to his, his eyes searching hers. "What do you mean, Jess? You said he didn't threaten you."

"Not tonight," she admitted, then faltered.

His fingers on her chin tightened. "Tell me, Jess." His gaze was relentlessly demanding. "Everything."

Everything? Not that, never that, she thought fuzzily. She cringed inside. The shame was too much to bear.

"Jess." Brody gave her shoulders a little shake.

She closed her eyes, unable to rid herself of the sickening feel of dread. "Eric was a justice of the state supreme court." Her lips barely moved.

"You already told me." Brody sounded impatient.

"His position was up for reconfirmation before the voters last November."

It was on the tip of Brody's tongue to say he knew this, too. Wisely he kept silent.

"I left him less than three months before the election. The press got wind that I was divorcing him and had a field day with it. It aroused questions—questions neither one of us would answer." Her voice was shaky. "That was why Eric didn't want me to leave him. He was afraid of what the publicity would do.... And it did. All the speculation ruined his bid, and he was defeated."

Brody's voice was sharp. "That's when he threatened you?"

She shook her head. "It was before, when I told him I was filing for divorce. He said I would regret leaving him. He said he'd make me sorrier than I ever dreamed." She let out a deep, shuddering breath. "He said he'd get even with me somehow, someday...."

Brody muttered a vile obscenity under his breath. "He wanted to scare you, Jess. The way he's trying to now." His attempt to draw her nearer met with resistance. Jess pushed away from him with both hands, staring up at him dully.

"There's more," she said, and withdrew from his arms entirely. It was the only way she could get through this.

There was such an air of vulnerability about her that Brody wanted nothing more than to take her into his arms and soothe and comfort her. But he let her go, sensing the violent upheaval going on inside her, knowing she wouldn't welcome his touch right now.

"Eric was right," she said suddenly. "I knew a divorce just then might ruin him, and I knew he didn't dare contest it for that very reason. I *used* him the way he'd always used me. And I didn't care what happened with the election one way or the other."

The air was suddenly thick and heavy with expectancy. Brody realized this was what he'd been waiting for, but suddenly he wasn't sure he wanted to hear it. He could almost see the tension invade her body.

Her lips trembled. "There was someone else, you see. There had been all along.... Someone I knew, someone I'd counted as a friend. And I saw them together in my own home—or rather Eric's home." Once started, she couldn't seem to stop. "Eric didn't know I saw them—he still doesn't—but there was no doubt that they were lovers. I was too bitter and too hurt to tell him I saw them together. I just wanted out.

"I was such a stupid, naive little fool. I actually believed all his excuses." Her voice caught on a sound that was half laugh, half sob. "But it certainly explained why we had separate bedrooms for most of our marriage. And all the evenings he spent away from home... It had nothing to do with stress, or a heavy docket or anything like that."

She wrapped her arms around herself, as if to ward off a chill. Her face was haunted, her voice raspy as the story emerged in hoarse, jagged bursts. "He wouldn't touch me for weeks at a time. He only made love to me in the dark. I actually believed it was my fault, that I was lacking whatever it took to keep him at home. I'd never dreamed of the real reason he was so indifferent. I already knew our marriage was over, but I could have coped with another woman, at least until after the election." She was crying now, with tears sliding unchecked down her cheeks. "I was such a fool.... He was an old law-school buddy. Their affair probably began long before Eric and I were married. Oh, God, it hurt so much to know that he only married me so no one would suspect..."

Comprehension came with a dizzying rush. In that one startling moment of clarity, Brody knew.

Eric Culver's lover was another man.

IT WAS A LONG TIME LATER when Jess finally laid Nathan back in his crib. Her mind was on Brody, waiting for her downstairs. Conflict waged a violent battle within her.

She had cried her heart out until it seemed there wasn't a drop of emotion left in her. All the while, Brody had held her, stroking her in comfort, not in passion, shielding her against all the bitterness and hurt. She was a little ashamed of her suspicions of him. He had shown her nothing but caring and sensitivity.

On the one hand, she was glad the awful secret was finally out. All this time, her pain and humiliation had been capped tightly in storage. But her feelings had finally escaped like a burst of steam from a kettle, and the pressure was gone; but on the other hand, not forgotten.

And she didn't want to acknowledge her shame and embarrassment over her weakness. She had barely sat up in Brody's arms, with the last tear only a memory, when Nathan awoke. And while she was feeding and tending to her son, she hadn't had to think about what she'd done. But now...

She sensed Brody's presence even before the shadow fell across the crib. Knowing that he was watching her, Jess was besieged with a dreaded feeling of inevitability. She inhaled deeply, inwardly bracing herself. Shame was a tangible force within her. She wanted to run and hide. Conversely, she craved the warm shelter of Brody's arms once again.

It had felt wonderful to be held, safe and secure, in his protective, comforting embrace. She was like a woman starved for affection. And surely it wasn't wrong to lean on someone else, just once.

"Jess." He spoke her name very quietly, alerting her to his presence.

Jess turned and met a pair of keen, watchful eyes. Brody's tone was even, his expression betraying nothing of his thoughts. She hesitated a moment longer, aware that her features reflected her uncertainty.

Brody's eyes roved over her tear-ravaged face. His sharp-featured reserve changed radically to concern as he absorbed her distress. Wordlessly he extended his hand.

Without conscious volition, her legs carried her forward.

Brody's hard, calloused fingers closed around hers. He pulled her to his side. Their eyes met and held once more. It was as if a silent, unspoken message had connected between them, and Jess experienced an overwhelming sense of relief.

"There's some coffee in the kitchen if you want it." With his free hand Brody brushed a loose strand of hair from her cheek.

The kitchen. Eric's face suddenly swam before her.

Brody's hand tightened around hers. "What is it?" he asked quickly.

Jess bit her lip. "Eric," she said, her voice very low. "I wish I knew for certain how he knew about you. And how he knew about Nathan—that he had a son. It gives me the creeps to think of someone snooping around behind my back." She thought for a moment. "Although he could have checked for Nathan's birth in the local newspapers or called Vital Statistics for the births recorded in this area last month. I don't suppose it would be difficult for him to figure out I'd moved back to Amity."

Brody cursed himself a thousand times over. He was going to have to tell her who he was—and soon. But not now. She was too emotionally raw right now. *Tell it like it is,* an inner voice chided. Yet he was afraid Jess would turn away from him. It was a very real possibility.

There was a brief pause. "I can't help but think maybe Eric's call to you was simply to get you riled up. Maybe he waited until Nathan was born to give you a false sense of security."

Jess frowned. "To scare me, you mean? So that I would react exactly the way I did?"

"Exactly." At least he hoped that was all it was. Brody intended to find out, one way or another.

"It's more than possible," she rationalized slowly. "Knowing Eric, it's altogether probable."

Uncomfortable with the conversation, Brody was relieved when Jess fell silent. He took the opportunity to study her. "You're tired," he observed with a frown. The skin beneath her eyes looked fragile and translucent, shaded with a faint tinge of purple.

"You've been through so much," he murmured. "The move into this house, adjusting to a new baby, starting the nursery..." He shook his head. His lips tightened as if in disapproval.

"I am tired," she admitted. "Tonight, of all nights, I wish Nathan would sleep through until morning."

A tiny smile grazed his lips. "Not very likely, eh?"

"No," she said dryly. "But he went six hours just the other night." She closed her eyes and lifted her face. "It was heavenly!" She sighed.

They both laughed, and it seemed to dispel some of the tension Eric's name had aroused. Brody's gaze drifted into Nathan's room. When it flickered back to Jess, he discovered her eyes upon him.

"Brody," She seemed to hesitate. "I—I'd like to say thank-you for everything you've done. And I'd like to apologize for being so suspicious of you earlier."

Inwardly he winced. "There's no need, Jess."

"There is," she insisted. "You could have walked away, but you didn't." Her voice grew husky. "That means a lot to me, Brody. Thank you." She placed her hands on his shoulders and raised herself up on tiptoe, then pressed her mouth to his. It was a gentle, passionless kiss, but all at once, the air between them was charged.

Jess felt an odd tightening in her chest. Perhaps it was the intimate silence of the night, or being alone with him, with Nathan tucked away for the evening. Whatever the reason, her body was almost painfully conscious of their closeness.

Little by little, she lowered herself, still gripping his shoulders. Brody's hands had settled on her hips. They, too, displayed a reluctance to leave her.

Her gaze moved to his mouth.

"Brody." She spoke his name in a breathy little voice that sounded nothing at all like her own. "Brody, don't leave me alone tonight."

His arms stiffened. Jess was so sweet, so willing...so scared and alone. For a moment he said nothing, caught squarely between heaven and hell. When he finally spoke, his voice was rough with the strain he was under. "Jess, you don't know what you're asking."

"I do," she countered immediately. Throwing caution to the wind, she recklessly pressed herself closer. She wanted him as she had never wanted anything in her life. She tried to ignore the insistent voice inside that called her wanton and reckless, far too bold and daring.

Her mouth was dry, her hands slid over his shoulders and down his arms. She could feel the tension in the muscles that bunched and knotted under her fingertips, and it filled her with a tingling excitement.

Inwardly shaking, she brushed his mouth once more. Against her, he stood rigid and frozen. Her lips parted. Her tongue came out of hiding and traced the seam of his

mouth. Her heart leaped to her throat as she slowly coaxed
forth a response. She was trembling . . . but so was he.

"I need you, Brody." The words slipped out before she
could recall them, and then she didn't want to. "I need you
to make love to me."

Hearing those words was sweet agony. Brody felt the layers of resistance being slowly peeled away. If he had an
ounce of honor, he would leave her alone and refuse what
she was offering. Conversely, he knew that Jess was the one
woman alive who could cleanse the darkness in his soul. He
had never been good at self-denial, and he was also a man,
and the primal male within hungered for her, for this
woman . . . for Jess.

She drew back slowly. "I—I thought you wanted me,"
she said, her voice wavering. A hot tide of color rose to her
cheeks. *Oh, God,* she thought frantically. *It's happening
again, just like Eric. . . .*

His breathing was choppy. Brody hauled in a huge breath
of air and tried to steel himself against the hurt he heard in
her voice, but it was no use. He watched the play of doubt
and fear chase across her face and felt something come un-
done inside him.

Jess needed him, and not once in his life had he ever heard
those words—"I need you"—addressed to him.

"I'm sorry," she choked out. "I didn't realize I'd mis-
understood."

She would have wrenched away but he grabbed her before she could take more than a step. Her eyes were red
rimmed and swollen, her face still streaked with tears. He'd
never seen her look more beautiful.

"Not want you?" With a muffled sound from deep in his
chest, he caught her to him fiercely. He wanted to protect
her, take away her pain. He wanted to possess her, heart and
soul. The warmth of her body softly cushioned against his

and the baby-fresh scent that always clung to her filled him with a possessive hunger.

"My God," he said hoarsely, "I'm going crazy with wanting you." And it was true. His whole being was filled with a desire so strong he could scarcely think.

Her eyes searched his. Her voice shook ever so slightly as she said, "You don't want to leave?"

"Lord, no," he whispered, tipping her face to his. His arms tightened, binding their hips together. He knew the truth was starkly written in his expression, as well as the burgeoning thrust of his desire. He kissed her then—a sweet, infinitely gentle kiss of promise. But all too soon, protection became possession. Tenderness became passion. They were both breathing hard when Brody finally dragged his mouth away.

He rested his forehead against hers. "You'll be sorry, Jess. I'm not good enough for you. I'm not—"

Her fingers pressed against his mouth, stifling his words. "Don't say that." Her eyes darkened. "Don't even think it. I'll have no regrets, Brody. I promise you."

For a timeless moment their eyes locked. A heady anticipation spilled through her as she took his hand and led him into her bedroom. But with the closing of one door, another opened, and out leaped the sordid hurts and empty failures of the past. Her courage, tentative at best, slipped away.

She had come to Eric an eager, willing bride, wanting nothing more than to please her husband. But all that she offered he held in disdain, intent on his own satisfaction and completing the act as quickly as possible. Her chest tightened as she recalled how many nights she had lain awake, yearning and unfulfilled, feeling as if her heart had been ripped out and desperately wondering what was wrong with her.

Guilt no longer plagued Jess, and the reasons why no longer mattered. But she couldn't stop her traitorous mind from silently asking if Brody would be as selfish a lover as Eric.

Her trepidation mounted as reality crashed down around her. Sex could never be a casual encounter for Jess. Her values were too traditional. In spite of everything, she still believed that making love could be—and should be—a meeting of souls, a melding of hearts. She wanted to believe that Brody felt the same—that he cared. But she'd also wanted to believe that Eric loved her.

Deep inside Jess knew that Brody shared her feelings. Deep inside she knew she had wronged him in even thinking twice about it. She was quickly discovering that rational thinking played a small part in affairs of the heart.

Along with that realization came another—one that was just as disturbing, and one that roused still another sleeping demon.

Brody was a strong, undeniably attractive man who was intensely sure of himself and his masculinity. Undoubtedly he knew his way around a woman's bedroom—and a woman's body. Jess retained no illusions that it might be otherwise. And wasn't he exactly the kind of man she needed? One who was man to her woman, male to her female, whole to her half. But her feelings of inadequacy continued to haunt her.

She moved to switch on the bedside lamp, needing time to deal with her emotions, which lay scattered in every direction. She grappled for control, desperately afraid of what Brody might think. That she was nothing but a tease. That she . . .

"What's wrong?"

Her hands locked in front of her. For a moment, speech was totally impossible. Jess fought the urge to fling herself into Brody's arms and bury her face in the temptingly warm spot between his shoulder and neck so that she didn't have to face him. She couldn't stand it if Brody looked at her as Eric had: so coldly, so dispassionately, so contemptibly!

Slowly she met Brody's gaze. His golden-brown eyes were gentle, questioning and concerned. Still, she couldn't erase the choking fear inside her.

"Know what?" Her lips trembled; she hated the quaver in her voice.

"What?" His hands settled on her shoulders. He pulled her to him with gentle firmness.

Jess could look no higher than the hollow of his throat. The wild tangle of hairs there kindled a mingled feeling of thrilling excitement and dismay.

There was a huge lump in her throat. "I'm scared," she whispered, wishing she could disappear into the night.

Silence seeped into the room. Jess felt Brody go very still. "Why?" He spoke very quietly, betraying nothing of what was in his mind.

Jess struggled to find her voice. "I know this is going to sound crazy," she muttered. "But even though I was married for six years, Eric never encouraged me to... I mean, it's not as if it's my first time, but I feel as if it is. It's not me I'm worried about," she hastened to assure him. Her tongue tripped over itself as she sought to simply have it out and over with. "I guess I'm not as experienced as you might think, and I—I just don't want you to be disappointed."

Disappointed? Brody would have laughed if everything she said weren't tugging at his heart. He wondered if she knew that his own fears were just as great as hers. He thought of Eric Culver's smooth, polished good looks. Sexual preferences aside, Culver was like a jewel of the finest cut, while he was nothing but a pebble in the sand.

Jess saw his fingers through a blur and felt their subtle pressure under her chin. Eyes like golden torches traced the delicate curve of her brows, the straight line of her nose, the enticing curve of her mouth.

"That won't happen," he said very softly. Then, smiling, he borrowed her words of the previous moment. "Know what?"

Jess gave an almost imperceptible shake of her head.

The smile faded, leaving only a soft blaze of clear gold in his eyes. "I'm scared, too," he confided, his voice very low. "I'm ashamed to admit my own needs have always come before anyone else's. But it's not that way with you. You—" he hesitated "—you're different."

Different. A prayer or a curse? "Are you trying to say that you . . . that you care?" The question emerged lightly. But the instant it was out, Jess held her breath, still afraid, but now for another reason entirely.

Brody stared at her, his throat unexpectedly tight. *Did he care?* God, yes. And it didn't even begin to describe what he felt for her.

But it was wrong, he thought helplessly, and suddenly he was being torn apart. His caring would only hurt her, and that was the last thing he wanted. God help them both, for he couldn't stop himself.

His breath caught sharply, and he rasped her name, feeling raw and broken inside. His tongue felt clumsy as he struggled to find his voice again. His fingers touched her cheek, her mouth. He was trembling, he realized. The choice was already made.

"I care," he whispered, and pulled her to him with an almost desperate strength. "I care," he said again, only this time the words were ragged and muffled against her mouth.

The kiss they shared was both hungry and fierce, reverent and tender. Brody's hands slid down and under the fabric of her blouse to the bare skin of her back, flooding each of them with heat. They were breathless and giddy when their lips finally parted, both of them achingly conscious of the pressure of her breasts against his chest. He tore off his shirt, wanting nothing more than to feel the delicious friction of skin against skin.

Alive with anticipation, Jess's pulses leaped when Brody's hand settled with precise deliberation at the top button of her blouse. She was certain he could hear her heart thundering wildly in her breast. When the last button was free of restraint, the air grew very still.

To Jess it seemed the entire world was holding its breath. Brody's hands began to lift to her shoulders, but all at once, he paused and looked deeply into her eyes.

He was waiting, she realized, waiting for her to take this last, irrevocable step. Jess edged slowly backward, just far enough so that she could see his expression. His hands released her, but not his eyes.

Jess's blouse floated down her arms to the floor. She shed her jeans almost as quickly. But her hands were shaking so that it took several attempts before the catch on her bra was released.

Brody could see the doubt and uncertainty in her expressive features, the anxiety mounting with each piece of clothing that slid to the floor. Reluctantly pulling his gaze away, he started to work on his own undressing, silently cursing Eric Culver for causing Jess to be so uncertain of herself and her womanhood.

She had no reason to be ashamed. When he turned back to her, his mouth went dry as he drank in the sight of her. Her skin possessed the gleaming luster of a pearl. Her body was as slender as a reed, the nipples crowning her breasts a dusky pink and begging to be touched.

Brody watched her slide beneath the covers. But the move she made toward the lamp was swiftly aborted; he reached out and caught her hand in his. A look of surprise flitted across her features, and he recalled that Eric had always made love to her in the dark.

"Leave it," he said quietly. "I want to be able to see you." His gaze held hers. "All of you," he added softly, deliberately.

His eyes were softer, warmer than she'd ever seen them. The mattress dipped as he got into bed beside her. She gave a startled gasp as he swept back the sheet and blanket, leaving her totally open to his vision.

The room was suddenly hushed. Jess counted the heartbeats, wanting to close her eyes but not daring to. They were both naked, separated by the width of a hand. The intimacy was unbearably sweet and tempting, but frightening, too.

Feeling his gaze slide over her filled her with mingled excitement and apprehension. Her stomach was almost flat, but not quite, and oh, how she wished it were! And her breasts were still so full from nursing, too full for the rest of her.

She wanted desperately to look at him, to seek the approval she prayed she would find. But what if he found her less than perfect? Less than a woman, less than he wanted?

She needed the closeness of another human being sharing what she felt. She needed to touch and be touched, to know what it was like to want and be wanted in equal measure.

What she needed was Brody. But she still needed to hear him say how much he wanted her, how much he needed her.

Her heart stood still as eyes like dark gold fire roamed her slender curves. Jess caught her breath at their brilliance.

He wasted no time in giving her his verdict. He breached the distance between them, reaching out to scale the slope of her shoulder with his fingertips. "You feel so good," he whispered, curling his hand around her neck to bring her nearer. "So damn good." His arms slid around her. He buried his mouth in the scented hollow of her shoulder. "I want you," he breathed into her ear. "I want you so much, Jess. Can you feel how I want you?"

Jess could, and the wonderful awareness of his arousal, heavy and tight against her belly, made her want to weep with joy. She arched into him with a breathless little cry that sent a jolt of pleasure coursing through both of them.

Slowly Brody raised his head to look at her. "God, you're pretty." His tone was deep and husky. His palm shaped the cushioned fullness of her breast, sending needles of sensation rippling through her.

"So pretty," he marveled. His forehead came to rest against hers. Seeing her like this, bathed in the soft light of the lamp, tore at Brody's control, but he forced himself to go slowly. "You're everything a man could possibly want, Jess—everything *I* want."

He kissed her then, but all too soon the kiss caught fire and raged out of control. He could taste the hunger in her mouth, a fiery desire that matched his own. With a groan, he molded the entire sweet length of her against him, imprinting her body with the hard, male feel of his.

In the back of his mind, a distant realization occurred. What was it Culver had said? He had warned him, warned him that Jess was sweet and innocent and eager. Eager? God, yes, Brody thought mindlessly. He'd have it no other way. Each contact of his hair-roughened skin sliding against her smoothness strained his willpower to the limit. Desire was a raw ache in his gut.

Jess was lost in a world made dizzy and breathless by the man who lingered over her, touching and exploring her body as if she were a priceless treasure. Over and over and over he kissed her; long, endless kisses that pulled her into a tempest of wild sensation where time and place ceased to exist. His hands followed the same path his eyes had taken, shaping and molding, tempting and teasing her breasts, the smoothness of her belly. When his mouth finally closed over the ripe, straining peak of one breast, Jess shuddered with pleasure. She threaded her fingers through the golden roughness of his hair as he bathed the quivering bud of her nipple with moist heat, tugging like a tide, all the way to her heart.

Never in her life had she felt more beautiful. Never in her life had she felt so cherished. She wanted his mouth on hers, feeding and stoking the hidden fires deep within. She wanted his hands on her breasts, the heated fullness of him deep inside to fill the empty void he'd created. She reveled in the hot, possessive light in his eyes; in the way he touched her as if he owned her. For this—this was what she had forever craved: this man, this moment of magic, this incredible feeling of wanting and being wanted in return.

And he did want her. Jess was both amazed and pleased at the extent of his desire for her. With his hand over hers, he invited her touch, her tentative exploration that began with shy clumsiness—but only for a moment. Her hands coasted down his chest, then sifted through the golden net of down that paved the way to lower regions. It was wonderful to be able to touch him like this, to be given free rein and know she could indulge her curiosity and longings without fear of rejection. His skin was hot and sleek like sun-warmed satin. A heady sense of power filled her at the way his muscles clenched as she continued her plundering journey. Brody inhaled sharply when her cool fingers discovered the thundering pulse of his lifeblood.

"You're a witch," he muttered, the sound half-laugh, half-groan. "A witch, and you're driving me crazy."

Jess merely smiled a smile both innocent and sensual, and let her newly discovered instincts take over, learning the shape and texture of him and glorying in the response he could barely control.

Brody bore her sweet torture as long as he could, then proceeded to turn the tables on her. He returned kiss for kiss, touch for touch, testing the limits of her control and his.

He raised his head to look at her, his features taut and strained. *I love you,* he almost said, but didn't. He wanted to tell her; the words were a burning ache inside his heart. Yet he didn't dare, because he was a coward. He was afraid, desperately afraid of what she would think when this was all over and she knew of his deception.

He was even more afraid to say the words he feared she couldn't say in return.

"Brody. Brody, please—"

He rejoiced in the sharp need he heard in her voice, knowing she could wait no longer. His hands trembled as he slid his palms beneath her and bound her hips with his. Tiny shivers of delight danced along his spine when at last he was fully clasped within the heated velvet of her body.

Her cry at the moment of possession tore at his control. Her face was filled with such joy and wonder that he felt himself humbled. She arched against him, and he closed his eyes against a pleasure so exquisite it was almost unbearable. He wanted to prolong the moment, make it last forever in his mind and heart. His body began the slow, sensuous rhythm of love....

His mouth was sealed with hers. He drank in each soft cry, each breathless whimper, each tremor of her quivering flesh clinging tightly to his. She whispered his name over and over, as if it were the last word she would ever say.

And all the while he told her, with his heart and his body, what he could not say in words. *I love you,* he whispered between each slow, rhythmic thrust. *I love you,* he cried with each thundering beat of his heart. *I love you,* he shouted as the fevered rhythm reached a shattering crescendo.

And when it was over, he kissed away the salty tears that slid from the corners of her eyes. Very gently his hand came up to cradle her cheek, brushing away the damp tendrils of hair and searching her eyes. "Why?" he asked softly.

Her smile was misty. "You can ask why? After what you've just given me?" She pressed her mouth into the warm roughness of his palm. "Thank you—" she began.

Brody placed his fingers against her lips. "No," he interrupted quietly. "I'm the one who should be thanking you."

Her eyes were wide and questioning on his face. "For what?"

He smiled at her, then kissed her tenderly, putting all his pent-up emotions into the caress. "For bringing me here," he whispered when her lips finally parted. And because for the first time ever, he knew what it was to find joy in someone else's pleasure.

But the happiness he found in that thought was dimmed by another: because Brody knew that loving her was both the easiest and the hardest thing he'd ever done in his life.

CHAPTER FIFTEEN

IT WAS A TINY SOUND that woke Brody very early the next morning, so faint he thought he'd dreamed it. He lay very still, watching the pale streamers of light fill the room. Then the sound came again, a faint mewling cry, and he recognized the source.

He glanced over at Jess. She was sleeping peacefully, one hand tucked under her cheek. She looked as innocent and childlike as the baby whose summons came from the room across the hall.

Sliding out of bed, he slipped into his jeans and walked barefoot from the room.

Nathan was squirming, trying to jam his fist into his mouth and whining fretfully when he didn't succeed. Brody hesitated, then lifted the child from the crib.

The touch of Brody's hands told Nathan he wasn't alone. His cries ceased. Brody stood awkwardly for a moment, then carried him over to the padded change table in the corner. He'd never changed a baby before, and he had a little difficulty locating all the snaps on Nathan's sleeper. Removing the disposable diaper posed no problem, but his hands were clumsy as he positioned a clean one beneath the baby's tiny bottom and tried to fasten the tapes.

Nathan gazed up at him trustingly. He made a soft little sound that Brody could have sworn was one of contentment. His hands stilled abruptly.

Nathan was so small, so totally dependent on someone else for all his needs. He thought of Jess and how she must feel, knowing that she was completely responsible for this tiny being. Most of all he remembered the radiance that surrounded her whenever she was with her son.

A feeling that was part pleasure, part pain shot through him. Never before had Brody thought of having a child, a wife or a family. Paternal instincts were alien to him. But he couldn't deny right now that he felt incomplete. Alone and empty.

It hit him with a devastating intensity that he didn't want to spend his life alone—like Murphy. Like his father. He wanted someone to share his days and nights, to love and to love him in return.

He finished changing the baby's diaper. He still felt awkward handling the child, but he no longer felt totally inadequate. Nor could he deny that holding Nathan gave him a warm sense of contentment.

Brody lifted the baby. "So, what do you say, Nathan? I think you and I do pretty well together." He settled the child into the crook of his arm, laughing softly when Nathan turned his head toward his chest. His tiny mouth was open, avidly searching. "But we can't get along without your mom, now, can we?"

Jess was just waking up when the pair moved back across the hall. Brody watched from the doorway, admiring the slender curve of her shoulder, recalling just how sweet the silky hollow at the base of her throat tasted and relishing all over again the way her pulse had quickened and throbbed beneath the agile thrust of his tongue.

But most of all, he thrilled to the leap of joy in her eyes when he murmured a good-morning.

Jess sat up slowly, pulling the sheet to her naked breasts. Brody still stood in the doorway, casually holding her son in one arm. Nathan seemed intent on the fist he'd managed to stuff into his mouth. Both looked amazingly nonchalant and immensely contented, as well.

A slight smile pulled at her lips. "I guess there's no need to ask why you're up," she murmured dryly. Her eyes fixed on Nathan. "Nor can I believe he slept through his two o'clock feeding."

"Maybe," Brody suggested with a decidedly wicked gleam in his eyes, "it's because he knew his mother was otherwise occupied."

Jess felt a faint warmth creep into her cheeks, and Brody's low, husky laugh made her heart turn over.

"However," he continued, "I think you might want to remedy the situation soon, before he loses patience with both of us."

Jess began to reach for the baby automatically, but suddenly remembered she wasn't wearing a single stitch of clothing. She knew she shouldn't have been so modest, particularly after last night, but she couldn't help it.

Brody tossed her the nightgown that was draped over the back of the chair, his eyes knowingly amused. Jess pulled it over her head, then reached for her son. She dismissed the idea of asking Brody to get a blanket from Nathan's room and concentrated instead on easing back against the pillow and readying herself for Nathan.

The nightgown was one specifically made for nursing, with two vertical slits hidden within its folds. The instant Nathan was settled in her arms, he thumped her breast impatiently, his tiny mouth avid and open. Brody laughed at his eagerness.

Jess leaned back against the headboard. "I'm sorry I didn't hear him wake up," she apologized.

Brody merely smiled. "You won't complain if his diaper falls off, will you?"

"You changed him?"

His expression changed to one of mock pain. "To the best of my ability," he said glumly. "It didn't take me long to figure out my hands are too big and his bottom is too small."

Jess's lips twitched. She started to tease him that saggy diaper or no, he was showing definite signs of being excellent father material. Yet the thought made her heart constrict. Whether her feelings were wanted or unwanted, warranted or unwarranted, she loved Brody Alexander.

But their time together was measured. A niggling little voice reminded her that soon, very soon, he would be leaving. His destination—if he even had one—was of little consequence. Whether it was back to California, or off to the ends of the earth, he would be lost to her forever.

He'd freely admitted that he cared. But did he love her? And last night . . . What did it *really* mean?

Jess didn't want him to leave—ever. Yet she didn't dare ask him to stay.

She was reminded of what Betty had said of Lucas a couple of weeks ago. *I want him to be with me because it's where he wants to be.* Jess suddenly understood Betty's meaning all too clearly.

She felt just a little shy and very much uncertain when the mattress dipped beside her. Brody was barefoot, shirtless and clad only in a pair of well-worn jeans. His hair was appealingly tousled. She loved the way the sunlight caught fire in the tawny strands. With his jaw darkened by a day's growth of beard, he looked tough, raw and very, very male.

A quiver shot through her as she recalled sliding her fingers through the rough mat of down that covered his chest. Even now, her fingertips tingled, as she remembered the feel of his skin against her palm, the straining ridges of his very well-developed biceps. And to her mingled delight and embarrassment, she remembered the thrilling excitement of being loved by him, the delicious way her body expanded to accommodate his straining fullness, the heated strokes that stole her breath and left her yearning for even more of him.

Beside her, Brody spoke softly. "What are you thinking?"

Jess turned her head slightly. They sat together on the bed, with only their shoulders touching. She hesitated, unwilling to risk anything that might shatter the magical spell that the night in each other's arms had cast. "Nothing, really," she murmured.

There was a moment's silence. "No regrets?"

Something in his voice caught her wholly off guard. She glanced up to discover an expression of wary hope on his rugged features. It seemed strange to think of Brody as vulnerable, yet Jess had the distinct impression that at this moment, he was every bit as susceptible as she.

Yes, she had doubts about tomorrow, but she had no regrets about having been with him last night. Because of him, she had recaptured what she'd thought Eric had stripped from her forever: the belief that she could be a desirable woman.

Leaning over, she placed her free hand along the bristly line of his jaw and kissed his mouth, very gently but very thoroughly. "I told you there wouldn't be," she said softly.

A part of Brody rejoiced, even while another part prayed that Jess wouldn't turn the question around on him, for what could he say? She had just given him the most wonderful night of his life. If only he could wipe the slate clean and start over again, this time with Jess. Yet because of Eric Culver, he was trapped by circumstances, caught squarely in the middle.

He sighed inwardly, idly running a finger down Nathan's chubby cheek. Nathan's mouth stopped working; he pulled away and gave a little grin aimed straight at Brody's startled face, then resumed his nursing.

Jess's eyes went wide. "Did you see that? He smiled—his first smile!" Her delighted laugh turned into a moan. "But it was at you, not me," she complained, frowning at Brody in mock indignation. "I'm beginning to think I'm just excess baggage around here."

Lord, no! Brody thought. Never that. He was the one who was an outsider, the one who didn't belong.

"That reminds me," he said lightly. "What's on the agenda for today, boss lady?"

Jess's eyes lit with an impish light. "How do you feel about giving the tractor a real test?"

Brody lifted his eyebrows inquiringly.

"Lucas should be here soon," she explained. "If the field behind the barn were tilled, I'd call today and confirm my order. Then we might be able to start planting the bare-root trees sometime next week."

Brody hesitated. "Better cross your fingers then, because I'm afraid I can't promise how long I can keep it running."

She chuckled at his skepticism. "Don't you have any faith in yourself? Why, you've already done the impossible. Even Lucas's friend Ray thought that tractor was destined for the junk pile."

"That's a loaded question, Jess. Believe me, Ray was right. It's a miracle I even got the damn thing started at all," he said with a grimace.

She remained undaunted. "All I ask is that we get that field done. Then I won't have to worry so much about the loan, at least until next year. And hopefully, by then I'll be in a better financial position."

Brody watched as she switched the baby to the other breast. When she glanced up again, her expression had turned rather serious. Her eyes had darkened, like storm clouds gathering on the horizon. Brody sensed her mind was once again on Eric's disturbing phone call yesterday. He squeezed her fingers reassuringly. "Don't worry," he said quietly. "I still think Eric was just out to scare you."

There was a protracted silence. "I expect you're right," she said finally. Her arm tightened around her son, but eventually she seemed to relax.

Brody wanted nothing more than to drive the darkness from her face. "Now that we have today all planned out," he said with a smile, "I have just one small request. While Lucas and I are hard at work here, I'd like you to make a little trip down to the hardware store."

"The hardware store!" She chuckled. "Brody, in case you haven't noticed, between my barn and Lucas's garage, we've got almost as much inventory as any hardware store within twenty miles of here."

"Not of this particular item, you don't."

Her curiosity was getting the better of her. "And just what is this particular item?"

"Paint."

"Paint! For my living room?"

He nodded. "And this room," he clarified.

Her smile lit her eyes to the clearest shade of blue he'd ever seen. "You don't like waking up to purple walls?" she asked pertly.

Brody's gaze trickled down her face and neck, feasting on her pink bareness. "I'll tell you what I do like." His tone was not without a hint of suggestiveness as he weaved his fingers through her free hand. "I like waking up next to you."

Jess felt her blood heat with the warmth of his expression. It was as if she were poised at the summit of a treacherous peak. She felt bold and daring and just a little fearful.

"The feeling is mutual," she confided, "and one I have no objection to repeating."

His gaze captured hers. Inside, Brody thrilled to the shy promise in her voice. "Is that an invitation?"

Light as his tone was, there was an underlying note of gravity in the question. Her heart leaped and soared. Down deep, Jess realized she'd been afraid Brody might take their night together for granted. She knew now that nothing could have been further from the truth.

Lifting their clasped hands, she rubbed her cheek against his strong brown knuckles. "It is," she confirmed happily.

The look deepened. "I don't want to make things awkward or difficult for you, Jess."

Two faint, tiny lines appeared between her slender brows. "You mean Lucas?"

Brody nodded. He knew how extremely protective Lucas was of Jess.

The lines disappeared. "I don't think either of us needs to worry," she said softly. "Lucas only wants what's best for me."

Brody's smile was enigmatic. He looked almost sad. "I know," he responded quietly. "That's what bothers me."

Jess shifted the baby to her shoulder, grasping his meaning immediately. She abhorred the self-deprecation she suspected he was experiencing. "You're selling yourself short," she told him, eyes sparking dangerously. "I've told you my secrets, you've told me yours. That makes us even, Brody Alexander."

No. Not by a long shot, Brody denied silently. When she found out why he was here... God, that didn't even bear thinking about.

His fingers tangled in her hair. He brought her close for a brief, hard kiss. When he pulled her back, Jess buried her face in the hollow of his shoulder. "You should have run while you had the chance," he muttered into the dark cloud of her hair.

He felt her smile against his chest. She lifted her head, smiling directly into his eyes. "If I were running," she countered softly, "it would be *to* you, not from you."

She lowered her head again, and Brody's hand tightened around the slender curve of her nape. Closing his eyes, he rested his chin on her bent head.

This was wrong, all wrong. Jess deserved a better man than he. He had nothing—nothing but a handful of dreams that he'd lost along the way.

And all at once he wanted the world. He wanted nothing more than to be granted the privilege of spending the rest of his life at Jess's side. He wanted to give Nathan a brother and maybe a sister.

He knew he could never let her go. Not now. Maybe never. Damn, he swore softly. *Damn!* If only he weren't here with her under false pretenses. What chance did they have with such a secret hanging between them? Yet Brody knew he would never forgive himself if he didn't tell her.

But if he did, Jess might never forgive him. He was well aware that his motives were selfish. He was afraid of her rejection.

Yet he knew he had to tell her, and soon.

But not now. It would shatter last night's memory as surely as night followed day.

But when Jess found out . . . Brody realized then that the choice really wasn't his at all. How he felt about his deception was inconsequential. It was all up to Jess.

And in that moment, Brody knew fear as he'd never known it before.

NO ONE WAS MORE RELIEVED than Brody when the workday came to a close. Miraculously their luck with the tractor held out and they had been able to get Jess's precious field ready for planting.

Nor, he discovered, was there any need to worry about Lucas's reaction to his new relationship with Jess. No one had said a word, yet every so often Brody saw the old man's eyes move speculatively between him and Jess. It was almost as if he could see the wheels spinning wildly in Lucas's mind.

But there was no doubt that Lucas had put two and two together. Just before Lucas left for the day, he asked, "You and Jess have anything planned for the rest of the weekend?"

Brody leaned against the hood of the weathered old truck. The pose of studied nonchalance was deceiving. "I thought I'd paint Jess's living room and bedroom," he answered as casually as he could, then cocked an eyebrow. "Why? You in the mood to handle a paintbrush, too?"

"I think I'll leave that to you," he answered cheerfully. Brody stepped back as Lucas clambered into the cab. An instant later, he rolled down the window and stuck his head out.

Glancing across the drive, Brody found that Lucas's grin had faded. In its stead, his seamed face reflected anxious concern.

Every muscle in Brody's body tightened. Several seconds passed before he heard Lucas's voice.

"Son?"

With an effort, Brody met his eyes.

"I know this ain't none of my business and you can tell me where to go, but there's something I have to say. Jessie's been through a lot this past year. I'd hate to see her hurt again." Lucas cleared her throat. "Especially by you. See that you take care with her, won't you, son?"

With that, the engine coughed and sputtered, then roared to life. Brody was left standing in the drive, shoulders stiff with tension. He had the strangest sensation that if he moved, his control would shatter into a million pieces.

He despised himself as every kind of heel. A coward. A weakling. He was glad—even grateful—that Lucas hadn't demanded any kind of response, for what could he have said? He could offer no promises, no assurances . . . at least not yet, and perhaps never.

Brody also knew a deep, angry despair that fate had singled him out so cruelly.

Happiness—true happiness—was a commodity he'd had precious little experience with. Somehow it had always managed to elude him, tantalizingly close but dangling just beyond reach. Murphy was the one good thing that had come into his life; Jess was the other. Murphy was gone, already lost to him. And he was desperately afraid of losing Jess.

But who was he trying to fool? Through a twist of fate, it was altogether possible that Jess was already lost to him.

A SHORT TIME LATER Brody slipped back to his motel room in McMinnville on the pretense of picking up a few things. He bitterly regretted deceiving Jess. This would be the last time, he promised himself.

His stride carried him straight to the phone. Seconds later, Eric Culver was on the other end of the line.

Brody got right to the point. "What the hell are you trying to prove?"

Culver's reaction was predictable. "I beg your pardon?"

Brody swore hotly. "Don't play innocent with me. You called Jess last night. I'm warning you, stay the hell away from her."

"So you're still there, eh? Frankly, I'm surprised." Culver's laugh was grating. "On second thought, maybe I shouldn't be. After all, you've got a good thing going for you. I must admit, though, you're certainly making things easier for me. Tell me, Alexander, is she as ho—"

"Shut up, Culver. Just shut up and listen." Brody spoke through clenched teeth, barely able to control his hatred. "I'm not asking you to forget this whole thing—I'm *telling* you. You may think you're getting back at Jess, but you've got me to consider now."

"Again?" Culver sounded bored. "Your threats don't scare me now any more than they did the other day."

Brody's face was a mask of stone. His voice went low and deadly. "I won't let you do this to her. I won't let you hurt Jess again."

"No?" All at once Culver's voice changed. "You can't stop me."

Brody thought of the secret Jess had told him. He also remembered that Eric didn't know that Jess knew about his homosexuality. The accusation trembled on his lips; it was only the fear that he might need the revelation as ammunition later that kept Brody from revealing it.

"Yes, I can," he said very softly. "And it's not a threat, Culver. It's a promise."

"She ruined me, dammit. Everything I ever worked for was gone—just like that."

"I'm not forgetting anything," Brody stated calmly. "Back off now, or you'll be sorry. You may think your career is over, but if you drive Jess into a custody battle, you'll get more than you bargained for." He decided to leave him with a final warning. "Think about it, Culver. Think about it, and I'm sure you'll see this whole thing is better off forgotten."

BRODY HAD BEEN just a little unsure of Culver's reaction to his ultimatum. He had half expected Jess to receive another phone call from Eric, but she didn't.

In spite of his apprehension about Eric, the next few days were among the best Brody had ever had in his life. On Sunday he and Jess had painted her living room and bedroom. Afterward they had shared a cold supper on the living-room floor in front of the fireplace, then spent the evening making love over and over again.

Was this the beginning of the dream he'd thought he'd lost? The new start he'd wanted?

The few doubts he'd felt had long since passed. There was nothing tying him down in California. He loved Jess; he wanted her by his side as his wife. Nor had he forgotten Nathan. Nathan was a part of Jess; because he loved Jess, he also loved Nathan. Eric would never be a father to the boy; Nathan deserved one, and Brody wanted to be that man.

As for Eric, there were a few times when Brody feared that doom lurked overhead like the darkest thundercloud. But Culver was a smart man. Surely he would see the wisdom in letting go of his crazy vendetta.

When a week had passed without incident, Brody began to breathe more easily, to believe in the future that had eluded him for so long....

It was a costly mistake.

EARLY MONDAY AFTERNOON Lucas and Brody finished planting the last of the trees and bushes. Jess was anxious to begin work inside the greenhouse, so as soon as Nathan was down for his afternoon nap, the three of them began transferring trays, peat pots and bags of sterilized soil to the greenhouse. It was on the last trip that Jess laid a finger on her lips in consternation.

"Forget something?" asked Brody.

She nodded. "The sand. We need to mix it in with the soil. I left a couple of bags in the house."

Lucas glanced over at her. "I need to go in and use the phone, anyway," he told her, and disappeared through the doorway.

Hands on his hips, Brody's gaze lingered on the hanging baskets he'd just hooked on an overhead bracket. He reached up and touched one of the trailing vines that spilled over the edge of the basket. When he caught Jess's eyes on him, one corner of his mouth turned up sheepishly. "It's so shiny and green," he murmured. "What is it?"

Jess couldn't have been more pleased. "It's commonly known as Swedish ivy," she told him. "But it's actually not Swedish at all, but Australian. And it's really not ivy at all, but a member of the mint family."

Brody nodded toward another basket. "That one is baby's tears, right?"

She feigned surprise. "I'm going to make a nurseryman of you yet, Brody Alexander."

Brody merely smiled and shrugged.

Jess's eyes were full of laughter. "Who do you think Lucas is calling?" she asked.

He chuckled. "Want to bet Betty's line is busy?" He shook his head as if in disgust. "He's got it bad, you know." His eyes softened. "Almost as bad as me," he added.

Jess wasted no time in sidling over to him and slipping her arms around his neck. "This mysterious 'it' that we're talking about seems to be contagious."

He kissed the tip of her nose. "You think so?" His head dipped slowly.

Jess thrilled to the feel of his hard mouth against hers. "I know so," she whispered, pressing against him in wanton boldness. Her breasts were cushioned by the hardness of his chest. Her legs were flush against his.

Brody groaned at the delicious sensation of warm, feminine softness cradling his masculine counterpart. She arched against him, the sinuous motion kindling an undeniably male response he couldn't control. His mouth locked against hers; he pulled her fully and tightly against him.

Jess felt a tiny tremor of excitement as the heat of his arousal radiated against her. Her stomach muscles clenched, even as her limbs turned bone-meltingly weak. Would it always be like this? she asked herself dizzily. She prayed that it would.

And she prayed that Brody felt it, too. Her heart was filled with hungry hope. Whether he made love to her with fierce abandon or as gently and carefully as the first time, there was an ever-present element of unselfish caring and giving... and something she dared call love.

She had yet to hear the words fall from his lips, though. Jess admitted to the slightest twinge of disappointment. Better not to hear the words at all than to fall victim to false promises. She told herself it was only a matter of time.

But wasn't she living on borrowed time already? Time was probably the one thing they didn't have.

She couldn't stop the question from spilling forth when their lips finally parted. "Brody... Brody, what's going to happen next?" Her gaze faltered and so did her voice. "I mean, we're almost finished here...."

Something inside him twisted. He knew what she meant. Her greenhouse was built; most of her nursery stock was in. There were a few minor repairs left on the shade house, but most of the work she'd hired him for was completed.

Leaving was the one thing he hadn't wanted to think about. With Jess it was so easy to forget everything but the new emotions she aroused in him.

One side of his mouth slanted up. "Are you telling me this is the end of the line, Jess?" His tone was teasing, but he was deadly serious.

"Don't joke," she whispered. Her gaze faltered and so did her voice. "What now? Are you—are you going back to California?"

All of a sudden he wanted to say so many things. But he'd never been aware of just how much he'd lost in life: his mother, his youth, Murphy, the career that he'd never really wanted but was all he'd ever really had. He couldn't stand to lose Jess, too.

"Do you want me to?" His smile vanished. His gaze was piercingly direct. "Do you want me to leave here, Jess?"

Her fingers touched his cheek. Her lips formed a tremulous smile, but her eyes were suspiciously bright. "It's not my decision," she murmured helplessly. "I need to know what *you* want."

Brody's arms tightened. His hold on her was almost desperate. No more lies, he promised himself. No more pretense. He was going to tell her exactly what he wanted from her and pray that she wanted the same.

But he never got the chance. Before he could say a word, another sound invaded the silence—the scraping creak of a door being slowly opened—or closed.

Jess stiffened in his arms. Her eyes flew to its source—the portable monitor propped against the wall, which alerted her when Nathan awoke.

"What the—" Brody clamped his mouth shut.

The creak came again. A second later, there was a muffled shout. The sound of running footsteps followed and then a dull thud.

Jess's eyes swung to Brody's in stunned shock. His look of dazed apprehension suddenly became taut and strained, reflecting sheer, blind panic.

Her heart jumped to her throat. Something was wrong. Something was very wrong.

CHAPTER SIXTEEN

THE GROUND SPUN CRAZILY as Jess tore wildly toward the house. Brody was already yards ahead of her. By the time she yanked the screen door open, her lungs were burning.

In the kitchen she hesitated, her gaze swinging wildly toward the stairs. Nathan's door was ajar. Had she left it that way? Her mind filled with a dozen doubts and nameless fears. A sickly dread spread through her.

There was no sign of Brody. And Lucas—where was Lucas?

Then she heard it. A voice—no, two—raised in anger, and the pitifully thin wail of a baby.

"Nathan! Oh, God, *Nathan!*" Her scream shattered the deathly quiet of the house.

She had no memory of stumbling back outside. The next thing she knew she was standing in the yard near the front porch. What she saw made her blood run cold.

A man—a stranger—thrust Nathan into the front seat of a late-model car parked in the drive.

Eric... He was responsible for this!

Brody grabbed the man's arm and whirled him around before he could slide inside. The stranger jerked his arm away. They stood facing each other, scarcely a foot apart.

The man began to inch away, stealing slowly backward. Don't just stand there! a voice inside Jess screamed frantically. He's stealing your baby!

Panic swelled in her chest until she could scarcely breathe. This couldn't be happening, Jess thought dumbly. But it was. It was! Someone was stealing her baby and all she could do was stand by helplessly, as if she were carved in stone.

Their voices receded into a dim haze, blurred and indistinct, like insects buzzing all around her. Neither man seemed aware of her.

Suddenly the stranger whirled and grabbed for his car door. Jess cried out sharply at the same instant Brody's shoulder jammed into his back, throwing him off balance. It was the only edge Brody needed. Vaulting forward, Brody's fist shot out and connected with the man's jaw. Then he retrieved Nathan safely from the car.

Jess began to run, her legs like deadweights beneath her. When she reached the pair, Brody relinquished her son back to her arms.

"Nathan! Oh, Nathan!" She gave a breathless little cry and clutched the baby to her chest. His cries ceasing, Nathan squirmed and frowned up at her. Reassured, Jess turned furiously on the stranger. His face was dark and flushed. One hand cradled his injured jaw, but Jess was in no mood to commiserate.

"Eric's behind this, isn't he?" she demanded furiously. "My God, what kind of man are you to try to steal a baby away from his mother!"

The man's gaze—cool and remote and utterly expressionless—met hers. He said nothing.

Jess was suddenly shaking with fury. Anger propelled her forward; exactly what she'd have done, she never knew. Brody grasped her arm firmly. "Let's talk inside," he said grimly.

All at once there was a new kind of tension. The two men stared at one another, each seeming to take the other's measure. For just an instant, Jess could have sworn they knew each other. Brody's lips were ominously thin, while the other man's gaze was openly rebellious. Her own anger forgotten, Jess held her breath, mentally preparing for open warfare.

"Don't even think it," Brody warned tightly. "You're not leaving here till I know what the hell you're up to." The man turned and strode toward the house. Brody and Jess were right at his heels.

But there was another surprise waiting for them inside the house.

With all the excitement outside, Jess and Brody had forgotten about Lucas. Brody was the first to enter the living room. A low exclamation broke from his lips. Her gaze followed his hurried progress across the room. What she saw there tore a sharp cry from her throat: Lucas was stretched out at the foot of the stairs.

White-faced and trembling, she couldn't look away. "Oh, my God!" she choked. "Is he—"

"Call an ambulance, Jess. Now!" Brody knelt down beside Lucas's prone form. He pressed his fingers against Lucas's neck, feeling for a pulse. It was there, weak but steady.

With Nathan still in her arms, Jess fumbled for the phone and shakily punched out 911. A minute later, she hung up the receiver. "They're on their way." If only it were a dream, she thought helplessly. She knelt down beside Lucas and watched Brody slide his fingers under the back of his head. Her stomach lurched sickeningly when they came away smeared with blood. "How bad is it?" Her lips were so stiff she could scarcely speak.

Brody shook his head. "He's got a hell of a goose egg back there."

Just then Lucas groaned. His eyes opened, heavy lidded and confused. His mouth opened but no sound came out.

"Don't try to talk. Just lie back and take it easy," Jess soothed. "There's an ambulance on the way."

His eyes fluttered closed again.

Brody's eyes swung back to the stranger, standing just inside the doorway. His mouth tightened. "You did this, didn't you?"

The man was pale. He shook his head quickly.

"He saw you take the baby, didn't he?" Silent as a panther, Brody rose slowly to his full height.

The stranger's eyes darted from Lucas's figure to the man hovering above. "I..." he faltered.

"Didn't he?" Brody's face was harsh and threatening.

"I'll admit he caught me upstairs, but I didn't touch him! I turned around and there he was, standing in the door. I pushed him aside and ran past him, but that's all...."

Brody swore hotly. Jess experienced a rush of alarm at his expression. He looked rigidly tense, yet she sensed the anger pulsing through him, as if he wanted nothing more than to tear the other man apart. "You expect me to believe you? Dammit, O'Hara, you of all people! Everybody knows how dirty you play."

"Not this time. It was an accident, I swear!"

But Jess scarcely heard. All her attention was focused on Brody. "O'Hara?" Her lips parted. "You know this man?"

Brody's reaction was puzzling. For a fraction of a second, she could have sworn he blanched. Then he nodded curtly. "His name is O'Hara. Martin O'Hara." There was a brief pause. "He's a private investigator from San Francisco." His gaze swung back to the man he called O'Hara. "You'd better not be lying," he warned tautly, "because if Lucas is seriously hurt..."

A dozen questions flooded her mind, but she was unable to capture any of them. The soft menace in Brody's voice was frightening. Nor was Jess the only one to feel it.

O'Hara gazed first at Brody, then at Jess. Then he whirled back on Brody, his voice desperate. "Don't you try and pin this on me!" he cried. "If anything happens to that old man, it's as much your fault as mine. This wouldn't have happened at all if it weren't for you. You're the one who botched the job in the first place. You were supposed to have her—'' he jabbed his head at Jess ''—eating out of your hand, not the other way around.''

O'Hara glanced around and caught the horrified expression on Jess's face. Brody's stomach knotted with sick certainty. O'Hara was quick to grab the opportunity with both hands. He was confident, sure of himself once more.

It was over, Brody suddenly realized. His mind spewed forth every obscenity he could think of, but the target wasn't Eric Culver or even O'Hara. It was all over, and he had no one to blame but himself.

Jess had difficulty grappling with the implication of O'Hara's words. Then stubbornly, willfully, she refused to acknowledge it. Slowly she turned to Brody. Say something! she pleaded silently. Say it's not true! Say he's lying!

But he didn't. He simply stood there . . . and everything inside Jess seemed to shrivel up and die.

"You didn't know, did you?" O'Hara directed the question to Jess, then gestured at Brody. "You want to know how he knows me, little lady? I don't know what line he got you to swallow, but he's a private investigator, too. And you're right about your husband—or your ex-husband. He hired me to steal your baby, after he—'' he pointed an accusing finger at Brody ''—decided to play Mr. Goody-Two-Shoes. He was supposed to dig up a little dirt on you. He's got no more scruples than me—or at least he didn't until he was suckered in by your pretty face.''

This couldn't be happening. No more, Jess prayed silently. No more. Stricken, she couldn't look away from Brody. She stared at him with eyes both accusing and pleading.

Time hung suspended. There was a strange buzzing in her ears. For a fraction of a second, the world tilted alarmingly, then abruptly righted itself. Some distant part of her mind registered the sound of a siren coming closer and closer. She looked at Lucas. His eyes flitted open, then closed again. She shuddered. This was no dream; it was a nightmare.

Her gaze was drawn to Brody. He didn't look away, but she saw his mask of cool control slip. For just an instant, guilt shadowed the depths of his eyes, offering a fleeting glimpse of his soul. He looked as desolate and lonely as she felt. He glanced away, and when their eyes met again, his were curiously blank.

The pain that streaked through her was agony. It was like a knife sliding into her, plunging deeper and deeper.

"No," she whispered. Her lips barely moved. "It can't be..."

O'Hara drove the blade home.

"No?" O'Hara's laughter was grating. "Lady, you're one hell of a fringe benefit. I don't blame Alexander for doing more than rub shoulders with a lady as good-looking as you. Besides, Mr. Culver told me how he was *supposed* to. Nothing like a tawdry little affair to complicate a custody case."

"Oh, God." A prayer or a curse? Brody wondered. A deep, silent despair washed over him. With every breath, with every heartbeat, Jess was being carried further and further away from him.

There was a pounding at the front door. Jess stared at it through wide, sightless eyes. All she could see were Brody's craggy features, etched with guilt. She felt curiously numb; her emotions were frozen. Only Nathan was real, his small body soft and warm as he tried to jam a tiny fist into his mouth. A part of her wanted to crawl away and lick her wounds in private.

But she wasn't to be allowed the luxury of self-pity. The knock came again. Drawing on the courage she'd thought already sapped, she pulled open the door. Amid the crackle and buzz of a radio, two paramedics hustled inside.

Jess stood silently as they worked over Lucas in an atmosphere that was tense and hurried. Lucas began to cough and sputter as a vial was waved under his nose. One of the paramedics looked up at her. "We should probably take him to Emergency and have the doctor there check him out."

She nodded. "I'll go with you."

The other paramedic went out to the ambulance for the gurney. Brody reached over and touched Jess's arm. Her guard went up like the rapid slamming of doors and windows. Quickly, before he had time to change his mind, he spoke. "The hospital is in McMinnville?"

"Yes." She might have been speaking to a stranger.

"It might be easier on you if you leave Nathan here, Jess. If something comes up and you need to stay longer..."

"No." Her arms tightened protectively around Nathan. "You're the last person I'd leave my son with, and I think you've got a hell of a lot of gall to even suggest it! But then I guess you've already proved that, haven't you?"

Brody flinched. He'd expected her rejection, but he wasn't prepared for the pure blue fire raging in her eyes.

His voice was very low. "You know I wouldn't hurt Nathan, Jess. I care about him almost as much as I care about you." He held out his hand and repeated quietly. "I care, Jess."

She stared with ill-concealed hatred at the hand extended to her. Suddenly all the fire seemed to go out of her, and Brody experienced a crushing defeat unlike anything he'd ever felt. He could deal with her anger. He could deal with her hatred. But the eyes that rose slowly to his were empty, void of any feeling whatsoever.

His hand dropped to his side. Jess followed the paramedics out of the house.

"Jess," Brody called after her.

She turned. Nathan was asleep, his cheek fat and plump against her shoulder.

"What about him?" He indicated O'Hara, who had followed them out and was watching the gurney being loaded into the back of the ambulance.

"What about him?" Her voice, like her expression, was flat and remote.

He gestured vaguely. "Are you going to file a complaint with the police? O'Hara could be charged with attempted kidnapping. Eric, too."

She smiled then—a smile that chilled his heart. "And what about you, Brody? Are you any less guilty than they are?" For a moment she looked as if she wanted to say more. Then her jaw closed abruptly.

She delivered her decision with cool efficiency. "All I want," she stated precisely, "is for him to be gone when I come home." Her eyes, cold and shuttered, met his. "You, too. And I pray to God I never see either of you again."

She turned her back and moved toward the waiting vehicle. Her withdrawal was complete and absolute. Brody's gaze followed her progress, noting the firm resolve in her slender shoulders, her rigid self-control. It struck him then that he'd never felt such pride in her... or such love.

He would have laughed at the irony of it all, if only his heart weren't breaking in two.

How Jess got through the next few hours, she never knew. In the ambulance, Jess clung tightly to Lucas's hand. He squeezed her fingers, but his eyes remained shut. He made no effort to speak.

When they arrived at the hospital, Lucas was wheeled away from her through a set of wide double doors. Jess had the strangest sensation as the doors swung shut. It was like watching a part of her being sealed away forever.

Perhaps it was inevitable that she should be reminded.... These past weeks with Brody might never have happened. She had given herself so completely—physically and emotionally. Then in one brief moment of bitter revelation, all that was wiped cleanly away.

But you received more than you gave. Far more.

But that was before I knew who he really was, why he was here....

That doesn't change how you feel about him. He gave you something Eric never could. He gave you back your self-esteem, your pride in your sex....

But what good was pride in the face of betrayal? The Brody Alexander she had come to love had never existed. It was all just a lie, an excuse to enable him to get close to her.

A wrenching pain ripped through her. The one time she had been leery of him, he had turned aside her suspicions so neatly. And she had been so gullible, so ripe for the picking—so damned eager!

Unbidden, his face swam before her, his features dark and lean and as full of heartbreak as her own. There had been no triumph, no flame of victory alight in his expression; only a kind of bittersweet resignation. She could have sworn he felt as hollow and beaten as she.

But what was the lie, and what was the truth? Jess no longer knew.

Her movements mechanical, Jess located a phone and called Betty. By the time Betty arrived at the hospital, Jess was almost grateful for the numbness that had slipped over her. Together they sat down to wait. A nurse came out a short time later and told them Lucas was being admitted as a patient. They were directed to yet another waiting room upstairs. Jess changed Nathan with a diaper provided by the nurse. After being fed, he fell asleep. Jess pulled him to her shoulder, loath to let him go.

It was then that some of the numbness began to wear off. What if Lucas had been seriously injured? she thought, agonizing. In the ambulance he'd been so still and quiet. Oh, God! What if he—

She couldn't complete the thought. To her horror, her vision began to mist.

Betty eased down next to her. "Don't do this to yourself, Jess," she said quietly.

"But it's my fault he's here." Jess had given Betty a brief rundown of what had happened earlier. "If he hadn't been there with me, helping me—" She choked back a sob.

"Lucas doesn't do anything he doesn't want to. He also doesn't do things halfway." Betty slid her arm around the young woman. There was an odd half smile on her lips. "Haven't you learned that by now?"

Jess swiped at the tear sliding down her cheek. "I still feel responsible. I couldn't live with myself if anything happens to him."

"Mrs. Culver?"

They both glanced up to find a young, white-coated man before them. "I'm Dr. Hansen."

Jess rose shakily. "How is Lucas?" Her voice quavered. She hardly dared to breathe.

"He has a slight concussion, but as long as he stays quiet for the next few days, there should be no aftereffects. His ribs are bruised in a couple of spots but we X-rayed to make sure nothing is broken."

Relief flooded through her. "He'll be okay?"

The doctor laughed. "A week from now he'll be good as new. And he's more than okay, to tell you the truth. I'd say he could run circles around me if he wanted." There was a twinkle in his eye for an instant. "I'm keeping him overnight, though, just for observation. Nothing to be alarmed over, just a standard precaution."

Jess glanced at Betty. "Can we see him?"

"I don't see why not. Not too long, though. He's just had something to help him sleep."

He directed them to a room down the hall. Lucas was lying back against the pillow, his eyes closed. They snapped open at the sound of the door opening. He was a little pale, and there was an ugly bruise on his forehead, but relief flooded his face when he saw Nathan in Jess's arms. "He's okay?"

"He's fine," Jess said softly. Betty was already at his side. As Lucas groped for her hand, she bent over and murmured something to him. Lucas gave a tiny smile, but in the next instant his eyes were once again on Jess.

His voice was anxious. "Jess, that man in your house—"

She read the silent question in his eyes. "He was hired by Eric."

Lucas's mouth thinned. "I knew it," he muttered. "I knew he had something to do with it. Damn, if only I hadn't lost my balance—"

"That's what happened? He didn't push you?"

"Pretty clumsy of me," he said with a grimace. "I thought I heard something upstairs. When I got there, he shoved his way past me. I turned to follow him and that's when it happened."

Jess hesitated. "There's more," she said finally.

His brows drew together fiercely. "Out with it then, Jessie. I'm not the fragile little blossom you all seem to think. I told the doctor that and now I'm telling you."

Betty's eyes met hers. A glimmer of amusement passed between them, but then Jess drew a deep, fortifying breath. Keeping all expression from her voice, she told Lucas what little she knew—that Eric had also sent Brody, apparently on a spy mission.

Lucas said nothing for the longest time. It was Betty who finally broke the silence, her gaze on Lucas. "I'm not trying to change the subject, but how are you feeling?'' she asked him.

"Fine and dandy, now that you're here."

Jess raised her eyebrows in silent speculation, wondering at the glance he and Betty exchanged. Whatever doubts they'd had several weeks ago certainly didn't seem to be plaguing either one of them right now.

Betty's gaze slid to Jess. "Should we tell her?"

"Might as well. We planned to tonight anyway."

They both looked at Jess. Lucas cleared his throat several times; Betty's cheeks deepened in color.

Jess smiled. "I must admit I'm getting curious."

Lucas finally placed a gnarled hand over Betty's. "Betty and I are getting married."

Jess's eyes widened at his gruff declaration, then traveled to Betty. "So that's what you meant when you said he doesn't do things halfway!" she said unthinkingly.

Betty smiled, and Jess found herself struggling to hold back a laugh as Lucas lifted his chin and glared at her almost defiantly. As best as she could manage with Nathan in her arms, she hugged Betty and pressed a kiss on Lucas's grizzled cheek.

"Betty made a good choice," she murmured, then raised her brows in warning. "Don't make her regret it!"

His eyes lingered on Betty. His face was softer than she'd ever seen it. "That's something I don't think you need to worry about," he said with a rare smile.

Jess decided to give them a few minutes' privacy. She moved toward the door, but Lucas's voice stopped her at the threshold.

The statement wasn't at all what she expected.

"Jessie." He paused. "Don't be too hard on Brody. The fact that Eric had to send someone else to finish the job speaks for itself."

Her back stiffened. Over her shoulder, their eyes met. He must have read her mind.

His forehead was creased fiercely. "I'm not defending what he did, Jessie. I always had the feeling he wasn't a rolling stone. And there's good in him, girl. I can feel it here." He thumped his chest.

She went back down the hall to wait for Betty. She laid Nathan on the small sofa and sat beside him, but only for a minute. All of a sudden her limbs felt heavy and weak, but she knew the cause was a spiritual kind of weariness.

She couldn't stop the wave of despondency that swept over her. Lucas was going to be okay, and for that she was grateful. She was also genuinely glad about Lucas and Betty. But what about her? She'd never felt so alone.... *Alone.* The word sounded almost like a death knell. Jess suddenly felt as if the walls were closing in on her. She stumbled to the doorway and sagged against the frame.

Her head jerked up at the sound of footsteps echoing down the long, dismal hallway. Then she saw him, coming straight toward her.

Only once did he falter, the break in his step so slight she might have imagined it. Then, all at once, he was there before her.

For an instant there was total silence. And so much tension, it seemed her nerves were pulsing with static.

It was Brody who broke the silence, his voice so low she had to strain to hear. "I had to come, Jess, for several reasons. I had to know how Lucas is."

There was no mercy in her, no hint of compassion. Jess summoned an icy strength and stared at him, allowing all her resentment to show through before she lifted her chin. "I don't see why."

Her tone was dismissive; she would have turned away if Brody hadn't grabbed her by the shoulders. Fury, raw and wild, kindled in her eyes. For just an instant, it was met and matched by his. "You don't think I feel responsible?"

"Considering why you came to Oregon in the first place, I fail to see how you could feel much of anything." Jess took a perverse pleasure in seeing him flinch.

"Dammit, Jess, I'm not asking for much." His voice was hoarse. "Just tell me how bad he is . . . if he's going to be okay."

He sounded so tortured, the frigid ice that encased her heart thawed a little. "He'll be fine," she said shortly. "He has a slight concussion and his ribs are bruised. He's being released tomorrow."

She wanted to ignore the relief that scored his features. His sigh was audible. She longed to pretend she hadn't heard.

Brody dropped his hands from her shoulders. Turning away, he ran his fingers through his hair. Then he glanced back at her. "Jess?"

She waited for him to continue.

The words were halting. "Does he know about me . . . my part in all of—"

She grasped his meaning immediately. "He knows" was all she said.

This time there was no denying the pain reflected in his tense features. It kindled a curious reaction in Jess. She felt a compulsive need to strike out, to hurt Brody as much as he had hurt her.

"You said you had another reason for coming."

"I did," he said very quietly. "Now—" he seemed to hesitate "—now I'm not so sure it matters."

"I suppose you're going to tell me how innocent you are," she challenged.

The words were no less than an indictment. Brody was overcome with a weary resignation. Why bother? he asked himself. In Jess's eyes he was already tried, convicted and sentenced.

He couldn't blame her. That was the hell of it.

Brody shoved his hands into the pockets of his jeans and stared at the sterile gray wall. "I told you," he said tiredly. "I told you I wasn't the man you thought I was." His voice revealed the strain he was under.

The silence spun out, taut and brittle. "That's it?" She sounded incredulous. "That's your excuse? Because you warned me, it's all my fault?"

Brody's jaw clenched. "Of course it isn't. Don't you think I know that? Believe me, Jess, this isn't any easier for me than it is for you."

Their eyes locked in a silent clash of wills. His expression was dark and relentless and piercing. Jess didn't back down in the slightest. Her face was a mask of sheer determination. Her eyes glittered like pale blue frost.

"That," she said very deliberately, her voice dangerously low, "is where you're wrong."

It hit him right in the pit of his stomach then just what he had done—and exactly what he was up against. Jess was strong—far stronger than she knew.

Brody closed his eyes. His shoulders sagged against the wall. He knew what was coming, and it was almost as though he were bracing himself for it.

There was so much he wanted to say. That he felt closer to her than he'd ever been to anyone. But he knew what Jess would think. Any and everything he might say would be no more than empty platitudes. *Excuses.*

And so he listened, while her eyes damned him silently. And he wondered if she knew she was tearing him apart, little by little, piece by piece.

"You lied to me, Brody," she said in a voice just barely above a whisper. "You pretended to be so noble, so concerned. All the while I was drinking it all in, feeling sorry for

you because you had no one. What was that? A ploy to gain
my sympathy?''

She gave him no chance to answer. "I still can't believe I
fell for it—all of it! And what was in it for you? Money?
And a cheap roll in the hay? You should have asked Eric. He
could have told you what a disappointing experience it
would be.''

Brody was both angered and hurt at what she was doing—
twisting the most beautiful time of his life into something
ugly and shameful. His gaze bored into hers. "You know
better than that, Jess.''

"Do I?'' Her laugh was harsh. "I trusted you, Brody. I
poured out my heart to you and told you things I'd never
shared with anyone. And it seems to me that I've been incredibly stupid. It never crossed my mind you were out for
a cold-blooded seduction. And I actually made it easy for
you. God, how you must have laughed that *I* was the one
doing all the chasing!'' Her voice was filled with contempt,
both for him and for herself.

"It wasn't like that, Jess. It was never part of the plan, I
swear. I admit Eric wanted me to capitalize on—''

"On what? The fact that I was falling in love with you?''
She scarcely realized what she'd just revealed; nor could she
see her way past her anger to the pleading in his voice. "Why
should I believe you?'' It was a cry of pure anguish. "Why
should I believe anything you say?''

He lifted a hand to her. "Can I say just one thing?''

She stepped back to avoid his touch. "Another tender
trap for me to fall into?''

Brody's hand dropped to his side. "For what it's worth,
Jess, I knew almost from the start that I couldn't go through
with it.''

All at once, her expression changed. It was like watching
the flame of a candle flicker, then die out completely. Brody
wished she would fly into another rage, rant and rave at him,

do anything but look the way she did right now. So beaten. So defeated. So shattered.

He stepped close and captured her chin in his fingers. "Nothing I can say will change your mind, will it?" he asked quietly.

It was all there, stark and open and glaring—the bitter hurt, the angry despair, the pain of betrayal stamped on her lovely features. He saw the tears spring into her eyes. He saw her struggle to contain them, her throat working convulsively.

"If you had come to me a week ago, or even yesterday, I might have said yes," she whispered. "But now—" there was a ragged catch in her voice "—now it's too late."

Brody nodded slowly. He started to step back, but the movement was suddenly arrested. A sad little smile lifted his lips as he ran his thumb over the satiny curve of her mouth. "I'll be going home now, Jess," he said very softly. "I won't bother you again." Quickly, lightly, he brushed his mouth against hers, a fleeting touch that was more breath than a caress.

Then he was gone. Eyes wide and unblinking, Jess stood perfectly still, feeling that if she moved, she would splinter into a thousand tiny pieces.

In some deep, distant part of her, she wondered if she would ever forgive Brody. Or if she would ever forgive herself.

And so she watched him walk out of her life...but not out of her heart.

CHAPTER SEVENTEEN

JESS NEVER KNEW HOW she survived the next week. Oh, she went through the motions—helping Betty to see that Lucas didn't overdo it kept her mind occupied for a while. But sometimes when she looked at them together, the painful catch in her heart ran swift and deep.

In spite of how happy Lucas was with Betty, there were times when there was a spark missing in Lucas, too. Jess couldn't forget his wounded look when she had told him Brody had gone. That was the last they had spoken of him.

Her heart was like a stone in her chest, cold and lifeless. Her mind was dulled by pain, yet the tears refused to come. She didn't understand how Brody could have been so tender, so sensitive and alive to all her needs. Her satisfaction, her pleasure, her fulfillment, had always come first. It was no act, she was certain of it. How could he be so completely unselfish, yet so full of deceit?

He'd said he had known almost from the start that he couldn't go through with Eric's plan. Why hadn't he told her then?

Maybe because he was afraid you'd react exactly the way you did.

But what other choice did she have? Eric had made a fool of her once, and now Brody. Both men had betrayed her; both had violated her trust.

She wanted to hate him. She wanted to lash out at him, let him feel the bite and fury of her anger. She wanted to resent him for his callous use of her—she did resent him! But she could never, ever hate him, because she loved him too much.

And that hurt most of all.

In the midst of all this, Lucas had gone out to use the tractor, only once again it wouldn't start. Then Jess had received a phone call from the loan officer at the bank. Her loan application had been turned down. Every time she thought about it, she choked back a sob. What more could happen? How much was she expected to take? She knew it was self-pity, but knowing that didn't help any.

"Dammit!" She slammed a fist against the counter. "Dammit, I won't cry!"

Then, early Sunday afternoon, there was a knock on the back door. Jess wavered, tempted to ignore it. She simply didn't feel up to facing anyone right now.

The knock came again, more insistently this time. Dry eyed and stony faced, Jess went to answer it.

"Surprise! I bet you never thought you'd see me again so soon!"

There was no time to respond. The door had no sooner opened than she found herself enfolded in a warm, welcoming hug.

Jess took one look at Maggie and burst into tears.

BRODY UNLOCKED THE DOOR of his apartment and pushed it open. He was home. Everything looked exactly as he'd left it—the newspaper dropped carelessly on the end table, the cup and saucer still in the sink.

But this wasn't home—not anymore. As he stood there, he was suddenly overwhelmed by a terrifying sense of isolation, a feeling that he'd been stranded and left behind with no hope of ever being found.

No, this wasn't home. This place belonged to a stranger. He wasn't the same man who had left here. Home was the bluest eyes he'd ever seen, eyes that were misty and shy and soft with a love given without question. Now he was a man without a home. And he wished he were a man without a heart.

Did time really mend a broken heart? Where the question came from, Brody didn't know. He only knew that he was hurting as he'd never hurt before. With devastating clarity, he remembered Jess teasingly calling him King Midas. But his touch was far from golden. Jess was one of the few good things that had ever happened to him, and look what he'd done. He'd managed to complete the job Eric had only started. In a way, Eric's deceit had managed only to prick her skin. But him? Brody knew he'd managed to leave her raw and bleeding inside.

You're giving up too easily, a voice inside prodded.

He should never have touched her. He had known what would happen. He couldn't plead innocence. He'd been fully aware that the only thing he could give her was more pain, and God knew, she'd had enough of that to last a lifetime. But he'd ignored whatever questionable shred of conscience he possessed, and now he was paying the price. He was destined to suffer through the hundreds of tomorrows without Jess, wishing hopelessly for what he could never have.

Jess deserved more. She deserved love, love that filled every nook and cranny of her heart. *He could give her that. All that she needed and more, more than she could possibly want....*

But that was the question. Did Jess want him? *Could* she ever want him again, or had he killed everything she felt for him?

She deserved trust and honesty, and he had given her neither.

I was falling in love with you. Again he heard her words echoing through his mind, pouring through his heart.

So why don't you go after her?

When he'd left San Francisco a month ago, he'd thought of it as a chance to start over. He'd told himself it was time to fight for his dreams, the dreams he'd lost somewhere along the rocky path of life.

And what about now? Did he dare take a chance, the chance of a lifetime? Maybe it was time to start the battle in earnest.

He wasted no time doing exactly that. Nine o'clock the next morning found Brody stepping off a crowded elevator in a plush Oakland office complex. There was no denying the resolute determination that marked his stride as he walked swiftly through one doorway and then another—right past a stunned Miss Matthews.

"Wait! You can't go in there!"

The cool, ever-proper Miss Matthews was flustered as she rushed to stop him. A welcome change, Brody applauded silently.

The room Brody found himself in was four times the size of the waiting area. An entire wall of glass afforded a bird's-eye view of San Francisco Bay. The last whispery traces of rain and fog had disappeared hours ago, leaving behind a world that glinted in the morning sunshine. The waters of the bay appeared as a shimmering sheet of silver.

It was a breathtaking sight—the sky a bold, brilliant shade of blue, the sun spreading its soft, yellow light over the Bay. The colors were striking and intense, not quite as colorful as an Oregon horizon, Brody decided, but pretty nonetheless.

This was where it had all started. This was where it would end. Brody intended to make sure of that.

Miss Matthews burst into the room behind him. "Do you want me to call Security, Mr. Culver?"

Brody's voice was deceptively mild. "Out, Miss Matthews." His gaze moved to settle on the figure seated behind the massive desk.

Culver shook his head and waved his secretary out.

Brody waited until the door clicked shut. "You've been expecting me," he observed lightly. Culver didn't seem at all surprised by his appearance.

He acknowledged with a nod. "The minute O'Hara returned, I figured it wouldn't be long before you showed up."

"I'm glad I didn't disappoint you." Brody smiled tightly. He expected a biting comeback to his gibe; what he got was something else entirely. Culver merely leaned back in his chair. He appeared tired, almost resigned. When he said nothing, Brody moved to sit on the corner of his desk. "You know," he added conversationally, "fate definitely isn't smiling on you in this vendetta of yours. I hope you didn't persuade O'Hara to give it another try."

Culver grimaced. "O'Hara isn't any more fond of a jail cell than I am. And after what happened, he let me know in no uncertain terms that I'd better find myself another patsy."

Brody clucked softly. "Not a smart move," he murmured. "Not a smart move at all. Because if you do, I'm afraid I'll have to let the cat out of the bag."

For an instant, Culver seemed confused. Then a look of wariness stole over his features. "I'm not sure what you mean," he said slowly.

"No? Then let me spell it out for you. Considering how the city's press seems to love seeing your name in print, I'm sure they'd love to sink their claws into this. After all, what would people think if they really knew the truth?''

There was a smug smile of satisfaction tugging on Brody's lips. Culver was a smart and selfish man. Brody had no doubt he'd see the wisdom in letting go. ''I can see it now,'' Brody went on, undaunted. ''Everyone would be shocked to discover that all the years your beloved ex-wife appeared on your arm, you had a lover waiting in the wings, a *male* lo—''

Culver went white. For a long, tension-filled moment, he stared at Brody disbelievingly. When he finally spoke, he was scarcely able to form the words. ''How...how do you know? I'm sure no one ever—''

Brody's smile vanished. ''How do you think I know?'' His fist crashed down on the desktop. ''Jess told me.''

Eric's eyes widened. ''Jessica?'' he echoed dumbly. ''Jessica knew?''

''Damn right,'' he told the other man harshly. ''Why do you think she left you? She couldn't stand the thought of how she'd been duped!''

''So that's why.'' Eric's voice was hardly more than a breath of air. He got up and began to pace the room. He ran his hand repeatedly through his golden hair. Finally he came to a stop and raised his head. ''It never occurred to me that might be why. I never wanted Jessica to know, I swear.''

The words were almost pleading. Brody's gaze was trained on Culver's slender form. He sensed the man's astonishment was genuine, but he continued relentlessly.

''Don't tell me it was because of your overwhelming concern for her,'' Brody sneered. ''Sorry, Culver, but I'm not buying it. You were probably just afraid she'd leave you and blow the whistle. Well, I have no such qualms. I have an ultimatum for you, Culver, so listen, and listen well.''

He got to his feet slowly, fists clenched at his sides. "It would be my pleasure to let the world know what you really are. And I definitely don't think that would be to your advantage, especially if you ever decide you'd like to make a judicial comeback."

Across the room their eyes collided. "How much do you want?" Culver asked tiredly.

How Brody stopped himself from smashing Culver's pretty face, he never knew. He was so angry he was shaking with it. "I don't want your goddamn money," he stated flatly. "You'll stay away from Jess and her son—permanently—or else. And counselor, there'll be no plea-bargaining on this one. If I even think you're up to any tricks, I won't hesitate to fight dirty. Believe me," he added feelingly, "with you it would be a pleasure."

Culver's hands hung loosely at his sides. His arrogant confidence was gone. He suddenly looked old.

After a moment he glanced up and confronted Brody's brittle stare. "I'm many things, Alexander, but I'm not a fool." His voice was very quiet. He sounded utterly weary. "I'll do as you ask. Jessica—and the boy—have nothing to fear from me."

HAZY SPEARS of late-afternoon sunshine spilled through the sheer, lacy curtains dappling the living room with spots of soft yellow light.

The rocking chair in the corner creaked in a haphazard rhythm. Jess sat within its cushioned comfort, quietly nursing Nathan. Tracing an idle pattern against his plump cheek, she glanced up when Maggie came through the doorway. Her eyes crinkled when she saw that Maggie held a laundry basket full of baby clothes. "I'll bet you wish you were home," she commented.

Maggie plopped down on the sofa and dropped the basket on the floor at her feet. "Are you kidding?" She gave an exaggerated groan. "Right about now, Tony's probably walking through the door. Pretty soon he and Anna will be fighting about who's going to help change bed linen this weekend. Typical Monday at the lodge," she finished cheerfully. "Only this time Josie gets to play mediator. Besides, I've only been here a day."

Josie and her husband Frank were the two live-in employees at Maggie's lodge, The Trail's End. Josie had a variety of jobs—cook, occasional maid, even part-time reception clerk—and was, in Maggie's words, generally indispensable. Jess watched Maggie begin to swiftly and efficiently fold Nathan's tiny undershirts. She eyed her for a moment, sensing Maggie's mind was on Anna.

A guilty sigh escaped her lips. Maggie had hedged a little when Jess had asked about Anna. She had the feeling Maggie didn't want her to worry. Of course it hadn't helped that in the twenty-four hours since Maggie arrived, Jess had spent the first few of them on her cousin's shoulder, alternately talking and blubbering like a baby. But Maggie hadn't said "I told you so" when she learned about Brody's deceit, and for that Jess was grateful.

It had been a week since the shattering scene had been played out here in this very room. At times Jess was so angry whenever she thought of Brody she could hardly see straight; other times, all she wanted was to have him back again. Still, it was getting harder and harder to hold on to her anger. But when Jess had awakened this morning eyes swollen, puffy and red rimmed, she had vowed there would be no more tears shed over Brody Alexander.

"Maggie, when Steve died, how long did it take before you stopped feeling so—" Jess stumbled, suddenly not sure why she was even asking the question in the first place.

Across from her, Maggie had gone very still. "So alone?" she finished quietly.

Jess bit her lip, nodding wordlessly.

Maggie's movements were almost carefully precise as she folded the last undershirt and placed it on the stack. Then she rose and walked across to the window behind Jess, staring out at the hills in the distance.

"It's funny you should ask that," she said after a moment. "Because there are times when I can think of Steve, and it doesn't hurt at all." Her voice dropped further. "And there are other times when I wake up in the middle of the night, and without even thinking about it, I'll reach out, expecting him to be there...." Her voice trailed away. She looked down at her hands. "I don't know, Jess. Maybe it's the way he died. Sometimes I feel so cheated and so empty, it's like I'll never be whole again."

Jess tried not to think of Brody, but what Maggie had just said so closely paralleled her own feelings, it might have been her voice instead of Maggie's. But when Maggie turned around, Jess found her heart bleeding for her. Her cousin's eyes were liquid, shimmering like misty green emeralds.

"Just what you need, Nathan," Jess laughed shakily. "*Two* weepy women in the house." She lifted the baby to her shoulder to burp him.

Maggie smiled through her tears. "Here," she said, reaching for him a second later. "Let me do that. Then you can go take a nap if you want."

Jess stood reluctantly, but then a tiny smile edged her lips. "You know what sounds even better? I think I'll run into town and pick up some more flats. Then maybe I'll go work in the greenhouse for a while." She started toward the door, then stopped short. "Oh-oh. Your car's behind mine. I'll have to move it."

Maggie was already rummaging in her purse. "Here." She tossed the keys to Jess. "Just take mine instead."

Her thoughtful gaze followed her cousin out the door. Work, Maggie decided, was probably the best medicine for what ailed Jess.

"The problem," she murmured, holding a wide-eyed Nathan up so she could see him, "is that the cure and the cause are one and the same." She tucked the baby into the curve of her arm and added in a fierce whisper, "Let me tell you, if I ever get within ten miles of Brody Alexander, he's going to have a piece of my mind."

Not that the prospect was very likely, and for Jess's sake, Maggie wasn't sure whether she should be glad or sad.

IT SEEMED AGES since Brody had last pulled his car into the drive. At least he wasn't sneaking in the back way, as he had the first time. No, this time he was taking no chances. He parked his car right behind Jess's Volvo. He wanted everything out in the open this time—no deceit, no pretense, no hiding behind half-truths. He couldn't afford any mistakes this time. Just being here was a gamble.

Quickly, before he had time to change his mind, he strode to the back door and knocked. He'd retreated to the last step, about to give up when he spotted a shadow from inside coming toward the door. It opened slowly.

A bright-eyed Nathan came into view, circled by the smooth curve of a feminine arm. His heart beating like a trapped bird's, he held his breath while his gaze moved to the woman holding the child.

"Who the hell are you?" The question slipped out before he could stop it.

"I could ask the same thing of you!" she snapped.

Brody blinked, his stunned mind struggling to assimilate this—this phenomenon. The woman was petite, with

smattering of freckles on her nose. Perhaps it was the com-
bination—the reddish cast to her strawberry-blond hair and
those flashing green eyes raking him up and down so
boldly—but Brody was immediately reminded of a firecracker.

"Well?" she demanded.

A firecracker about to go off, Brody amended silently.
He'd opened his mouth to explain, when the realization
suddenly hit him. "Hey," he said suddenly. "I know you."

"I don't think so." Determination was etched in every line
of the woman's body as she stepped back and started to
close the door.

"Wait!" Brody's hand shot out and stopped its progress. He hadn't known he could move quite so fast, but he
stuck his shoulder in the narrow gap between the door and
its target. "I do," he said quickly. "Really. You're Maggie.
Jess's cousin Maggie. You own a vacation lodge in the
southern part of the state. Two kids. Anna and—" his mind
groped frantically for a name "—and Tony." Brody was
tempted to mop his brow. He couldn't remember when he'd
needed to rely on such quick recall. He only hoped the hell
he was right.

Again the door opened slowly. This time she regarded him
with a mixture of wariness and confusion.

"Jess talked a lot about you," he explained. "Is she
around, by any chance?" He glanced back at his car. "I've
driven all day just to see her."

Maggie's eyes followed his. Brody nearly groaned when
he saw them linger on his California license plate. He was
half prepared to hear another gibe similar to the one Lucas
had first taunted him with, but all at once comprehension
washed into Maggie's elfin features.

"So you're Brody," she murmured. "Come in, Brody. Jess isn't here right now. She ran into town but I don't think she'll be gone long."

Maggie ushered him into the kitchen, her manner all gracious hospitality. Brody had just begun to relax a little when he caught a glimpse of her eyes. They were lit with an almost feral gleam. She looked like the cat who had swallowed the canary, and Brody wondered if he would be next.

She put Nathan in his swing, then turned to face him. "You know," she stated bluntly, "I think you've got a lot of nerve coming back here after what you've done."

Brody had been about to sit down, but he changed his mind abruptly. All at once he had the feeling that if it was up to Maggie, he wouldn't be staying, after all.

His eyes narrowed. "You know?"

Her chin tilted. "Everything," she said flatly.

His jaw tightened. "I don't much care for people meddling in my business, Maggie."

He didn't have to wait long to discover she had every inch of backbone he suspected she had.

"And I don't much care for the way you've hurt Jess." Her tone was downright nasty. "The minute she told me about you, I had the feeling you were trouble—trouble with a capital *T*. I'm not about to rub Jess's nose in it, but you're a different story. I wasn't surprised to find that Eric was behind all this, but you? You didn't even know her!"

A spasm of pain etched Brody's hard features. "Believe me, there's nothing you can say that I haven't already told myself," he said bitterly. "I'm a liar, a cheat. I knew there was a chance Jess might get hurt, only—only I never thought it would happen the way it did." There was an unbearable tightness in his chest, and it was a moment before he could go on. "I'm not defending what I did," he said roughly, "but in a way, I was just as much a victim as Jess."

The words kindled an unexpected reaction from Maggie. Brody half expected her to complete the job she'd started, raking him over the coals and nailing him to the wall. Then she confounded the hell out of him.

"Then tell me," she said quietly, "what you intend to do about winning Jess back."

He stared at her, convinced he hadn't heard right. "Let me get this straight," he said slowly. "You want me to try to patch things up with Jess? You don't want me to leave—now—before she gets back?"

"Leave?" She looked horrified. "Why would you want to leave? You haven't even seen Jess yet."

His mouth was set grimly. "It's not just a matter of what I want. I want what's best for Jess."

Maggie's expression softened. "So do I, Brody. And that's why I wouldn't dream of letting you leave so soon."

They had been facing each other across the width of the kitchen, Nathan in the baby swing between them. But now Maggie sat down at the table, silently indicating that Brody take the opposite chair.

Brody hesitated. He'd let Maggie have her say, because he knew damned well how guilty he was. Still, a man could only take so much. He watched as Maggie folded her hands on the tabletop.

She didn't speak until he was sitting across from her. "Obviously I'm not going to try to pretend that what you did was right."

Both eyebrows rose. "Obviously."

"I'm sorry I spouted off at you." She gave an apologetic smile. "My husband always said I was like a stick of dynamite."

Her expression suggested that she was far, far away for a moment. Seeing it, hearing her words, Brody experienced a strange empathy.

Her smile ebbed. "Jess said you told her you never intended to go through with Eric's plan." She searched his face. "Is that true?"

"It is," he confirmed heavily. "But Jess clearly doesn't believe me."

She frowned. "What makes you say that?"

"She told me to leave, Maggie." His voice was very low, betraying the strain he was under. "She said she hoped she never had to lay eyes on me again."

"Jess had a right to be hurt and bitter," Maggie said quietly. "You should have told her who you really were, Brody. Why didn't you?"

"Because I was scared," he answered truthfully. "I wanted her right from the start, and Eric Culver didn't have a damn thing to do with it." For an instant his voice turned harsh. "But I was afraid that if I told her, she'd turn away from me. Then later, I knew I had to find a way to protect her and Nathan from Eric."

"And did you?"

He smiled grimly. "I think it's safe to say he won't bother her ever again."

"Is that why you came back?"

"That's one of the reasons," he admitted. "I wanted to let Jess know she had nothing to fear from him anymore."

"And the other?"

Curiously, Brody no longer felt any resentment at Maggie's questions. He knew her only concern was Jess. Nor did he feel any shame in opening his heart to this woman.

Yet mere words escaped him. He could find no way to express the turbulent emotions roiling inside him. Jess was so many things to him—his rescuer, his salvation. She had given light to a world that until then had held only darkness and shadows. She had taught him how to dream again, and to believe in those dreams.

Then finally, his eyes came to rest on the asparagus plant hanging near the window, abundant and green with fresh new growth. It was like her precious, newly planted seedlings, so fragile and delicate, which she nurtured and tended, giving them life—just as she had given him life; just as *she* was his life.

He rose and walked over to stand before it. "You see this plant?" he asked quietly. "It was nearly dead when Jess found it. Anyone else would have tossed it out as worthless."

He reached out to touch the trailing tip of a delicate, pale green frond straining toward the sun. "But look at it now. It's alive, and it's thriving because Jess took the time to care for it and bring it back to life. That's what Jess did for me, and I came back because I had this crazy idea that if I told Jess how much I love her, it might make a difference." His sigh was a lonely, wistful sound. "All the difference in the world."

Behind him, Maggie smiled. If he'd seen it, Brody might have wondered about that secretive smile.

But then he heard a voice, a voice that made his heart leap and his mouth go dry with fear.

"I think," Jess said very softly, "it already has."

CHAPTER EIGHTEEN

BRODY FROZE, a coil of tension slowly tightening his stomach. He was suddenly paralyzed, knowing Jess was here—knowing she was watching him. He wanted nothing more than to see her, to snatch her into his arms. And yet he was afraid—desperately afraid—of what he might find when he turned around.

Slowly he turned to face her. The force of emotions rushing through him was enough to bring him to his knees.

Maggie rose from the table. Neither Brody nor Jess seemed to notice her movement. Their eyes were riveted on each other.

She pulled Nathan from the swing, unable to wipe the smile from her face or keep the amused satisfaction from bubbling over in her voice. "Let's grab your diaper bag and go over to Lucas's house for a while, Nathan. Maybe we'll even put you down for a nap there." Nathan wrinkled his brows and gave a tiny grin. Maggie chuckled. "Sounds good, huh?"

When she was gone, there was a heated rush of silence. It was just the two of them now.

Jess found herself torn by a hundred different feelings. She ached to sweep back the dark gold strands that lay on Brody's forehead. She longed to smooth away the taut lines of strain etched beside his mouth. She wanted to pinch herself to see if this moment was real or imagined. Was Brody actually here, standing no more than ten feet away from her? Or was he only a mirage, conjured up out of her own desperate yearning?

He'd said he loved her. *He loved her.*

She wanted to say something but couldn't. Her tongue was glued to the roof of her mouth. Her heart had set up a clamor in her chest that was deafening.

He was looking at her, as if his face were carved out of stone. How could a man who appeared so strong, so disciplined and controlled, be so vulnerable?

"Is it...is it true?" Her voice quavered. Jess scarcely recognized it as hers.

Brody held his breath, hardly daring to breathe. "What?" he asked softly.

Her knees were shaking. That she could stand at all was a miracle. "What you just said." *Oh, God, let it be true.* If it was just a misunderstanding—a mistake—she wanted to die.

She began to count the heartbeats. One, two...

Silently he beseeched her, begged her forgiveness. *I love you.* He said it again, with his eyes.

Then once more aloud: "I love you, Jess." It was an urgent whisper, a fervent prayer, a promise and a plea. It was all there in his eyes, in the hoarseness of his voice—the fierce, stark yearning, the depth of emotion he couldn't hide and didn't want to.

Something inside her twisted and then broke free. It was like a bird taking flight, floating with the wind, soaring higher and higher.

"Brody," she choked out. "Oh, Brody." She was laughing; she was crying.

She was in his arms, pressed against his heart, right where she belonged.

He buried his head in the fragrant silk of her hair, keenly feeling her pain and his own. She clung to his neck and sobbed out her joy, wetting his shirt with tears of relief.

"Jess." His hands weren't entirely steady as they smoothed her hair. "Jess, please." His heart wrenched. "Hush, love," he implored raggedly. "You don't know how it hurts, knowing I've made you cry. . . . I'll never make you cry again, I swear. I love you, Jess. I love you."

His fingers cupped her nape. His hand slid around to gently guide her face to his. His eyes were as misty as her own.

She pressed her mouth into the warm roughness of his palm.

Brody's heart contracted with the pure, sweet pleasure he felt. He held her tightly, allowing himself to bask in the wonder of having her near once more. "Oh, Jess," he murmured finally. "I have so much to explain. So much to—"

Her fingers against his mouth silenced him. She shook her head, unable to speak.

"You heard?" His tone was very quiet. He searched her face intently.

She nodded. Her trembling lips curved in a shaky smile. "Almost all of it," she confided. "I couldn't believe it when I saw your car here. I felt—oh, God—I don't know how I felt. I wanted so much to be angry all over again. And then I came in and heard you with Maggie—" Her eyes squeezed shut. When they opened, they were shining, filled with more emotion than he'd ever dared hope to see.

"When I married Eric, I thought he loved me. It wasn't until much, much later that I realized I needed to be wanted for myself and not for what I could do for someone else." For just an instant, pain and regret laced her voice.

His voice low and intent, he spoke before she could say any more. "Don't you think that's how I love you? Believe it, Jess, because I promise I'll never lie to you again." His eyes grew bleak, his tone rough. "I know I had no right to come here. I know I have no right to ask anything of you—"

"Brody." Inside she was trembling uncontrollably. "Brody, will you please just get on with it?" She hardly dared to hope. She hardly dared to breathe.

He stared down at her. "It doesn't matter?" he asked slowly. "It doesn't matter what I've been, what I've done? I have nothing to offer you, Jess. No home, no—"

She wanted to pound her fists against his chest in pure frustration. But he sounded so tortured, so utterly unsure of himself that tears brimmed anew. "All I want," she whispered brokenly, "is for you to love me."

His eyes darkened. "I do," he said fervently. "God knows, I do."

The heartfelt emotion, the raw conviction in his voice, filled her heart to near bursting. But through her tears she smiled, a poignantly sweet smile that made Brody's breath catch.

His arms tightened. His head began to lower, thrilling her with the sweet promise of hard lips smothered against her own.

With infinite gentleness, he wiped away her tears. Then he kissed her eyelids closed, gently probed the corner of her mouth with his tongue. "I want you, Jess," he whispered. "Now. Tomorrow. Forever. And I have just one question: Do you love me, sweet?"

Her eyes snapped open. Brody would have laughed at her riotous disappointment, except everything inside him was tight with anticipation.

Thank heaven she chose not to make him suffer any-more. She drew back just enough so that she could see his face. "I love you more," she said softly, "with every day that passes."

"Is that a promise?"

"It is."

It was his turn to smile against her lips. "Then marry me, Jess. Marry me just as soon as we can."

Her "Yes" was lost somewhere in an endless kiss that sent a surge of aching sweetness through her veins. She clung to him, caught up in an overwhelming intensity of emotion that consumed them both.

Finally Brody lifted his head. His arms tightened; he cra-dled her close and buried his mouth in her hair. "I do love you," he murmured.

Her eyes opened, as pure and bright as the summer sky. Her heart was singing. "I know," she said softly.

And she did.

IT WAS BRODY who suggested they go to Lucas's to join Nathan and Maggie. Now that he was back, Brody had a compulsive need to see for himself that Lucas hadn't suf-fered any serious harm from his fall.

Betty's car was parked in front of the house, as well as Maggie's. Brody and Jess exchanged glances as he pulled the keys from the ignition. "Now that wedding bells are in the air, think we'll need a minister willing to do two for the price of one?" he asked with a grin.

Jess's eyes lit up. Brody chuckled at her expression.

She wrinkled her nose at him. "Don't laugh," she said loftily. "There's a distinct possibility. Lucas already asked Betty to marry him." It was her turn to laugh when Brody's eyes widened.

Betty greeted them at the door and led them into the living room. Nathan was napping, asleep on the sofa cushion next to Maggie. Maggie took one look at Jess's glowing face and let out a peal of laughter. "I almost said it before I left, but I thought I'd better wait just to be sure. Welcome to the family, Brody!"

Brody smiled, but his eyes were sober as he moved across the room toward Lucas, who had risen to his feet. He paused, once again unsure of himself. "Lucas, I . . ."

The old man never let him finish. "Don't say another word, son. What's done is done, and I know I'm not the only one who's glad to have you back."

Brody's throat was curiously tight. Male pride be damned, he thought to himself, and he embraced the older man in a fierce hug. He swore there was a suspiciously bright sheen of moisture in Lucas's eyes; there was no doubt about the shimmer in his own.

But when he stepped back he saw Lucas's worried gaze move between Jess and himself. "You are staying, aren't you?" He cleared his throat. "I mean, you're not going back to California, are you?"

Brody slipped an arm around Jess and brought her closer. For an instant, his mind went back to the time he'd first met Jess and Lucas. How things had changed since then—how *he* had changed. "Jess did threaten to make a nurseryman out of me." He smiled into her upturned face. "I think she's succeeded."

EPILOGUE

BRODY AND JESS were married on a glorious, sun-kissed afternoon in the middle of May. And as Jess had teased, theirs wasn't the only wedding to take place that day in Amity's tiny, flower-bedecked church. The ceremony was a simple one, attended by those closest to the two couples. Neither bride had ever been happier; neither groom had ever been more nervous.

Brody still couldn't believe his luck. All of his dreams—all he had ever wanted—were wrapped up in the woman who was now his wife. Oh, there were a few times when he still harbored doubts about what he had brought to this marriage; about his ability to give Jess everything she needed.

But a vague idea had begun to nag at him just before he'd returned to Oregon for the wedding after tying up loose ends in San Francisco. It was Lucas who had told him the tractor they'd worked so hard to repair had finally breathed its last.

Of course, with the hurried trip back to California there had been no time to do anything about it. Then there was the wedding and the week they'd spent at the coast. They'd originally planned to spend only their wedding night away since Jess had been reluctant to leave the nursery for any length of time. But Maggie, who had come for the wedding with Anna and Tony, had offered to watch over things so they could take a proper honeymoon. But now they were home again...

Brody sat on the rough wooden planks of the back porch. Jess was inside with Nathan. The moon cast a faint sheen of silver on the roof of Jess's greenhouse. The night sky was cluttered with dozens of winking stars, and a strong breeze whipped the tree branches, but he felt as if the sun were shining.

The screen door opened. Jess stepped outside.

Brody got to his feet. It was strange—*he* was the one who felt like a kid on Christmas morning. "Nathan's all settled in for the night?"

"Yes." She smiled up at him and slid her arms around his neck, lifting her lips for him to sample.

"Oh, no." He chuckled playfully. "There's time for that later. Right now I have a surprise for you."

Jess looked startled. "A surprise?" Her eyes began to glow like hundred-watt light bulbs.

"Yes. Now close your eyes." He took her hand and began to lead her toward the barn.

"Brody! Brody, what on earth...!"

"Shh. We're almost there." His hand on her waist, he guided her across the yard.

With every step that he took, excitement and apprehension mingled. What if she hated it? What if she thought it was crazy and unromantic and... Maybe this wasn't such a good idea after all.

The barn door creaked noisily when he opened it. Brody's heart was thudding so that he scarcely heard. Jess was shielding her eyes with her hand. He pulled her inside and flipped on the light.

"Okay," he said quietly. "You can open your eyes now."

She did. For the space of a heartbeat, there was complete and total silence.

"Well?" Brody's voice betrayed his anxiety. "What do you think?"

Jess gazed at the sleek new tractor in front of her. She moved forward as if in a trance and reached out to touch one of the huge rear wheels.

"Brody," she breathed. "Brody, what is this for?"

The wonder on her face was something to behold. "It's for you, Jess. A wedding present." He smiled crookedly. "I know you probably think it's odd—"

She turned and propelled herself into his arms. "It's not! At least now I know why Betty was so insistent on dragging me off shopping this afternoon." Suddenly she was both laughing and crying. "I...oh, Brody, I don't know what to say. I can't think of anything you could have given me that would make me happier. But it's not just for me," she said, raising her face to his. "It's for us. Because we're in this together."

Together. He liked the sound of that, and nothing she could have said would have pleased him more. He raised her chin to look into her face. "You sure you're not disappointed?"

"No! Only I know what a machine like this costs." A faint frown appeared between her finely arched brows. "How on earth did you manage to..."

It was a pleasure kissing her mouth closed. "It's ours free and clear, sweetheart," he told her a moment later. He reminded her about his nest egg, the money he'd saved during his years in the service. "I always thought of the money as Murphy's," he said softly. "I guess that's why I never touched it even after he was gone."

For the first time Jess looked a trifle hesitant.

Brody had no trouble reading her mind. "I wanted to, Jess." He ran the tip of his finger down her nose. When her mouth opened, he laid his finger against her lips. "No arguments, love. And I know Murphy would be pleased."

He was lost in quiet reflection for a moment. "Remember I told you about that place in the sun Murphy always wanted? I'd like to think he found it. I'd like to think he's there now, in a place just like this.''

Her eyes wandered tenderly over his face. ''And what about you?'' she asked softly.

''I've found my dream, too.'' He rested his forehead against hers and smiled. ''Right here.''

CALLOWAY CORNERS

Created by four outstanding Superromance authors, bonded by lifelong friendship and a love of their home state: Sandra Canfield, Tracy Hughes, Katherine Burton and Penny Richards.

CALLOWAY CORNERS

Home of four sisters as different as the seasons, as elusive as the elements; an undiscovered part of Louisiana where time stands still and passion lasts forever.

CALLOWAY CORNERS

Birthplace of the unforgettable Calloway women: *Mariah*, free as the wind, and untamed until she meets the preacher who claims her, body and soul; *Jo*, the fiery, feisty defender of lost causes who loses her heart to a rock and roll man; *Tess*, gentle as a placid lake but tormented by her longing for the town's bad boy and *Eden*, the earth mother who's been so busy giving love she doesn't know how much she needs it until she's awakened by a drifter's kiss...

CALLOWAY CORNERS

Coming from Superromance, in 1989:
Mariah, by Sandra Canfield, a January release
Jo, by Tracy Hughes, a February release
Tess, by Katherine Burton, a March release
Eden, by Penny Richards, an April release

Have You Ever Wondered If You Could Write A Harlequin Novel?

Here's great news—Harlequin is offering a series of cassette tapes to help you do just that. Written by Harlequin editors, these tapes give practical advice on how to make your characters—and your story—come alive. There's a tape for each contemporary romance series Harlequin publishes.

Mail order only

All sales final

TO: ***Harlequin Reader Service***
Audiocassette Tape Offer
P.O. Box 1396
Buffalo, NY   14269-1396

I enclose a check/money order payable to HARLEQUIN READER SERVICE® for $9.70 ($8.95 plus 75¢ postage and handling) for EACH tape ordered for the total sum of $_____*
Please send:

[ ] Romance and Presents   ☐ Intrigue
[ ] American Romance   ☐ Temptation
[ ] Superromance   [ ] All five tapes ($38.80 total)

Signature_____

Name:_____
                                            (please print clearly)

Address:_____

State:_____ Zip:_____

* Iowa and New York residents add appropriate sales tax.

AUDIO-H

TEARS IN THE RAIN

STARRING
CHRISTOPHER CAVZENOVE AND
SHARON STONE

BASED ON A NOVEL BY
PAMELA WALLACE

PREMIERING IN NOVEMBER

TITR-1